The Window Trilogy

By Carol Shackleford

The Underwater Window

Carol Shackleford

CHAPTER 1

"What were you doing in the Yellow Zone?" the man in the uniform asked Jacob again. He had started the questions in a nice quiet voice but it was starting to get louder and more intense. Jacob didn't know what to do. This wasn't like the regular police that he had seen around town or when he went to see his Uncle Richie at the police station where he worked as an investigator. This man had on a gray uniform with yellow stripes down the sides. Jacob was so scared. He could feel his heart pounding. Even though he knew it was wrong to lie, he was too afraid to tell the truth.

"I want to talk to my parents." Jacob said.

The uniformed man replied, "I'll see what I can do after you tell me why you were in a restricted area. Don't you know that trespassing is against the law? I could arrest you right now. How long were you in the water?"

Jacob was starting to feel dizzy and sick to his stomach. "Just for a minute. I don't really remember. It happened so fast." Jacob hesitated. "Can I go home now?" he asked quietly. The man in the uniform slammed his hand down on the table in front of him so hard that it knocked over the glass of water that had been put there for Jacob earlier.

"You aren't going anywhere until you tell me why you were behind the fence. That fence is there for a reason young man. Not so little troublemaking brats like you can break through it. I know you didn't climb over it because you would have been cut by the barbed wire. So how did you do it? Cut the fence with wire cutters?" His eyes were like little slits as he glared at Jacob.

"No sir," He answered. "I was walking my dog and he got off his leash and went through an opening where the dirt was kind of low. I was just trying to get my dog. Honest. That's all."

The man had been pacing the room and slowly turned and put both hands on the table in front of Jacob. Leaning down he put his face right in Jacob's face and said, "If you were there to get your dog, why did you end up in the lake? And where is your dog?"

Jacob could smell his breath as he breathed heavily in his face. "I was chasing him and I tripped on something, a rock or something, and I fell. There was a hill and I couldn't stop falling. I don't know where my dog is. That's why I have to go home. My mom and dad are going to be wondering where I am and I have to find my dog before he gets too far away."

Staring at Jacob he slowly and angrily asked, "How long were you in the water?"

"Just for a minute. Someone came and pulled me out. And now I'm here. I'm not sure what's going on." The man kept staring at Jacob and Jacob could tell he was trying to see if he was lying or not. Jacob sure couldn't tell him what he had seen. He didn't think anyone would believe him if he did tell them anyway. He knew his mom always told him she could tell when he was not being honest. He was really hoping that maybe only his mom had that ability.

Before he could say anything, the door to the room was thrown open and crashed into the wall. Jacob's Uncle stood in the doorway. Jacob had never been so happy to see anyone in his whole life! "Jacob," he said, "How long have you been here?" Jacob wanted to get up and run to him but was still afraid of the man in the uniform. There was another uniformed man right behind his uncle. The man said, "I'm sorry sir, this man barged in and I couldn't stop him. He says he's the kid's uncle. He's with the city PD sir." The man in the uniform was looking from Jacob's uncle to Jacob. He finally said, "Thank you, Bill. That will be all. Shut the door behind you when you leave."

Jacob's uncle reached out to shake hands with the man in the uniform. "My name is Richard Mansell. I'm an investigator with the Blue Water Police Department. I would like to know what you think you are doing keeping a minor here without contacting his parents. Has he committed a crime?"

The man in the uniform looked at Richard's hand and stood a little taller as he put both of his hands behind his back and clasped them together as he started to pace the room again. Jacob had been so nervous that he hadn't even noticed where he was. He started looking around. It was a fairly large room with just a table and two chairs. The walls were cement and painted a dull gray color. Kind of like the color of their uniforms. There was a big mirror on one wall. He wondered if it was one of those mirrors where someone was on the other side watching them. This whole thing didn't seem real. It seemed like something he would watch on tv.

The man in the uniform said, "Mr. Mansell, my name is Commander Thomas Leclead. I am the overseer of The Yellow Zone. Your nephew was caught trespassing. This is a serious offense. One of our guards saw him in the lake and pulled him out. I am trying to get to the bottom of his reason for being behind the fence. I'm sure you understand that we cannot tolerate any disobedience."

Richard looked Jacob over. "Jacob, are you alright? You didn't get hurt, did you?" Jacob shook his head. "Why were you behind the fence? You know the Yellow Zone is completely off limits."

Jacob could feel his eyes getting hot, like he might start to cry. Well, he certainly could not cry in front of anyone. He had to be strong. So he closed his eyes for a second to clear them and looked at his uncle. "I already told him that I was walking Bosco and he got loose. You know that he runs if he gets off his leash. Well, he got under the fence and I knew if I didn't get him, he might get hurt or lost. Jillie would kill me if I lost the dog. I tripped and fell down a hill and landed in the lake. That's all I remember until they pulled me out."

Richard looked at Commander Leclead. "Well, that sounds reasonable to me. Is there anything else you need before I take my nephew home? We need to make sure he didn't get hurt falling down that hill. "

The Commander shook his head but said, "I will need his address and phone number along with yours in case we have any further questions."

"That's not a problem." said Richard as he wrote the information in a notebook that was on the table. When Jacob got up from the table, his ankle gave way and he almost fell to the floor. He had been so nervous that he hadn't even realized it hurt. Richard came over and helped him walk out. Being so big, Jacob was sure he could have just thrown him over his shoulder and carried him out. Richard helped Jacob to his car. Richard waited until they were both in the car before he turned to Jacob and shook his head. "Buddy, this is a big deal. No one has ever been behind the fence. With all of the guards I don't even see how you could have made it in there. Let me see that ankle. Do we need to go to the doctor?" He had Jacob move his foot up and down and roll it in a circle. "I think it just got twisted. It should be fine in a few days."

"Uncle Richie, how did you know where to find me?" Jacob asked.

He just smiled and said, "I know everyone in this town. It didn't take long for the word to spread. We need to get you home before your folks find out and start an all-out manhunt looking for you."

Jacob leaned back in the seat. Should he tell his Uncle Richie what he had seen? Would he believe him? Maybe he had just imagined it. Maybe he had actually hit his head and it made him hallucinate. He felt around his head but it didn't feel sore anywhere. Richard looked over at him. "You ok? Did you hit your head?"

"No, I don't think so." He replied. "Uncle Richie, do we have to tell my mom and dad? They are going to be really mad at me. They will be mad enough that I lost the dog."

"I think they will just be happy that you are ok. Your sis might be a little ticked about the dog though. Let's drive by The Yellow Zone and see if we can find him on the way home. How does that sound?"

"Thanks." He said with a slight smile on his face. "Did you or my mom ever do anything to get in trouble like this when you were growing up? My mom tries to tell me that she never did anything wrong and everything was your fault but I think she may be remembering it wrong."

Richard laughed. "Well, she was the good one but you can ask her about washing the car with an SOS pad and see what she says."

"No way! Did she get in trouble?"

"I don't think so. She was just trying to help by washing the car. Hey, show me where you got through the fence. We're getting close to it now." Richard slowed the car down so they could look at the fence. Jacob was trying to remember where it was. "I wasn't really paying attention when I was walking Bosco." They drove the whole section that he had walked past. Most of the lake was surrounded by woods that the fence wove through but there was one section that you could walk along. They usually tried to stay away because the guards were always watching. The lake couldn't even really be seen from up here. Jacob didn't know it was so big until he was falling down the hill. He was starting to wonder if the guards had anything to do with what he had seen in the water. No place could be found along the fence that would have allowed him to crawl under. Maybe they had already filled it in. It was kind of rocky and had hard clay along the bottom of the fence. After just a few minutes of looking, Richard thought it would be a good idea to get Jacob home.

Jacob was just starting to worry about what his parents would say when they drove up to the front of the house. Richard helped him out of the front seat and held on to his arm as he hopped up the sidewalk. Jacob's mom, Anne, came to the front door. Just as she was opening the door, they heard a bark and turned in time to see Bosco running around the side of the house. He ran up the steps and right in the door his mom had just opened. Well, that was one less thing for him to worry about. At least his sister wouldn't kill him now! His mom came outside and down the steps. "What in the world happened to you? I was just starting to wonder where you had gone off to. What happened Rich? How did Jacob end up in your work car?"

Richard chuckled, "As usual you don't let me answer before you have ten questions out there! Is Wray home from work yet? It would be easier to tell you both at once."

Anne's eyes narrowed as she got a worried look on her face. "Seriously? Should I be worried? You know how much I worry. What's going on? Let me go get Wray."

Richard chuckled again. He looked over at Jacob. "You're going to give your mom some major gray hair dude. We don't need to stress her out by giving her too many details. Just the facts, ok?" Richard and Jacob walked into the house and went to sit at the kitchen table.

Anne came into the kitchen followed by her husband who still had water dripping from his hair after being interrupted in the shower. Wray always tried to fit in a quick workout and shower before dinner. "Do you want something to drink?" Anne asked everyone. They all shook their heads.

Wray pulled out a chair and asked, "What's got your mom so upset Jacob? Did something bad happen today? It's not every day your uncle has to bring you home. Were you at the police station?"

Jacob looked over at his uncle. Richard nodded his head to encourage him to tell the story.

Jacob began with walking the dog and when he got to the part where Bosco got off his leash and went under the fence, he could see his mom's face turn white. "Please tell me you didn't try to follow him under the fence." She said with anxiety in her eyes. Jacob gave her a weak smile. "I just reacted. I didn't even think about where I was." When Jacob got to the part about falling down the hill into the lake, his mom stood up and started pacing the room. "Do you know what could have happened?" She put her hand up to her forehead and closed her eyes. "Jacob, did you get hurt? Are you ok? Let me see you." She came over and started looking him up and down. "I'm fine. I just twisted my ankle but it doesn't even hurt much anymore, see." He said as he moved his ankle in a circle. Jacob continued with the story about someone pulling him out of the lake and taking him to the Yellow Zone Headquarters. At that, his dad started to question Richard. "Why didn't they call us? What do we even know about those people? This whole thing with them has been so bizarre for so long. Has this ever happened before?"

Richard smiled and said, "Slow down, you've been hanging around your wife too long. One question at a time. I don't know why they didn't call you. As far as I know, no one has ever been past the fence so this is new territory for all of us. But I think it should all work out ok. They have your phone number and address in case they have any questions but I don't see what they could possibly want. There was no harm done and it's not like Jacob saw any kind of secret activity or secret missions going on, right Jakey?"

Jacob let out a strange laugh. "No. Nothing. I didn't see anything. I already told them that."

Richard laughed to ease the tension in the room but his investigator instincts were kicking in. He could tell that Jacob was not telling them everything.

Anne looked at her son as she tilted her head. "You're not being honest about something. You can't lie to your mother. What aren't you telling us?"

Jacob got up from the table and went to the cupboard for a glass for water. He needed the distraction. "Mom, you're reading too much into this. I'm just freaked out about what happened. The guy was interrogating me like I killed someone or something. Please don't start in on me too."

Anne went over to give her son a big hug. "Please don't ever do anything like that again."

Wray got up and walked over to tussle Jacob's hair. "Buddy, you better start doing extra chores around here and maybe making some cash to save up to use for bail money if you keep it up!" Anne playfully hit him in the shoulder as she rolled her eyes and said, "Well, that better never happen. Honestly! You two are going to make me crazy! Supper will be ready soon. Will you be able to go to baseball practice with your ankle being sore?"

"I think so. It's already feeling better."

"Ok. Well go clean up. Put those clothes in the laundry room. They have all that mud and stuff from the lake on them."

Jacob looked down at his clothes. He hadn't realized how filthy he was. He would be more than willing to get these clothes off and pretend like this whole day never even happened. But as he stood in the shower with the water hitting his face, all he could see was the window. The window under the water.

CHAPTER 2

Lincoln lay in bed with his hands behind his head as he stared up at the ceiling. He had been laying there for what seemed to him to be all night. This had been his bedroom for as long as he could remember. Nothing had changed in here for 11 years. He didn't mean to feel restless and wish his life was different. This was really all he knew but he had always sensed that there was more. More out there that he didn't know about. He sometimes had vague dreams of blue skies and green grass. He had seen pictures in books and supposed that was where his dreams came from. His favorite dream was the one of him running on the grass with no shoes on. He imagined it would be soft and maybe tickle the bottoms of his feet. He ran and ran and he could see grass for as far as his vision allowed. His life was just drab and boring. Everything was gray and dull. He knew he had no right to complain. He had heard stories of what the world had come to. The sickness and the death and the unknown. He had heard about the preparation to protect everyone here. He was safe and he was thankful. But was this really all there was? His days were very routine. The same every day. His mom, Clara woke him up for school with a gentle knock on his door. He got dressed and went to the kitchen for breakfast. She was always singing songs she said were from "her younger years". After breakfast he would meet his friend Simon for school. There were a few other kids at school but Simon was the only one he would really call his friend. Lincoln wondered if he should confide in Simon and tell him what he had seen. After some thought, he decided that Simon would think he was crazy and wouldn't believe him anyway.

Out of the quiet of the house, Lincoln could hear his parents talking. Their house was very small so it was easy to hear noises if someone was moving around. It was the middle of the night. What could they be discussing at this hour? He couldn't make out what they were saying but he thought he heard his dad say something about it being safe to leave. Leave where? What was he talking about? He didn't sound angry or anything. Lincoln had very rarely seen his dad, Samuel, get mad about anything. His dad had always told him that he had seen enough violence for a lifetime and saw no reason to ever get worked up about situations that he had some control over. It had made sense to him. But why were they up so late? Lincoln slowly and as quietly as he could, slid out of his bed. He tiptoed to the door and put his ear against it in the hopes of hearing better. He knew he shouldn't be eavesdropping but he couldn't help himself.

Samuel said, "Clara, I just don't feel like they are being honest with us. I'm beginning to wonder if maybe it's safe to go back. When we are here, they have complete control of everything. What would be the benefit of telling us the truth and allowing us to go?"

"I just can't believe that would happen. They are the ones who helped us find this place to keep us safe. I trust you, Samuel, but are you sure about this? Where is your information coming from?"

"It's just a gut feeling. I guess I still carry some of the Army with me."

"Well, what are you going to do? Have you mentioned your theory to anyone else?"

"I don't think it would be well-received. This is a very close community. I don't want to stir up unnecessary problems."

"Well, Honey, I would sleep on it tonight and maybe in the morning, you'll have a clearer picture of what direction to go. I'm behind you whatever we decide to do." Clara hugged her husband and knew that whatever his decision was, it would be for the best of the family.

*****

Lincoln crawled back into bed. He couldn't believe it. Did he hear them right? Was it even possible that they may be able to leave? Were the dangers gone? He wondered if there really was grass he could walk on. He began to wonder if he could possibly tell his dad what he had seen. As Lincoln drifted off to sleep, he started dreaming of a sky filled with stars like he had seen pictures of. Maybe, just maybe, it was real.

Jacob woke the next morning completely worn out. He didn't sleep well the night before. He tenderly moved his ankle around and it was still sore but not as bad as he thought it might be after baseball practice last night. He was glad it was Saturday so he didn't have school. All night he had thought about what had happened. He had nightmares about the uniformed man throwing him in jail and no one knew where he was. He heard the doorbell ring and quickly jumped out of bed to throw on some clothes to see who it was. As he walked down the hall, he heard his mom open the door.

"Good morning, Michael. How are you this morning?" Asked Anne.

"Morning Mrs. Lindstrom. I'm fine. Is Jacob here?"

Jacob rounded the corner and waved at his friend. "Mom, is it ok if Mike and I go for a bike ride? I promise I'll pick up my room when I get home. Please?"

"Ok. But your room better be cleaned before your game or there will be trouble."

"Thanks mom. It will be."

"Oh, and Jacob? Stay out of trouble today, ok?"

"Haha, very funny mom."

Jacob grabbed his baseball cap on his way out the door. They started down the slight hill in front of Jacob's house. They were laughing as they started racing each other. All of a sudden,

Jacob skidded his bike to a stop. Mike stopped and turned around. "What's wrong?" he asked.

"Do you see that guy over there? I think I know him. Does it seem like he's watching us?" Jacob asked as he looked over at the black SUV with dark windows. The man in the driver's seat looked exactly like Commander Leclead from the interrogation room yesterday. But why would he be parked here watching his house?

"I don't think so. Why? You look kinda freaked out. Who is he?"

Jacob didn't know if he should tell Mike about his adventure from the day before. He was afraid that if Mike's mom found out, she might not let her son hang out with him anymore. Mike was an only child and she seemed really protective of him. "I might be wrong. Let's keep going and see if he follows us." They continued down the hill and quickly turned the corner and rode as fast as they could until they got so out of breath they had to stop.

"What's going on? I don't think I've ever ridden my bike that hard!" panted Mike.

Jacob was watching the road behind him. He didn't see any sign of the SUV. "I had a little run-in with the officers from the Yellow Zone yesterday and that looked like the guy that was asking me questions."

"Dude! You're kidding me! I heard about that. Everyone was talking about it last night at the neighborhood picnic. That was YOU?"

"Yep. What did they say about it?"

"Just that there was a kid that crossed the fence and fell down the hill. Where did they take you? Man! I can't believe it was you! Why were you behind the fence?"

"Bosco got loose when I was walking him and I chased after him hoping to catch him before he got too far away. I didn't even really think about it until I was falling down the hill and fell in the lake."

"You fell in the lake? You can't swim very well. What did you do?"

Jacob was starting to feel sick to his stomach talking about it again. "A guard pulled me from the water. It was no big deal. We better get going. I have the game tonight and I still have to clean my room."

"Ok. Are you all right? You seem really nervous or something."

"Sure. I'm just nervous for our game. We play the Tigers and they are really good. Hey, can you do me a favor and not tell anyone it was me? I just don't want to answer a bunch of questions. Plus your parents won't be too happy about it. They might not let you come over any more."

"Yeah. I won't tell anyone. I'm not doing anything tonight. Want me to come to your game?"

"That would be awesome. We will need all the fans we can get. It's at 7:00."

"Ok. See you there." The boys waved to each other as they went separate ways to their houses. When Jacob turned the corner to go up his street, the SUV from earlier was gone. He was starting to feel like he was being paranoid. He thought he must be imagining things.

*****

Lincoln had a long day of wandering around and thinking about what he heard his parents say the night before. He walked every inch of the place he called home. The places without lights were dark so he had to take his flashlight. Although he knew he wasn't supposed to wander out into the cave, he couldn't help himself today. He imagined what it would be like to have sunshine to light his path and warm his face. He spent a long time looking out the big window. It was the only way to see if it was daytime or nighttime. If the water was light and you could see into it, then it was day. Otherwise, at night it was dark and you could only make out the shadow of a swimming fish if it was really close by. There were 37 small homes in his underground town. It was a town built inside of a huge man-made cave. It was the only town he remembered. His parents told him they moved there when he was 2 years old. It was a nice place to live. His dad was the town doctor. His mom worked at the little food market when he was in school. He had often wondered if his parents had ever wanted to go anywhere else. There must be other towns like this. Maybe bigger ones. Lincoln had always wished there could be a big window in the ceiling so it could let in sunlight. He had learned to be content and happy. But after hearing his parent's conversation last night, he started to wonder if there was something more out

21

there. Especially after what he saw in the window. His mind was going everywhere. As he was doing his wandering, he ran his hand along the rough wall of the cave. It felt cool to his touch. He started wondering where the opening was. He had never thought such things before. But he realized there must be a way in and out. How else would they get food? Nothing was grown down here. Where did their food come from? How about supplies like what they used for school and medicine? He was beginning to become determined to figure it out. As he continued thinking, he didn't realize how far he had walked. He didn't notice until his flashlight suddenly blinked on and off a few times before totally going out. It was so dark, he couldn't see anything. He could sort of see a glow in the distance which must be the town lights. He was about to start walking toward the glow when he heard two voices. They were not very far away. He saw the rays from a flashlight. He squatted down low to the ground. There was no place to hide so he had to just hope they didn't shine their light in his direction.

"They pulled him out in just a matter of a minute. It seemed like he didn't know how to swim. There is no reason to believe he saw anything. We're going to keep an eye on him for a while though. He's just a kid so I don't think we have anything to worry about."

Lincoln couldn't believe his ears. They were talking about the boy he saw through the window yesterday. He didn't imagine it! Why was there a boy in the water? Where did he live? There couldn't really be people living out there, out in the sunshine, could there? How could he find out? So many questions to think through.

The men were now gone. Lincoln was turned around. He didn't know which way they had come from or where they went. But that also meant he didn't know which direction his home was. He sat on the ground and closed his eyes and let his mind wonder about the boy he had seen in the water. It was for just a couple seconds but it was enough time to get a pretty good look at him. He looked to be about the same age as himself. And he was wearing a chain around his neck with a pendant on it that had somehow seemed familiar to Lincoln. Where had he seen something like that before? He opened his eyes and felt around him for the wall. He thought his best bet would be to just keep his hand on the wall and start walking. It would eventually lead him back to his town. At least he hoped it would.

CHAPTER 4

Richard sat at his desk and tried to keep his anger from taking over. The encounter with the Yellow Zone official yesterday was really bothering him. These people had a lot of nerve to keep his nephew in an interrogation room without anyone there on his behalf. The city police had never had any trouble with the Yellow Zone officials. They kept to themselves and didn't require any assistance from the BWPD. He felt that his nephew was not telling him the whole story about what occurred. Jacob was a good kid. He didn't think his nephew would ever do anything on purpose to break the law or cause trouble. He was going to have to talk to him again and see if he could get any other information. In the meantime, he thought it would be a good idea to have a discussion with the Chief to see exactly what the history of the Yellow Zone was.

*****

Anne went in to check on Jacob. He had come home from his bike ride with Mike and went right to his room. She opened his bedroom door and was shocked to see that his room had been cleaned. She usually had to tell him at least three times before he finally got to it. He was laying on his bed and staring up at the ceiling. She sat on the bed next to him and asked, "Care to share what's on your mind?"

He gave her a faint smile. "Just thinking, I guess."

"Something must be up because your room looks great and I didn't even have to yell."

"I was just thinking about yesterday. Are you and dad mad at me?"

"Jacob, why would we be mad? I was worried but I am so thankful that you didn't get hurt."

"I'm sorry. I didn't mean to cause any trouble."

"You didn't." Anne tipped her head to one side as she observed her son's anxious face. "Are you sure you're ok? "

"Sure. Just nervous for the game tonight. Are we eating supper soon?"

"Now there's my boy! Always wondering when his stomach will get fed. It will be ready in about 40 minutes. Your uniform is in the laundry room. You have to be there 30 minutes early to warm up?"

"Yeah. Thanks mom."

Anne got up and walked to the door. She turned and looked at her son staring at the ceiling. Something happened yesterday that he wasn't telling them about. She was going to have to get to the bottom of it. She didn't like to see her boy so distracted and obviously upset. Maybe she would talk to her brother. He and Jacob had always been buddies. Maybe Jacob would confide in him.

Jacob stared at the ceiling. He had to know if what he saw was real. Was there really a boy standing behind a glass window under the water in the lake behind the fence? If there was, why was he there? Did it have something to do with the Yellow Zone? The only way he knew to find out for sure was to somehow get back in that lake. But how could he do that with all of the guards? They probably were extra careful now to make sure that no one would get past the fence. There had to be a way. He would figure it out somehow.

*****

Lincoln had been walking for what seemed like hours. His hand was sore from running it along the wall to feel his way back home. He didn't know how long he had been gone and hoped no one had been looking for him. There weren't a lot of places to look for someone and they would know he had been wandering in the cave which was something that was not acceptable. He wondered where the entrance for the cave was and what time people came and left? It must be at night when everyone was sleeping so no one would ever question anything. He started making a plan to sneak out of the house to try to find out more information. There certainly wasn't anyone he could ask to help him. He thought again of the pendant the boy in the water was wearing. It was so familiar. But surely that was impossible. He didn't know anyone from outside their small town. Up until now, Lincoln didn't know if there were other towns like his or not. Now he had proof that indeed there were other towns. And they weren't underground. He started to wonder if the boy he saw was ok. By the look on his face, he had been very scared. Why had he been in the water in the first place? Other than an occasional fish or two, no one had ever seen anything in the water before. All of a sudden, Lincoln heard voices. He had been so deep in thought that he didn't notice he had almost arrived back at the town. Abruptly stopping, he stood very still hoping no one had heard him coming.

"Well, we have looked for him everywhere. It's so strange that he just disappeared. He has to be somewhere. I'll go back and check in with his mom to see if she has heard anything. I just hope he hasn't wandered into the cave. Some of these young folks are getting a bit rebellious. It's better for everyone if they just mind their own business and follow the rules." Lincoln recognized the voice of the man who ran the food market his mom worked at.

"It wouldn't take much to start some problems. It seems to me lately that people are getting restless. I think some of the townsfolk are going to start asking questions soon. I'm not sure what we will do then." As he turned to walk away, Lincoln could hear keys jingling on a keychain. It must be the town security officer. Lincoln always wondered why they needed a security officer when nothing bad ever happened in their small community.

The relief Lincoln felt by finding his way home and not being caught was temporary as he began to think of where he was going to tell his parents he had been for so long. Scanning the area around him, he ran along the back of the houses and through the neighbor's side yard to the main road. He didn't see his friend Simon watching him from behind the town's water tank. Simon knew everyone was looking for his best friend. He was afraid of the trouble Lincoln would be in when they found out he had been in the cave.

CHAPTER 5

It was the bottom of the 5th inning and Jacob was up to bat. Although his team was winning, his mind wasn't on the game. In the very top row of the bleachers was a man he had never seen before at any of his games. The sun was starting to set and it seemed strange that the man was still wearing his dark sunglasses. Jacob felt sure that the man was watching him. His team was cheering for him as he swung for his second strike. He could hear his dad telling him to keep his eye on the ball. It was a cool night but he could feel the beads of sweat on his forehead. He knew it wasn't from the weather. His anxiety about the stranger watching him was making him feel sick to his stomach. The next pitch nearly hit him in the leg and his delayed reaction caused him to almost fall over. He looked up into the bleachers. The man in the sunglasses had just a hint of a smile on his face. Jacob felt almost angry at the intimidation of this man. He hadn't done anything wrong. Why was he being followed and watched like some kind of juvenile delinquent? As the next pitch was thrown, Jacob put all his frustration and irritation into swinging the bat and he knew as it connected with the ball that it was going to bring home his teammate currently on second base. Jacob had hit the ball out of the park. It was only the second time he had ever accomplished that and even though his team was going crazy cheering and yelling along with the parents of the home team, he was distracted as he ran the bases. As his foot landed on home plate, he looked up into the stands to where the man with the sunglasses had been sitting. He was gone. His teammates were slapping him on the back and congratulating him. He tried to act excited and as normal as possible but all he wanted to do was go home.

Wray and Anne were watching their son as he ran from base to base. They looked at each other and knew they were both thinking the same thing. Something was definitely wrong with Jacob. It was something other than a sore ankle or being worried about being in trouble. What exactly had happened yesterday?

*****

Lincoln made it to the back of his house when he heard the neighbor, John, yell to him. "Lincoln, where have you been? Almost the whole town has been looking for you!"

Lincoln could feel his face turn red. He hadn't thought of what he was going to say yet. "I, uh, fell asleep behind Simon's house." He knew he sounded like he was lying. His brain was spinning trying to think of how to get out of this mess.

"Really? I thought we had looked everywhere. Funny no one saw you." John said suspiciously.

Lincoln was starting to feel anxious. He had never had to cover up something before and he wasn't sure how he was going to make a story believable. "Well, that's where I was. I guess I better go in and make sure my mom knows I'm home. "

"She is out looking for you. I would have thought Simon's house would be the first place she would've looked."

Frantic to get out of this conversation, Lincoln started to turn around to walk into his house when he heard Simon speak to the neighbor. "It's my fault. I knew where he was but I didn't say anything." Lincoln looked Simon in the eye and knew that he had seen him come out from the cave. He held his breath. Simon said, "He was sleeping in my backyard. No one probably saw him because I started building a fort back there and he was behind the supplies."

John shook his head. "You kids are getting more out of control every year. Your parents should rein you in a little." He turned and stalked away.

Lincoln watched as Simon walked closer to him. "So," Simon said, "Anything you want to share with your best friend?"

Lincoln just blinked a few times. He knew he could trust Simon with the truth. He just wasn't sure Simon would believe him.

"Come on, man! Nothing exciting ever happens around here. Where were you and what did you see in the cave?" Simon was looking at him with energy and excitement in his eyes.

"You're not going to believe me if I tell you."

"Why would I not believe you? You've never lied to me before. Is it something big? Are you in trouble with your parents?"

"No, of course not. You have to swear that no matter what, you won't tell anyone."

Simon's eyebrows drew together. "This sounds big. I don't understand. What could have possibly happened that is such a big deal?"

"Let's go inside. I don't want anyone to overhear."

They went inside the house and Lincoln checked to make sure his parents weren't home. Simon followed him into his bedroom and he closed the door and turned on his radio. He started talking really quietly so Simon had to lean in to hear him. "I went to the window yesterday. The water was pretty clear and I was just thinking about what's on the other side of that window. All of a sudden, the water got all...." Lincoln was waving his hands around. "It got all shook up. And I saw a boy. In the water." He looked at Simon's face. "See, I told you that you wouldn't believe me!"

Simon was slow to answer. "Soooooo, what happened?"

"He looked at me and his face looked scared. Then he just disappeared. Like someone yanked him up and then he was gone. I think he's from another town. A real town. On the outside."

Simon was staring at him. His mouth kept moving like he was about to ask a question but didn't know what to ask. Then he started shaking his head. "Are you sure? Maybe you dreamed it."

"No. I know it was real. That's why I went to the cave. I went to think about it and I started wondering if I might be able to find the way out."

"Are you crazy? What if they found you out there looking?"

"My flashlight went out and it was so dark. But I heard people talking about the boy. So I know it's real. They said they didn't think he saw anything but I know he saw me. What if he tells someone? What would they do to me? If I can get out for just a little while, I might be able to find him. And I might be able to see what's out there."

CHAPTER 6

There was a knock on Jacob's bedroom door. Jacob wanted to pretend to still be sleeping since he wasn't in the mood to talk to anyone. He was tired of everyone asking him questions and checking to see if he was ok. His Uncle slowly opened the door and stuck his head inside. "Hey, buddy. Your mom said you were still in bed. I've never known you to sleep past 7:00."

"I guess I'm just tired from that incredible home run I hit yesterday."

Richard smirked. "Yes, that was impressive. Your athletic skills obviously come from your dad. Your mom never could hit a baseball and she was afraid of getting hit in the face so she couldn't catch one either." He was trying to lighten the mood and hesitated before asking, "Can I ask you why you seem so distracted lately? You know you can talk to me about anything."

Jacob looked at his uncle. He did trust him and he really wanted to talk to someone. He kept quiet and looked down at the floor.

Richard sat on the edge of the bed. "You know you aren't in trouble about the lake. It was an accident. Wasn't it?"

"Of course. I already told you I was trying to get Bosco and fell."

"Then why haven't you seemed the same since it happened?"

34

Jacob looked around nervously. "Do you remember the man in the uniform from the Yellow Zone?"

"Yes. Commander Leclead. Why?"

"I'm pretty sure I saw him watching me at my game yesterday. And I thought I saw him watching me from a car when I was riding my bike with Mike."

"Really? Where was he sitting and what was he wearing?"

"The top row of the bleachers. He had on sunglasses and a hat so I couldn't really see his face. I know he was watching me though. I could feel his eyes on me. And earlier he was in an SUV parked outside the house part way down the hill."

Richard could see the anxiety all over Jacob's face. He could feel his own anger rising to the surface. Why would Leclead be watching his nephew? This was an open and shut case of simple, innocent, accidental trespassing. Why would the Yellow Zone still be concerned about it? He tried to look relaxed to put Jacob at ease. "Hey, buddy, I think you might be watching too many spy movies on tv. They would have no reason to keep an eye on you. I'll tell you what, you just relax and let me worry about everything. I will go by their offices later and make sure it's all wrapped up. OK?"

Jacob looked at his uncle with relief all over his face. "Thanks, Uncle Richie. That really would make me feel better."

"No problem. You just keep your focus on that winning streak in baseball." Richard reached over and messed up Jacob's already messy hair. He loved this kid and it angered him to see the stress he was feeling. Why in the world would they be watching Jacob? He would have to get to the bottom of it.

*****

Simon had not slept at all. He and Lincoln had been interrupted before Lincoln could give him any details. It was impossible to believe what he had been told. He knew his best friend would never lie to him though. He was a mixture of excitement and fear. Lincoln would be in so much trouble if they ever found out he had been in the cave. It was just an expectation that no one ever questioned. No one Simon knew had ever been there. Not even the adults. No one even talked about it. And seeing a boy in the water. That was just too much to take in. There was a sudden, quiet tapping on Simon's window. He knew without looking that it was Lincoln. He went to the window and slid it open. Lincoln climbed through and leaned on the wall as he glanced around the room. "Are your parents here?" Lincoln asked.

"No, they went to a meeting of some kind."

"Mine did too. Do you know what it's about?"

"No, I don't think they knew what it was about." Simon responded. "Why did you come to the window instead of to the door?"

"I didn't know if you wanted to talk to me after covering for me yesterday or if your parents would let me see you or not."

"Of course I want to see you! I have so many questions! I couldn't even sleep last night. Are you serious about all that stuff yesterday? I can't believe it! Start from the beginning. My head is spinning with so much information!"

"Yes, I am totally serious." Lincoln began to explain exactly what had happened and Simon just stared at him with his mouth hanging open.

Lincoln was glad he had someone he could tell his story to. But he wondered how much Simon really wanted to get involved. If anyone found out he was going to try to sneak out of the cave, there would be some pretty big trouble. He had wanted to try his plan to escape last night but his parents had been so worried when they couldn't find him yesterday that they had stayed up talking quietly most of the night. He had tried to listen in by the door but they were too muffled to hear this time. He was afraid that this town meeting the security officer had called on such short notice was probably about him. He promised Simon to keep him completely informed before he tried to do anything and left to go back home. If he wasn't in the house when his parents got home today, they might not be so understanding.

*****

The town meeting was just getting started and no one really knew why they had all been called together. The security guard was nervously jingling his keys. The mayor had not given him any indication of a problem so he was anxious to know what was going to be discussed.

"It has come to my attention that there has been an incident in the lake and there is talk of closing off the window." The mayor's statement was met with everyone talking at the same time.

"But that's the only light we get down here."

"We need more than clocks to tell us day from night."

"That's the only connection we have to our old lives."

"What kind of incident would close the window?"

The mayor held up his hand to try to silence everyone. "I know it seems extreme." He took a deep breath. He couldn't tell the people about the boy in the water because they didn't know there was life right outside their underground town. "I am doing everything I can to see that it remains open."

Samuel spoke up. "Sir, I think it would be very damaging to everyone's frame of mind to take away the window."

The mayor responded, "Yes, I agree, but it may not be our decision. The Yellow Zone has informed me of their request."

"Did they give you a reason why?"

"No. But I can tell you that I will do everything in my power to keep the window open. I just thought it would be best to hear it from me so you can prepare for the possibility of it happening."

The school teacher stood up and said, "Is there any news from the Yellow Zone about the outside? We haven't gotten an update in such a long time. Maybe it's safe for some of us to go check it out."

John stood up and said in a harsh, loud voice, "Maybe you all had better just settle down and quit asking so many questions. You know they will let us know as soon as they have new information. I think you should worry about keeping your kids under control and let the Yellow Zone worry about the outside." As he finished speaking and sat down, he looked directly at Samuel. Samuel was surprised at the look of disapproval on his neighbor's face.

*****

Richard sat down at the kitchen table with Anne and Wray and a cup of steaming coffee. He could see the concern on their faces.

"Did he tell you anything, Rich?" Anne asked with anxiety.

"No. He says he's fine. I think we all agree that he isn't telling us everything. Something happened the other day. I will tell you that I'm sure it was terrifying for him to be interviewed by the Yellow Zone. They are intimidating even for adults. But he does seem to be hiding something. Has he said anything at all to either of you?"

Anne and Wray exchanged looks and both shook their heads no.

Richard looked across the table taking turns looking each of them in the eye. "We need to keep a close eye on him. Something happened and he wants to tell someone. I don't anticipate any trouble, but if the Yellow Zone comes to talk to him, make sure you call me before you let them take him to ask any more questions."

Anne drew in a sharp breath. "Is that a possibility? Why would they need to talk to him again? Rich, should we be worried?"

39

"No, sis. Just be cautious."

*****

Lincoln heard his parents come home after their meeting but pretended to be asleep. He could hear them talking in hushed tones again. His heart was beating fast as he thought about how to get to the outside. At least now he could count on Simon to have his back. Did he dare put his best friend in such a dangerous situation? What if they got to the outside and couldn't get back in? He eventually fell into a fitful sleep filled with dreams of swimming underwater.

*****

Samuel and Clara sat close on the couch in order to speak quietly just in case Lincoln awoke so he couldn't overhear their conversation. Samuel felt like getting up to pace the floor but knew he had to remain calm. "I just know they are holding back information from us. Clara, what if we can go back? What if our families are still there? It makes absolutely no sense to close the only connection to the outside world. Something happened that they aren't telling us. But what would it have to do with the window?"

Clara sat slowly shaking her head as she thought about everything her husband was saying. Her hands were clasped tightly in her lap. Things were changing quickly and she had not let herself think about getting back outside in such a long time. Could she start letting herself hope again? "What do you think we should do?"

After sitting quietly for several minutes, Samuel got up and took a few steps before turning around to face his wife. "I am going to talk to the mayor tomorrow morning and request a meeting with the Yellow Zone. We need some answers and they are the only ones who know what those answers are."

Clara stood up and slowly let out a big breath as she wrapped her arms around Samuel. "It's time."

*****

Jacob stared out his window as he started planning in his mind how he was going to get back to the window. He couldn't remember where he had gotten into the fence so he certainly couldn't find the exact spot in the water either. If there was a window under the water that meant there was a room under the water too. There had to be a way to find that room without going in the water again. Tomorrow he would ride his bike around the wire to see if anything looked like a possibility. Maybe it was time to talk to his uncle. One more day and he would think about confiding in him. Until then, he would see what he could find out on his own.

CHAPTER 7

Richard had set a meeting with his Chief first thing Monday morning. As he waited outside the Chief's office, he thought through the last few days since his nephew had fallen into the lake. He didn't know much about the Yellow Zone. He had started working for the police department shortly after the plague had hit the area. Many people had fled or just seemed to disappear. The Yellow Zone had organized almost overnight. It took a few years, but things got back to normal and now no one gave much thought to it.

Chief Fletcher opened up his door and called Richard into his office. Richard sat on the edge of his chair as the Chief walked around the big desk and sat down. He leaned back in his chair and looked at Richard over the rim of his glasses. "So, I hear your nephew is the talk of the town."

Richard heard the teasing tone in the Chief's voice. They had always been friends and the Chief was proud of how hard Richard had worked over the years. He was an excellent officer and vigilant about things being done correctly.

"Yes, sir. I have to say, I am incredibly surprised at the procedures, or lack of procedures, that the Yellow Zone used while interrogating Jacob. They seemed overly edgy about the whole thing. I was just wanting your opinion about them and to see exactly what you know about them as a whole."

"Well, Richard, to be honest, they keep to themselves and we don't have that much interaction with them. It's always been kind of an unspoken rule that they mind their business and we mind ours. Personally, I have always thought they seemed a bit extreme."

"Have you ever seen them cross the line like they did with Jacob?" Richard asked as he leaned back in his chair anxious to hear the answer.

"No, I can't say that I have." Chief Fletcher responded.

"There is definitely something going on. I think we need to patrol the area more and see if we can hunt down some more information about who exactly they are."

"I agree. I'm on it. I'll let you know what I find out." The Chief let out a big sigh with a shake of his head. He knew the day would come when the Yellow Zone would become a problem. He supposed that day was today.

*****

Lincoln saw Simon at school across the yard. He hollered to him as he ran across the artificial grass in front of the school. Simon looked up in surprise as he watched Lincoln run over to him. He seemed really nervous and edgy. His eyes kept darting around as if looking to see if he was being watched. Simon leaned in so he could hear Lincoln as he spoke quietly. "Hey, I have a plan and I might need your help. I don't want you to get in trouble but I don't know if I can do it alone."

Simon got a big smile on his face. "I was hoping you would include me in this crazy adventure. You aren't going to do anything stupid though, are you?"

"I'm going to get out of here and find out what's going on out there. Let's meet up after school at my house and I will tell you my plan." He watched Simon as his eyes got a little bigger and he noticed his friend glancing around and biting his lip as if deep in thought. Lincoln said seriously, "I would understand if you just want to stay out of it. I can figure something out on my own."

"No way! I'm in. I'll see you after school. We're doing this!"

*****

As Jacob was walking in the hallway, an older kid bumped into him and knocked his folder with all of his science notes out of his hand. They scattered all over the floor. The two boys who were with the older boy laughed and stepped on his papers as they kept walking. Jacob bent down to pick up his now dirty notes and was happy to see Mike walk up to help him. Mike looked him in the eye and said, "Hey, are you still worried about that guy following you? Are you jumpy or just clumsy?" He said it with a bit of humor. He was worried about his friend and didn't like to see him so distracted.

Jacob chuckled, "I just wasn't paying attention and someone ran into me. I haven't seen that guy since my baseball game so I guess he got bored with me."

Mike was serious when he said, "I have been watching for him and I haven't seen him either. Don't worry, I've got your back."

Jacob smacked him lightly on the shoulder as they started back down the hallway, "I know you do and I appreciate it."

The teacher's voice seemed far off in the distance as Jacob sat in class staring at the wall and planning his night. Tonight was the night he would go out to look around the fence by the water. He had already found all dark clothes to wear and he knew with a storm coming in, it would be cloudy and dark.

*****

Wray and Anne were sitting at the kitchen table eating a quick lunch before Wray headed back to work. He didn't often get to come home for lunch but he fit it into his schedule so they had some time to talk about Jacob without worrying about him or Jillian overhearing their conversation. Wray leaned back in his chair and crossed his ankles in front of him. "He seemed okay at breakfast, don't you think? Maybe we are worrying too much. It was an intense ordeal for him but he's a tough kid and I think he seems better."

Anne got up to refill her husband's water glass and then kept pacing. "He's just not himself. He seems jumpy and nervous all the time. Sometimes he catches himself and tries to act fine but I know he's not. I just wish I could get my hands on that Yellow Zone official that was so awful. I would wring his neck!"

Wray just smiled at his wife. He knew she was overly protective of her family. He loved that about her but he also didn't want her losing sleep over it. He tried to reassure her by giving her a wink and a calm smile. "I think we just need to keep a close eye on him for a while. Watch his grades to make sure they aren't slipping. And make sure he still does what he enjoys like baseball and being with Mike and bugging his sister. Let's find out if your brother has heard anything new about the investigation." He got up from the table and went to his wife.

Anne leaned her head on her husband's shoulder and sighed. "You're right. Let's just give it a little more time. I'll check with Richie after he gets home from work tonight. Thanks for coming home for lunch. I packed you some brownies to take with you back to work."

Grabbing the little sack with the brownies, he chuckled as he said, "This is why I have to work out every day. I can't resist! Thanks. See you after work."

Long after Wray went back to work, Anne sat at the table trying to imagine what her son was feeling.

*****

Samuel sat in the front office of the City Hall waiting for the mayor to return. After several hours, Samuel left another message with the receptionist and headed back to work feeling frustrated about being ignored once again. His questions were adding up and he was beginning to realize that he was not going to get answers any time soon.

CHAPTER 8

Simon knocked on Lincoln's front door. He was excited to hear what Lincoln's plans were. Every day was the same and he was ready for some action. Something unexpected. Lincoln opened the door and looked around outside as Simon came in. He felt like everyone could read his mind and knew he was planning something but of course he knew that was ridiculous. Simon sat on the couch and waited for his friend to sit down. Lincoln paced the floor. He had been thinking about his plan and there were so many unknown obstacles. As he started laying it out for Simon, his emotions fluctuated between excited and nervous. After Lincoln explained it in detail, Simon went home and waited for the clock to reach midnight.

Lincoln had already made sure his flashlight had new batteries and he had an extra set in his pocket just in case. He didn't want a repeat of last time. He had heard his parents go to bed a few hours ago and it was so quiet in the house. As he crept toward the front door, the floor in front of the couch squeaked. It sounded so loud that he stopped and listened for any indication that one of his parents had heard it. After a few seconds, he finished his quiet journey out of the house. As planned, good old Simon was waiting for him by the large planter with a tree growing wildly out of it. Lincoln had never really noticed how creepy that tree was before. Although, he reasoned, he had never tried sneaking out of the house in the middle of the night before either. There weren't many places to hide or take cover but they did the best they could as they made their way to the edge of town. It was a good thing no one was allowed to keep a dog outside at night. One bark would have given them away.

As quietly as they could, they crept up to the window of the city hall. They had to find out how to get out of the cave and the mayor seemed like the most likely one to have the answers. It wasn't a big building but it seemed daunting in the quiet of night. They tried both doors and were not surprised to find them locked. Then they proceeded to go window to window hoping that one had been left unlocked. They were all sealed up tight. Not willing to give up so easily, they went back to the door which didn't face any houses. They had brought along a screwdriver and a small putty knife. Knowing they had to be quiet and not leave any traces of damage, Lincoln took the screwdriver out of his pocket and handed it to Simon. Simon tried to wedge it in the door frame but it was too big. He handed it back and took the putty knife from Lincoln's slightly shaking hand. The putty knife slipped between the door and the frame. Simon slowly slid it down around the door knob area. After what seemed like hours even though it was merely minutes, he felt a pop and when they tried the knob, it turned and the door opened! They quickly and quietly entered the building and shut the door behind them.

They got to the mayor's office and scanned the room. Lincoln pointed to the file cabinet and headed over to it while Simon went to the large desk in the center of the room. They each began rummaging through their allocated spots not really certain what they were looking for. Lincoln was surprised to see file folders with each resident's name that lived in the cave. He found the file with his name on it and quickly scanned it. There was every bit of Lincoln's history in it. How could they possibly know so much? It showed that he was born in a town called Lancer. How did they know where he was born? He didn't even know where he was born. How was it that it had never come up in conversation with his parents? He whispered to Simon, "Simon, where were you born?"

Simon quit sifting through the middle desk drawer for a second. He looked up to the ceiling as he thought about it before answering, "I think a town called Lance or something. Why?"

Lincoln held up the paper with his information on it. "Lancer? That's where I was born too. Crazy. Have you found anything yet?"

"No. Not yet. You?"

"They have everyone's information in here. They know everything about us. I wonder why?"

Simon suddenly gasped as he pulled his hand out of the drawer. He had jabbed his finger into a stack of thumb tacks. As he jerked his hand out of the drawer, he hit the inside top of it and felt it move. "Lincoln!" He said so loudly it sounded like it echoed in the room. They both stood still as statues for a few seconds before Lincoln shut the file cabinet drawer and went over to the desk. Simon knelt down as he pulled the drawer out as far as it would go. He reached up and moved the top piece around until it fell into his hand. A slip of paper floated to the floor. Lincoln quickly grabbed it and shined his flashlight on the number written in black ink. 190649. It had to be a code for getting out of the cave! It's exactly what they were looking for. They had already made the decision to memorize what they learned so there was no evidence to be found later. They both repeated it to themselves several times. Simon slid the paper back into the secret cubby and jiggled the secret door around until he felt it snap back in place.

Their hearts were pounding as they checked the room to make sure they hadn't left anything different than when they came in. They slipped out of the office and down the hall to the door they had entered. As they went back outside, they were surprised that the whole excursion had taken less than 20 minutes.

As Lincoln and Simon exchanged glances, they gave each other the thumbs up sign and Lincoln ran off into the cave while Simon hunkered down behind a sign with the town's warning of no trespassing outlined for everyone to see on the edge of town. Everyone knew you didn't go into the cave. It was not allowed.

*****

Jacob looked at the clock on his nightstand for what seemed like the hundredth time since he came to bed. His palms were sweaty and his stomach was in knots. He climbed out of bed just as a big clap of thunder shook the house. He jumped and almost yelled. What if the storm woke his mom up? She was always a light sleeper. He didn't know for sure but he imagined she probably came in to check on him whenever she woke up at night. As a quick after-thought, he grabbed the dirty clothes out of his hamper and wadded them up under the covers so it sort of looked like someone was laying in the bed just in case she did peek in. He quickly put on his dark clothes before he gave himself the chance to change his mind.

As Jacob snuck down the stairs, he heard a soft thud from his sister's room. Oh no! He didn't take into account that Bosco might hear him. Sure enough, after jumping off the bed, he came trotting to the staircase. His collar making slight jingling noises. He stopped and stared at Jacob. Jacob whispered quietly to him to go back to Jillian's room but as he continued down the stairs, he heard Bosco right behind him. He was so mad at himself for not thinking this through better. He hadn't even gotten out of the house yet and he was already messing up. After thinking about it for a minute, he just continued down the stairs and hoped the dog wouldn't give him away. Bosco followed him all the way to the side door where Jacob slipped out between the lightning flashes. Luckily, when he peeked in the window, he saw the shadow of a small dog heading back to the staircase. He grabbed the wire cutters he had hidden behind the wood pile earlier that day.

Jacob jogged along the houses to stay out of plain sight. It was so dark and he was already soaking wet from the huge drops of rain. He had to hurry because it was quite a way to the lake. He didn't dare take his bike because surely someone would see him.

Out of breath partly from jogging and partly from fear, Jacob was coming to the edge of the lake. He had to cross the street and it was well lit around the Yellow Zone. What was he thinking? He must be out of his mind to think he could get away with this. If he was caught, there was no telling what would happen to him. He thought back to the boy he saw behind the window. He had to continue on. He just had to know. He waited until the next big flash of lightning lit up the sky and it became dark again before sprinting across the street into the edge of the woods. His heart was pounding and he could feel his pulse in his eardrums. Starting along the inside of the trees, he snuck from tree to tree. The branches were wildly swinging and smacking into him. Fortunately, he had pulled his hoodie up to help from being seen so it was protecting him from most of the lashes.

As Jacob approached the lake, he was calculating how far it was to the window area. He would have to crawl quite a ways to reach it. The storm was getting worse and the wind was picking up. It was now or never. He took the first step out of the woods and was about to run to the fence when he felt a large hand cover his mouth and strong arms pull him back into the woods.

CHAPTER 9

Lincoln ran into the darkness until he started getting his sense of direction confused. He stopped and turned around to check if he could see anything from town. He could just barely make out a faint glow. He turned on the flashlight and waited for a few seconds to see if Simon gave him the signal that he could see it. No signal was given so he left the flashlight on and ran to where he remembered approximately where the door was. It seemed to take forever but he eventually found the door. Upon closer inspection, he found a keypad next to the door. With shaking hands and his heartbeat pounding in his ears, he entered the number they had found in the desk. 190649. He waited. Nothing. He tried it again. Staring at the keypad, he started wondering if he had remembered the number wrong. No. He was good at remembering things. He was sure he had it right. Maybe it was a number for something else. A safe or something. But surely it had to be the number to get out. He looked closely at the keypad. Maybe there was an enter button. No enter button but there was a star and a pound sign. He tried 190649*. Nothing. One more chance and then he didn't know what he would do. He hit 190649# and held his breath. The door handle made a buzz noise. He opened the door and stepped out into a drenching rain.

*****

Jacob was dragged a few feet back into the woods before a familiar voice said into his ear, "Are you absolutely out of your mind?" He was so relieved he almost cried. "Uncle Richie. What are you doing here?"

"What am I doing here? Saving you from the worst choice you've ever made, that's what!" Richard said angrily. He was upset with himself for not confronting Jacob earlier. He knew there was something wrong. He should have pressed him harder for more information before now.

"How did you know I was here?" Jacob was looking at his uncle and could see the anger in his face with each flash of lightning.

"Because I knew you were holding out on me. I was out patrolling and saw you leave your house. Do you have any idea what could have happened if anyone but me saw you?"

Jacob put his head down and shook his head feeling defeated. "I'm sorry."

Richard put his hand on his nephew's shoulder. "We need to get you home before anyone sees us."

Jacob knew he was in no position to argue with his uncle. As they started darting through the woods to head for home, they didn't notice that Jacob had dropped his wire cutters when his uncle had startled him. They lay on the ground at the edge of the woods with the lightning shining off of it with every flash.

*****

It was taking longer than Lincoln wanted for his eyes to adjust to being out of the cave. He had to try to get his bearings so he would be able to find his way back. As he turned around to look at the door he had just exited, he was thankful that he had thought through getting back in so he hadn't let the door close behind him. He looked around and found a small rock he could reach with his foot and he stepped on it to drag it closer. Reaching down, he grabbed it and put it at the bottom of the door and slowly let it close. It almost shut but didn't latch so he let out a big sigh of relief that it had worked like he planned.

His eyes slowly scanned the area. It was hard to see very far with the dark sky and rain hitting him in the face. Already drenched, he began to trek through the trees that were blocking his view of anything. He had only walked a few minutes when he came to a clearing. As the lightning lit up the sky, his mouth dropped open at the sight before him. A town sprawled out in front of him. There were buildings and houses and cars everywhere. He saw lights on in a few houses and the streets were lit up with lights on big poles. He had been right. There was life outside the cave. Now that he knew it for sure, he should turn back and get to the cave before too much time passed. But his curiosity was so strong that he couldn't help himself from squeezing through a small opening between a tree and a large metal fence. He ran out of the trees and across the street to one of the buildings that had lights on. Peering into the window, he noticed an elderly man lying in a bed watching a box that had moving pictures on it. Lincoln was mesmerized as the box showed a family sitting at a table eating dinner. When Lincoln returned his gaze to the elderly man, he was startled to see the man staring at him. The man lifted his hand in a sort of wave and Lincoln smiled at him and waved back. Just then, a woman walked into the room and spoke to the man. Before the woman could see him, Lincoln ducked down and raced along the building. As he came around the corner, he ran head on into a man that was about to enter the building by a side door. Looking up into the man's eyes, he felt all the air come out of his lungs and he felt dizzy. The man grabbed him by the arms to keep him steady and catch his balance.

"What are you doing out in this storm?" asked the man in a curious but not unfriendly way.

Lincoln took a step back, turned and ran in the opposite direction. He was certain he had just looked into his own father's eyes.

*****

As Wray entered the hospital, he was still somewhat stunned by the boy he had just seen. The poor kid looked like he had seen a ghost. He didn't have much time to think about it as the nurse came out of a room down the hall. "Doctor, Mr. Ellison still needs your attention but it's so strange, when I went into his room just a few minutes ago, he seemed to have turned a corner and was actually responsive and even smiling."

CHAPTER 10

Lincoln had slowed down to catch his breath. He was still shocked by what he had seen. Seeming unable to concentrate, he stopped to take note of where he was. He was on a street lined with houses. Some were completely dark while others had outside lights on and a few even had lights on inside. Realizing he had better get back to the cave, he started to jog back towards the woods. From the side of a house, a large German Shepherd came charging towards him barking loudly. Not knowing whether he should be more concerned about being attacked by the dog or of someone hearing the dog and coming to see what it was barking about, he started sprinting. Somewhat expecting to be chased by the dog, he ran full speed into the woods. It wasn't until he felt a slash across his cheek that he stopped running. He had been hit by a large tree branch and even though his adrenalin was pumping, it was enough to make him stop and catch his breath and take notice of his surroundings. The weather had started to calm down a bit and it wasn't lit up by lightning as much. Although it was still windy, it wasn't blowing quite so hard. Being pretty sure he was close to the cave entrance, he started paying more attention. He was just about to go through the line of trees to where he was certain he needed to go when he heard a tree branch break and heard voices. He stopped in his tracks and crouched down to the base of a large tree.

The Yellow Zone guard hated working during storms. He sang to himself to pass the time. Having to check the cave entrance was his least favorite part of the job. It was so dark and he was already soaking wet. He wanted to go back to base and get a cup of coffee. He just needed to check the door and he would be on his way. Just as he reached for the door handle, his radio went off.

Lincoln knew if the door was opened, the official would know it hadn't been shut all the way and would not only investigate it but would make sure it was locked when he left. If that happened, Lincoln wouldn't be able to get back in.

"Base to Yellow Three."

"Yellow Three here."

"We have a report of suspicious activity near the Southwest corner of the fence."

"Roger that. Will investigate right now. Out."

The guard quickly started heading in the direction of the reported activity. Lincoln was holding his breath as the guard went within 5 feet of him. Luckily there wasn't a flash of lightning or the guard definitely would have spotted him.

Lincoln ran to the cave door and remembered to move the little rock that kept it from shutting all the way. He made sure the door was secure before turning on his flashlight and heading for home.

*****

Jacob and Richard stood in the kitchen dripping wet. Jacob went into the bathroom to grab some towels to use to dry off. His mind was spinning over the events of the past hour. Just as they pulled out the chairs at the table, the light was turned on to brighten the room. Standing in the doorway in her bathrobe with her hands on her hips was Anne. Jacob and Richard exchanged glances knowing they were about to be bombarded with questions.

Slowly and deliberately walking over to the table to join them, she was taking in the scene sitting in front of her. She pulled out her chair, sat down and placed her hands on the table in front of her. "Which of you would like to start?" Anne asked with aggravation in her voice. She felt like they had been keeping secrets from her and she didn't like it one bit.

Richard held up his hands in defeat. "We were just getting around to discussing what happened. Maybe Wray should be here too." Richard looked over to see the worried look on his nephew's face.

"Wray was on call and had to go to the hospital. I don't know when he will be back so go ahead and start." Anne couldn't wait for her husband to get home. She was determined to find out why her brother and son were sitting at the kitchen table getting puddles all over the floor. This was the biggest storm they had had in many years. She was actually very surprised that the power was still on with all of the wind they received.

"Well," Richard started, "I was out on patrol when I spotted a certain young man crossing the street to head over to the Yellow Zone."

Anne could feel her face starting to flush. "No, you didn't." She looked over at her son who was staring at the table and whose hands were fidgeting in front of him. It was one of his nervous habits. He was wringing his hands together so hard she figured they would be hurting him soon if he kept it up.

After a minute with no response, Jacob finally looked up. His glance went from his mom to looking his uncle in the eyes. He started breathing a little faster. "I saw something."

Richard kept eye contact with him. "In the woods? It was pretty dark."

"No." Starting to rock forward and back just a little, he bit his lip. Another two of his nervous habits. What in the world was happening to her son? Anne looked at her brother and one look from him made her keep from asking questions. This was his territory. He knew what questions to ask. She trusted her brother one hundred percent. It was so hard to keep her composure when she could tell how visibly upset her boy was.

"No, not in the woods?" asked Richard.

"No, it wasn't tonight. It was on Friday."

Richard couldn't help but feel frustrated. He had known something was wrong the other day but he gave Jacob some time to come to him to talk about it. He should have pushed him harder and gotten some information from him days ago. "What did you see?"

"A boy. About my age."

"Where did you see him?"

"In the water."

Creasing his brow in confusion Richard asked quietly, "You saw the body of a boy in the water?"

"No. I saw a live boy behind a window under the water. And he saw me too."

After a few moments of startled silence, Jacob began telling them about chasing the dog under the fence, falling down the hill and ending up in the water. When he was finished with his story, they all just sat there looking at each other. No one knew where to go from here.

*****

Lincoln's dad, Samuel, was starting to pace frantically. He had woken up and been unable to fall back to sleep. After getting up to get a drink of water he quickly peeked into Lincoln's room. Lincoln had never given them any trouble at all. He was a good kid and they were so thankful for that. But lately he had been acting strange. Fidgety and unusually quiet and even a bit jittery. The bed was empty. Panic started to take over before he realized there weren't very many places he could have gone. It was extra concerning after the incident just a few days ago in which no one knew his whereabouts for quite some time. He had ended up being at Simon's house but it was after that when he started acting extra strange.

Not wanting to wake his wife because he knew how much she would worry, he quickly checked the house. There were not many places in the small structure for a boy to hide. He had known he wasn't hiding. He was much too old for those kinds of games. Quietly he left the house and began a search of the neighborhood. He was starting to feel discouraged when he spotted Simon sitting behind the No Trespassing sign at the edge of the cave. A quick sweeping glance of the area proved that Lincoln was not with him. With a feeling of dread, he quietly whispered Simon's name.

Simon whipped his head around and was relieved to see that it was Lincoln's dad.

Samuel could tell by the look on Simon's face that there was something wrong. "Simon. Tell me. Please."

"Lincoln found a way to the outside and he snuck out to see what was out there. He was supposed to be gone for just a short time but he's been gone for over an hour. Something went wrong."

His mind racing, Samuel tried to keep his composure. "Simon, I will stay here and wait for him. You need to get home before your parents notice you're gone. Lincoln or I will come to see you in the morning so you know he is ok."

"Ok. I'm sorry. I should have talked him out of it."

"Let's not worry about that. We both know Lincoln can't be talked out of much if he has his mind set on it. Make sure you are quiet so no one notices you going home."

After Simon left, Samuel sat down by the sign and stared out into the cave. The possibilities of what could have happened to Lincoln were scrambling through his already busy mind. How did he find a way out? And what was out there?

*****

Leaving the hospital, Wray was feeling upbeat about the quick turnaround of his patient. He was fearing the worst when he received the emergency phone call tonight. It wasn't until he walked out the door into the damp, foggy air that he remembered the boy that ran into him earlier. The rain had stopped and the road was littered with leaves and small tree branches. It was a little surprising that there hadn't been more damage from the strong storm. It was something to be thankful for. He wondered why the boy had been out in the rain. He had seemed to be in a hurry. As he pulled his car into the driveway, he was surprised to see the kitchen light on. He could see there were people sitting at the table. Since it was the middle of the night, he felt his pulse race thinking that there must be something wrong. He quickly put the car in park and ran into the house.

Sitting at the table were his wife, his son and his brother-in-law all looking shaken up and worn out.

*****

Lincoln could see the dim light coming from his town. He quickly turned off the flashlight as he kept jogging toward the light. He was so tired and sore. He wasn't used to running so far. As he came closer to the edge of town, he knew Simon would be upset at how long he had been gone. As he slowed down to a walk in order to catch his breath, he noticed a man standing where he had left Simon. Knowing he didn't have anywhere to turn and surely didn't have the energy to run again, he took a few more steps as the man started walking towards him. Relief washed over him as he saw his dad walking in his direction. Samuel grabbed him into a big hug for just a moment before pulling him back to arm's length. He reached into his pocket to grab his handkerchief and held it up to Lincoln's cheek. Reaching up to touch it, Lincoln began to realize his cheek was burning and when his father took the handkerchief off to get a closer look, Lincoln saw the blood and almost started feeling sick.

While applying pressure to the wound on Lincoln's cheek, Samuel quietly said, "Let's go home and get a good look at this." Eyeing him with concern, he added, "And have a little talk."

Walking silently together in the stillness of the small underground town, they both knew the day was going to be a long one. As they walked through the front door, neither of them noticed their neighbor, John, watching them through his dark window.

CHAPTER 11

Richard was waiting at Chief Fletcher's office when he arrived in the early morning hours. The Chief chuckled when he saw him and said, "Come on man, I haven't even had my coffee yet!" Seeing the seriousness on Richard's face, he quickly turned his full attention to what he had to say.

As Richard laid out the full story about his nephew and the prior evening, the Chief kept shaking his head in disbelief. How could this be happening in his town? He was supposed to be protecting the people in Blue Water.

After discussing their plans for over two hours, Richard left feeling relieved that they had decided how to proceed but very hesitant knowing they would receive plenty of resistance from the Yellow Zone. He fully anticipated a confrontation ahead.

*****

The Yellow Zone official was making his hourly rotation checks when he noticed the sun glinting off an object lying on the ground. Walking over, he reached down and slowly lifted the wire cutters from the grass. He wondered how long they had been lying there. Hesitantly turning them over in his hands, he didn't notice signs that they had been out in the elements for any length of time. There was no rust or built-up dirt. This was not good. The Commander would not be happy. It was his job to find anything or anyone suspicious and report it immediately. With a sense of dread, he carried the cutters with him as he checked the door to the cave and then headed to the Commander's office.

*****

Anne was busy finishing up folding a load of towels she had just taken out of the dryer when she heard a loud pounding on the front door. As she went to answer it, Jacob appeared at the top of the stairs and they made eye contact. "Jacob, stay upstairs. Call your dad." They had all been jumpy today and Wray had not wanted to leave for work but he had patients to see and there wasn't anything they could do until Richard had talked to the Chief.

Opening the door, Anne stood looking through the screen door at a very stern-faced man. "Mrs. Lindstrom?" the man demanded in a powerful voice.

"Yes. And you are?"

"Lieutenant Commander Ellison of the Yellow Zone. I need to speak to your son." He leaned toward the door in an intimidating manner.

"Well, you will have to do that with my husband and brother present." Anne knew her voice sounded shaky but she was surprised with her courage to talk to him instead of closing the door in his face.

"I don't have time for games Mrs. Lindstrom. I have reason to believe that your son planned to use these wire cutters to vandalize and trespass on Yellow Zone property." He held up the wire cutters and although she couldn't be sure they belonged to

66

her husband, she did know he had a pair just like them. She started feeling her heart beat harder.

"Ok. Well, you can discuss it when my husband and brother get here. If you give me just a minute, I will call them."

In a demanding, loud voice he replied, "Your son needs to come with me NOW!" He reached for the door knob.

In a quick movement, Anne shut the door and locked both locks as the Commander started pounding on the door.

Jacob came running down the stairs after hearing the conversation that just took place. He was relieved to look out the front window and see that his uncle had arrived in his squad car. Looking into his mom's pale face, he walked over to her and said, "That's the man that pulled me out of the lake."

*****

The mayor was in his office sitting at his desk when he received a phone call from the Outside. They thought there may have been an attempted breach of the Yellow Zone perimeter. As he was discussing the potential threat to their community, he noticed a small, dark spot on the top of his desk. It looked like a drop of something. He rubbed it gently and held his finger up. It looked like blood. Why would there be blood on his desk? Opening his desk drawer, he felt for the secret door. He maneuvered it open and pulled out the piece of paper with the door code on it. In the top corner of the paper was a smudge of blood. Leaning back in his chair, the mayor started rubbing his jaw. Their time in the cave may be coming to an end. He made a phone call and began the process to cover up the window.

*****

Clara heard a knock on the door. She started wringing her hands together. There was so much going on right now. She had been so startled to see Lincoln after Samuel woke her last night and gave her a brief rundown of what had happened. They had agreed that she would stay home with Lincoln today. Samuel was working on a plan but it would look too suspicious if both of them stayed home. She went to the door and slowly opened it just a small bit and looked out. Their neighbor, John was at the door.

"Hi Clara! How are you today?" He asked cheerfully.

"I'm just fine, John. How are you?"

"Doing well. I'm surprised to see you home. You don't have to work today?"

"No. I took a day to get caught up around here. Can I help you with something?"

"Well, I was wondering if I could talk to Lincoln?"

Trying to keep her hands from shaking, she clasped them together in front of her. "I'm sorry, John, but he is still sleeping. He is feeling a bit under the weather today. I can sure give him a message for you though."

From behind his closed bedroom door, Lincoln was listening to his mom's conversation with the neighbor. The stinging pain in his cheek gave him a constant reminder of why he had to stay hidden. There would be no way to explain how he had

68

received the cut on his cheek from the tree branch. His dad had stitched it up but it would take time to heal.

John's eyes narrowed as he glared at her. "No message. I will be back shortly to talk to him. It's important."

Closing the door to John's retreating back, Clara began to pace the small space of their living room. As Lincoln opened the door to look out at her, she glanced up and in a quiet voice said, "Lincoln, I think we had better start packing up a few of our things. We are going to have to leave sooner than we thought." Clara went to the closet and took out a duffle bag. She was going to have to make some quick decisions of what was important enough to take into their new life. Digging into the back of the bottom drawer of her dresser, she pulled out a picture of a family gathering from over a decade ago. She would give anything to talk about her troubles with her best friend and sister-in-law. She still felt such a deep ache at the loss of their family and everyone else that was so dear to them.

*****

Simon had gone to school that morning after a quick talk with Lincoln's dad. Lincoln had made it back safely but had cut himself so he had to lay low until his parents could figure out what to do. Simon still couldn't believe Lincoln had made it to the Outside. He had so many questions for him but he had to act like everything was normal. As he walked to school, he heard some commotion over by the park. Taking the long way around the town, he saw some of the neighbors boarding up the window. He walked close enough to overhear their conversation.

"I don't know. It's by order of the mayor."

"It doesn't seem right that they can just close and cover up the only real light we get. Not even an explanation for it."

"Especially after that meeting last week. Everyone seems to be so edgy lately. It makes you wonder what exactly is going on that we don't know about."

Simon began to sweat. Did the Mayor find out they had been in his office? That was impossible. They had been so careful. Interrupting his thoughts, he realized someone had been talking to him.

"Simon, you are going to be late for school. Better get a move on. When you see your dad, would you tell him that some of us would like to talk to him?"

"Um, yeah, sure." He turned and quickly started walking to school.

*****

John walked into the mayor's office without knocking. "Mayor, we might have a problem."

The mayor frowned and replied, "Tell me something I don't already know."

John started telling him about seeing Samuel and Lincoln walking into their house in the middle of the night. "It just seemed suspicious to me. I think that kid is trouble. He is the one who went missing last week then out of nowhere just showed back up."

Crossing his arms over his chest, the mayor sighed deeply and said, "John, I think things are about to get interesting. Stay in touch. Things will move fast."

Nodding in agreement, John turned to leave the office mumbling to himself, "That's what I was afraid you would say."

*****

Staring out of his bedroom window, Jacob was worrying about what would happen to him if the Yellow Zone was allowed to take him from his house? He didn't want to go back to that interrogation room. And he couldn't tell them the truth about what he had seen. Even his uncle agreed that the Yellow Zone had to know about what was under there. That must be what they have been protecting all these years. He had to trust that his uncle and the Chief would work out a plan.

Coming into his room, his mom handed him his phone. "I heard it ringing. It looks like Michael has been trying to call you. Go ahead and call him back."

Looking at the clock, he realized that he and Mike would normally be at lunch right now. Assuming that he was in school, he called quickly before class started. Mike answered on the first ring. "Hey! Where are you?"

"I had kind of a long night." Jacob quickly gave a run down on the prior evening.

"Oh my gosh! You must be kidding! I'm coming over right after school to get all of the details."

71

"No. You better not. The Yellow Zone officials have been here already. I don't want you to get involved and have them on your case. Call me tonight and I'll give you an update."

"Don't let them intimidate you. Stay strong. I will call you later."

"Thanks. Later."

*****

Telling his staff he was going home for lunch, Samuel left his office and went home to make some final plans to get Outside. He was shocked to walk through the door and see that three bags were already packed and ready to go. Clara met him at the door almost in tears. "We have to leave now. John came over and was acting really strange wanting to talk to Lincoln. He said he is going to come back soon. What would I tell him? We need to go."

Putting his hands on his wife's shoulders, Samuel spoke calmly, "Clara, we need just a little more time. We can't leave in the middle of the day. Someone would see us and stop us."

Lincoln walked into the room. "Did you talk to Simon's parents this morning?"

"Yes. They know the plan and they will be prepared. I will try to think of some way to leave early. Be ready to go the second you get my signal."

Lincoln and Clara nodded in agreement. Hugging his wife as he slowly scanned his home, he knew they had slept their last night underground.

CHAPTER 12

Richard and Chief Fletcher had their team all set to go. They had put in a request with the state agency for a team of divers who had just shown up. Richard had no doubt they were about to find this window his nephew had described to them. As the team pulled up to the area in front of the lake, they were shocked to see the whole fence being protected by armed Yellow Zone guards.

Chief Fletcher glanced at Richard and they knew they were in for a confrontation. The Chief slowly exhaled and said, "Richard, stay in the car unless you see me signal. Make sure everyone knows to stand down. We don't want this getting out of control and it looks like it wouldn't take much for that to happen."

"You got it Chief. Be safe out there. I got your back." Richard responded as he watched the Chief get out of the car and head to the row of guards.

Richard noticed that as the Chief walked forward, a man in uniform started walking up to him from the South area by the tree line. Not completely surprised, he recognized Commander Leclede. The Chief handed him the search warrant for the lake and surrounding area. Not even looking at it, the Commander folded it and put it in his front shirt pocket. The Chief slightly shook his two fingers toward the ground. That was the signal for the team.

Piling out of their vehicles, all of the officers took their positions. Some were behind the stationary vehicles, some were fanning out toward the North and South.

The Yellow Zone guards lifted their weapons in response. The tension in the air was felt by everyone. Not sure who would be the first to make a move, the officers were taken by surprise when dozens of dark SUV's came roaring up behind them and more Yellow Zone guards took up position against them.

Making eye contact, Chief Fletcher and Richard knew they were outnumbered 4 to 1. They had no idea there were so many Zone officials. They must have been brought in from everywhere. They didn't have knowledge of other areas with a Yellow Zone presence. Nodding his head, the Chief turned to speak to Commander Leclede. After a brief exchange, the Chief headed back to the car where Richard waited.

Signaling his officers to cancel the mission, he climbed angrily into the car slamming the door behind him. As Richard drove away, the Chief called into the state requesting the aid of SWAT and the National Guard.

They would be back. And they would be ready for anything.

*****

From their front window, Jacob and his mom were watching the two cars placed in the street just outside their house. One on the top of the hill and one on the bottom. Anne didn't say anything to Jacob but it angered her that they weren't even trying to be discrete about it. She had called Wray and he just reminded her that no one was to go out or be let in. Luckily Jacob's sister, Jillian, had not minded being in her room instead of going to school today. She said it felt like a free sick day without being sick. Knowing how anxious her son must be feeling, Anne sat on the couch with her back to the window. "Dad will be home soon and Uncle Richie knows how to handle all of this." Trying to distract him, she started to talk about his baseball team and school and even though she knew she was rambling on and he wasn't really listening, she didn't know what else to do.

*****

The Mayor and John were pounding on the door. Clara and Lincoln stayed quiet on the other side. Peeking out the window from the other room, Clara could see that they had the town security officer with them. Uncertain how to keep them from breaking down the door, she was surprised to hear a ringing sound followed by the mayor's voice. After just a few brief words, everyone left quickly. Just as she started to relax, Clara heard a key in the door. Feeling panic sweep over her, she was filled with relief when Samuel walked through the door.

"I saw the mayor, John and Bill just leave. They were in a hurry somewhere. Luckily, I had seen them by the house and hid so they didn't notice me. Grab your bags, we have to leave right now. I'm afraid this may be our only chance."

Grabbing their duffle bags and backpacks, they all quickly scanned the home they had lived in for over a decade. Not having the time to even go over their plan one more time, they opened the front door, checked to make sure no one was around and all started running for the dark cave. It soon became so dark they had to stop and get out their small dim light. Since Lincoln had been here twice already, they let him lead the way while staying close together.

*****

The mayor had just gotten word from the Commander that Operation Relocate was to be set in motion. Rushing back to his office, the mayor gave John his orders. Sitting at his desk he put his head in his hands and started rubbing his temples. There was no going back after this. Knowing he had no choice, he got the key out of the back of his desk drawer and walked over to the picture of a mountain that was hanging on the wall beside his filing cabinet. Taking a moment to stare at the picture for the last time, he remembered leaving his home near that beautiful mountain to come and be in charge of the town. Shaking his head to clear his mind he refocused on the task at hand. This was not going to be easy.

He took the picture off the wall and using the key he had retrieved from his desk, he opened the small safe. Without hesitating, he pushed the red button inside the safe and could hear the alarm go off from every corner of the cave.

*****

Surprised to hear the town alarm, the people gathered in the City Hall conference room. They were talking among themselves trying to figure out what the emergency would be. The only other time they had been summoned here was during a fire at the cafe but that was quickly extinguished and they were able to leave in a short time. The room was air tight and fire proof and was considered to be a complete safe zone.

John was in the corner of the room taking inventory of each town member. A few people were still wandering in. All of the children from school were accounted for except Lincoln and John knew he had been home today. Scanning the room, he started specifically looking for Lincoln and his parents. He saw the staff from the clinic and asked the nurse where Doctor Samuel was. She said he had left the clinic shortly before the alarm had gone off.

Leaving the conference room, John radioed the mayor and told him everyone was accounted for except Samuel, Clara and Lincoln.

The mayor responded, "Go to their house and get them to the conference room within five minutes or you will have to get rid of them by any means necessary."

"Understood." John answered as he left City Hall.

*****

The only one in the room who wasn't completely surprised by the commotion was Simon's dad, Ron. After his conversation the morning with Samuel, Ron knew something was going on. He had been feeling apprehensive about the town lately. When he saw them boarding up the window, he knew things were about to change. He had told Simon to quietly prepare to leave at a moment's notice if necessary. Samuel had promised he would be back with help.

Ron noticed Simon had been reaching into the pocket of his jacket all morning. He didn't know that inside that pocket were 4 blades of grass that Simon had found inside of an envelope taped to his window that morning.

*****

Calling everyone to attention, the mayor asked people to take a seat and the meeting would begin shortly. Gesturing to the security guard and looking at his watch, the mayor walked out into the hallway and the officer shut the door behind him.

Radioing John, the mayor demanded, "Where are you? Time's up!"

Sounding out of breath, John answered, "They're gone. I've looked everywhere."

"Well, we don't have more time. If you find them, you know what to do."

"Yes, Sir."

Getting a cell phone out of a pocket inside his suit jacket, the mayor made a call. "Commander, Operation Relocate ready for Phase Two."

Each going to their own homes to pack a few personal belongings, they were not in the building when Ron tried to leave the conference room to find the mayor in hopes of asking some questions. Both doors out of the conference room were locked. Ron started banging on the door and hollering to the mayor.

When he turned around to look at his neighbors for their thoughts on being locked in, he saw some of the children with their heads bobbing down like they were falling asleep. Everyone's eyes were getting really heavy and some were laying on the ground. He ran over to an air vent and tried to cover it with his shirt. Before he could really get a grasp on what he was seeing, he started concentrating on making himself breath very slowly. The last thing he remembered was looking over to see his son laying on the ground next to the school teacher.

*****

Lincoln was at the keypad and had tried the code 4 times. He remembered that he had to push the pound sign but it still wasn't working. Looking at his dad, Lincoln's eyes held fear.

"It's ok. I was wondering if they would change the code. I'm sure they know about us missing by now. Let's just think this through for a minute. Obviously, we can't go back at this point." Samuel said calmly.

Seeing the hint of a light in the distance, they knew someone had come looking for them. Staying together, Samuel led the way using the wall as his guide. He tried to get as far away from the door as possible before they were seen.

Getting as far as they thought necessary, they all laid on the ground to be less visible if someone were to shine a light around them.

Hearing the sound of buttons being pushed, they almost gasped when after the click of unlocking, the door opened and sunlight streamed into the cave. They noticed John standing in the doorway looking around outside. His voice echoed in the cave as he spoke, "No sign of them outside. How should I proceed?"

The mayor answered, "Keep looking. And if you find them, make sure they don't leave your sight."

Continuing to stay low to the ground and trying to figure out a plan, Samuel, Clara and Lincoln were taken by surprise when the door opened and dozens of people in gray uniforms came running in and headed toward town. Once it was quiet for several minutes, they began to whisper to each other. Getting the code from Lincoln, Samuel snuck back to the door and tried the code again. He tried the door handle. Starting to hear voices carrying through the cave, he ran back to his family and they snuck deeper back along the wall.

The uniformed officials were coming back and each official had one of their neighbors thrown over their shoulder.

*****

Ron could feel his body being jostled around. He was feeling so groggy. Trying to open his eyes, he remembered being in the conference room and knew that he had to remain still so the person carrying him didn't realize he was almost awake. Opening his eyes just a slit, he realized it was dark but not the kind of dark from town. It was really dark. All of a sudden, a bright light assaulted his eyes and he closed them tightly. It was a brightness he wasn't used to. And he could feel air on his skin and smell things he hadn't smelled in a very long time. It smelled like grass and trees. Getting more familiar with the light, he peeked his eyelids open a crack and looked around without moving his head. He saw behind him a man carrying his neighbor. They were quickly making their way through some woods and no one was speaking. Considering their heavy loads, the officials were barely making a sound. Ron knew this was part of a plan. They were being taken from their homes. Feeling his mind getting foggy again, he closed his eyes and tried to memorize the sounds and smells around him.

*****

Once everyone had been removed from the conference room, the mayor got the order from his Commander. He and John started taking the files from the file cabinet and removing all of the information from his office. As they were leaving the building, he radioed headquarters and gave the all clear to begin Phase 3. Without speaking, John and the mayor left the town behind and followed the beam from the flashlight to the door. Neither of them realized they were about to come across some familiar faces.

*****

Knowing they didn't have much chance to get out of the cave, Samuel, Clara and Lincoln thought about heading back to their home to see if they could come up with another plan. Getting close to the door, they saw the flashlight shine and they rushed forward to get to the door. Just as the Mayor and John opened the door to the bright sunshine, they noticed Samuel rushing towards them. They got out of the cave and had the door securely shut just before Samuel reached them.

John spoke with some satisfaction, "Well, that made it easier to know they will be taken care of."

The mayor sighed deeply. "Yes, I believe you are right."

*****

There was a loud beeping noise off in the distance. It was coming from town. No one was there to see it, but as the time ran down, the underwater window began to crack. As it broke, the water started rushing in and washing everything toward the back of the cave. Samuel heard it first and grabbed his wife's hand. Yelling at Lincoln to run, they all started running as far away from the door as they could. The dim light from Lincoln's flashlight bounced off the ground. They didn't have any idea how far back they could go but they ran as fast as they could. They could hear the sound of rushing water closing in on them.

*****

Chief Fletcher just received notification that the National Guard had been deployed and SWAT would be arriving shortly. He and Richard headed back to the lake. Upon arrival, they were confused by the lack of Yellow Zone officials. In fact, there were none. As Richard stepped out of the car, he was aware of a vehicle coming up behind them. Turning to see who it was, he looked through the front windshield into the face of Commander Leclede. He had a smug half smile on his face. He got out of his SUV and walked up to Richard and the Chief. Just as he was about to speak, the National Guard troops arrived from every direction along with the SWAT team. The Commander waved his hand in the air toward the lake. "Be my guest." He stated with some amusement in his voice. He turned and got back into his vehicle and drove away.

Immediately Chief Fletcher called in the divers. Within moments the area was a swarm of activity. The National Guard started searching the surrounding land. Richard had a bad feeling about this. Why would the Commander just walk away after such a big show of power earlier? It made him even more certain there was something very serious going on around here.

*****

Samuel could feel the water around his ankles and he fell forward. The water was rising quickly and there was so much debris being forced at them. Lincoln was a few steps ahead and just as the water was about to take him over, his flashlight shone on a ledge in the wall. He yelled to his parents as he jumped toward it. Clara started to move in the direction of the beam of light when she got hit in the back of the leg with a large piece of wood. It knocked her over and the water engulfed her. Samuel lunged toward her as a metal post from a fence smashed him in the shoulder. He was able to get his bearings back in order to pull his wife from the water. He started making his way toward Lincoln who propped the flashlight up against some items he had pulled from the water. He jumped back in the water to help his dad get his mom safely up on the ledge. Once they were all on the ledge, they watched as the water kept rising. They were seeing items from their town being swept by in the current of water. Not sure how much time they had before the water might overtake them, they looked around for items that might be used to float on. Just as they were about to give up hope of finding something and as the water was almost to the ledge, they noticed that the water had started to level off and wasn't rushing at them as fast. Using the extra time they had been given and not knowing what lay ahead, Samuel quickly looked over his son and wife. Asking if they were hurt, he received a shake of the head from Lincoln. "I'm ok, dad." Looking at his wife, he noticed her face was pale. She glanced down at her leg where she had gotten hit by the piece of wood. It was deeply cut and bleeding intensely. Taking quick action, Samuel removed his shirt and felt around her leg for breaks. He had Lincoln hold the flashlight on her leg as he tied the shirt around the cut and held pressure on it. Just as they were about to be relieved that the water wasn't rising any longer, Lincoln's flashlight went out.

*****

After a long exploration of the water and surrounding area, the teams had come up with nothing. This did not come as a surprise to Richard. But that was impossible. He had no doubt that his nephew's story had been accurate. If it had not been, the Yellow Zone wouldn't have been covering the area so well earlier. But how could they move a window? That didn't make any sense at all. After a discussion with the Chief, they agreed there was no reason to keep everyone here. The National Guard and SWAT were dismissed. Unwilling to leave the scene, Richard stayed and continued to walk around thinking about the possibilities of the window.

CHAPTER 13

As the Townspeople began to come to, they groggily woke to find themselves in a big metal building. There were cots set up where each person had been laid down. It was a large area with bedding on one side and a kitchen with tables and chairs on the other. A few people started wandering around to see if there was a way out. The kids started gathering to talk about what they thought had happened. Simon just sat on his cot staring off into the distance. He was worried about Lincoln. Had he and his family made it out safely? He reached into his pocket to feel the grass Lincoln had left for him. He knew Lincoln would try to find him. If he was able to.

Ron pulled aside a few of his most trusted neighbors to begin the long explanation of what he knew and what he had seen as they left the cave. He was surprised at how many of the neighbors expressed their recent concerns that things had noticeably changed and there had been a restlessness among them to start getting answers. They all agreed to take things slowly and not to openly talk about their plans. Someone or possibly many among them could not be trusted. He warned them all to watch out for their neighbor John. No one had seen him since being in the building. After his strange and aggressive behavior with Simon, Ron knew he was definitely a part of whatever events were happening.

*****

Richard was sitting in the kitchen at his sister's house. She was trying to insist that he eat something but he could hardly get any food down. Jacob was sitting across from him replaying everything he knew as requested by his uncle. It was frustrating for Richard to have been so close and come up empty handed. Surely he was missing something. As Jacob was again describing the boy he had seen in the window, he noticed his dad's forehead was creased and his eyes were squinting as if to see something. Richard noticed it too.

"Wray, what's up?" asked Richard.

"Hearing Jacob describe the boy made me remember something. The other night when I was called in for an emergency at the hospital, a boy came running around the corner of the building and ran right into me. When he looked at me it seemed like he might have recognized me. I thought it was just a friend of Jacob's or one of the kids from baseball but now that I think about it, he did look like the boy Jacob is describing. It didn't make sense why he was out in the storm."

Richard leaned back in his chair and bounced his leg up and down which was an old habit when he was concentrating. Crossing his arms across his chest, he reached up to scratch at the stubble on his face that had been growing for several days because he was too impatient to shave in the hurry to get back to work. "How did he get out?" Tapping his index finger against his lips, he looked at his brother-in-law. "Which way did he go after he ran into you?"

Wray looked from Jacob to Richard. "He ran in the direction of the woods. By the lake."

Richard jumped up from the table. After reminding everyone to stay put and not let anyone in, he ran out the door and with lights flashing on top of his car, he headed for the lake.

*****

It was complete darkness in the cave. Lincoln could hear his parents breathing. It had become quieter once the water had quit rushing around and hitting items into each other.

"I'm not totally surprised that the mayor had something to do with this. I should have acted sooner on my suspicions. I need to see if I can find a way out of here." Samuel said.

Clara was concerned. "You don't know what's in the water and it's so dark you might not be able to find your way back."

"I'll be fine. Your voices should carry pretty far in here. I'll stay by the wall and see how far back it goes. Lincoln, no matter what, stay with your mom."

"I will. Be careful." Lincoln reached over to his dad. Once he could feel his shoulder, he squeezed it and felt his dad's hand cover his in a protective gesture.

After kissing his wife and feeling her leg for swelling, he felt around to the edge of the ledge and slowly slid into the water. Keeping his hand on the wall, he began his journey further back in the cave in hopes of finding a way out.

*****

Two members of the Yellow Zone were continuing their orders with closing out Phase 3. They had quietly snuck back to the entrance of the cave and were starting to put the explosives near the door. They were just about finished when they began to hear voices and quickly tried to sneak off in the opposite direction. One of Richard's officers heard the break of a twig and took off in the direction it came from. After a few minutes of chasing them through the woods, the officer caught one of them. Richard had moved his search from concentrating mainly around the water to further into the woods and it looked like it had already paid off. With one Yellow Zone official in custody, Richard's team continued to search for the other one that had gotten away from them.

After interrogating their suspect for over 30 minutes, Richard knew he was wasting his time. They had found explosive equipment on him. Since Richard didn't know if there had been other YZ officials sent for this same task that may be more successful, he immediately called in the bomb sniffing dogs.

It took no time at all for the dogs to trace the explosive site. It was hard to imagine that there was a door right here in the middle of the woods. It was so camouflaged that it was doubtful anyone would ever have come across it. After dismantling the bomb, they got a team in to get the door open.

No one could have guessed what they were about to see when they opened the door.

*****

Simon and his dad sat at one of the tables in the kitchen area of the huge building where they were being housed. There was no way out. All of the doors were securely locked. It made no sense. A few of their neighbors were starting to get edgy and nervous. No one was in charge and it was quickly getting out of control with theories and guesses as to what was going on.

Ron moved his chair closer to his son. In hushed tones he said, "Simon, you have to be prepared to move and go when I give you a signal. I don't know when it will be but I know the opportunity will come. Look at me." Ron put his right hand on his left shoulder and slid his hand down to his elbow and back up to his shoulder. "That's the signal. You got it?"

"Yes. I'll be ready. Will it be everyone or just us?"

"I don't know yet. We have to be prepared for anything." Ron met his son's eyes. "We're in this together."

Simon's face showed some signs of relaxing finally. He gave his dad a partial smile. Slightly nodding, he said, "I know. And we'll be fine."

*****

The team swung the heavy door open and shined light inside. It was a huge cave that went well beyond the ray of light. Everywhere the light shined was water. Why would they try to explode a door to nothing? Standing in the doorway, Richard caught sight of something in the water. Reaching down to grab it, he stood up holding a baseball cap.

Radioing to the chief, he arranged for the dive team to come to the scene. He was unsure where this would lead. It must be important if the Yellow Zone was willing to destroy all traces of it.

Richard leaned into the frame of the door. He could swear he heard voices. Unsure if he was making too much of the baseball cap, he hollered into the dark water, "Hold on! We are on the way to help you!" Why would a ball cap be in the water if there were no people down here?

*****

Lincoln yelled to his dad to make his way back to the ledge. They had seen the glow of a light in the distance. They thought they heard someone say something from far away. Lincoln continued to talk loudly so Samuel could follow his voice back toward them. They didn't know whether to be relieved that someone might come to help them or to be nervous that the mayor and John might be coming back to take them where they had taken their neighbors. Or were they coming back to get rid of them since they knew too much?

*****

The dive team had inflated several boats and Richard occupied one of them as the team slowly made their way into the dark abyss. With plenty of lighting, they could now make out the scene further in front of them. Everyone was shocked to see all of the items floating in the water around them. Thankfully no one had spotted any bodies yet. Where did all of this come from? It was piece after piece of household items and parts of houses.

91

Parts of tables and articles of clothing. They slowly made their way through the debris. Continuing to call out at regular intervals, they would then be still and listen for an answer. The boats split up to cover different directions. Richard's boat slowly made its way following along the cave wall. The water seemed to be getting deeper and the debris was becoming harder to navigate through. With a gasp, one of the divers pointed at a doll floating on the water. Deciding to stop and investigate further, the divers put their remaining gear on and slipped into the water. Richard stared into the water at all of the items. It looked like the remains from houses. It made sense that what Jacob had told him about seeing the boy was indeed true. He must have lived down here. But why couldn't they find the window from the lake?

*****

Samuel, Clara and Lincoln sat on the ledge and started hollering louder as they could see lights heading their way. As the lights came closer, a sudden beam of bright light fell right on them and within minutes there was a boat just ahead of them. Relief washed over all of them when they realized that they were going to get out of the cave. Lincoln was going to see the trees again. And feel the rain. Maybe the sun would shine and he could walk on the grass and see the stars in the sky when it was not flashing with lightning. But no matter what, he would find the boy he saw in the window and make sure he was ok.

*****

Richard received a radio call from one of the other boats. They had found three people. One was in need of medical attention for a wound on her leg. So, he hadn't imagined hearing voices. There were indeed people down here.

Richard answered the call, "Attention all who are on this call. No one is to know this information. Do you understand? As far as anyone knows, we don't even know this place exists."

Everyone responded in agreement.

CHAPTER 14

Jacob was pacing the floor in his room. He was going crazy not being able to leave the house. He checked out his window and it appeared as if the cars that had been watching the house had left and not been back in several hours. His parents had gone to bed hours ago. He had tried to sleep but there were so many questions in his mind he couldn't rest. He grabbed his baseball from the corner of his room and went downstairs. Laying on the couch, he tossed the ball up in the air catching it as it came back down. He had to smile when he thought of all the times his mom got after him for doing it. She always told him he was going to miss the ball and it would knock his teeth out. Holding the ball and rolling it around in his hand, he eventually began to get tired and started to doze off.

*****

As Richard stepped back into the woods from the cave, he saw the family sitting on the ground looking around in wonder. Richard walked over and introduced himself. It was interesting to him that they seemed so familiar. Almost as though he knew them. That was a crazy notion since they had literally been living in a cave.

"I know you have just as many questions as I do, but I think the first thing we need is to get you somewhere safe to get out of those wet clothes and check on that leg." Motioning for the officers standing nearest to Clara, they went over to put her on a gurney to start the trek out of the woods. Staying quiet, they made their way to the clearing and Richard instructed them to take her to his car. He drove the family to his sister's house. It was the only place he knew they would be safe.

As Richard pulled his car into the driveway, he suddenly realized how he knew this couple. Pulling to a stop by the garage, he slowly turned to look at his passengers. He could not believe what he was seeing. It was incredible.

Taking the key from the dark hiding place behind a rock in a wall, Richard let himself and his companions into Wray and Anne's house. He knew his sister and brother-in-law wouldn't mind. They had an extra bedroom and bathroom in the basement where they would be comfortable until Richard figured out how to proceed. Samuel helped Clara into the house and she sat at the kitchen table while Richard turned on the lights and closed all of the blinds so no one could see into the house. Samuel knelt down next to his wife to get a closer inspection of her injured leg. It was swelling and looked like it might be infected. Glancing over and noticing her leg, Richard said, "I will go up and get my brother-in-law. He is a doctor and he can look at it."

Samuel smiled appreciatively as he responded, "I am a doctor also but I wonder if he has any medication here for an infection along with some sterile dressing?"

"I will find out and then we will get you all taken care of and comfortable for the rest of the night."

"Thank you so much. I don't know what would have happened if you hadn't found us. I have so many questions."

Richard chuckled. "You and me both, my friend. I will be right back."

As Richard started up the stairs to wake Wray and Anne, he didn't notice Jacob getting up from his slumber on the living room couch. Jacob sleepily wandered into the kitchen wondering who was awake with all the lights on. Coming around the corner rubbing his right eye, he looked at his family's kitchen table with three strangers sitting at it. Startled, he was about to turn around and run to get his dad when his eyes locked with Lincoln's. Lincoln's breath caught in his throat as he sat staring at the boy he saw from the window. Jacob cocked his head to one side. He must be dreaming. Why would the boy he saw in the window be sitting at his table? He shook his head as if to clear his mind. He took a few hesitant steps in their direction.

"It's him." said Lincoln.

"I don't understand. Who are you?" Jacob asked quietly.

Slowly, Samuel got up from the table and walked over to Jacob reaching his hand out to him. Tears formed in his eyes. He put his fingertips on the medallion around Jacob's neck. Pulling his shaking hand away, Samuel asked Jacob in a whisper, "Where did you get this?"

"It's my Grandpa's." Jacob answered quietly. He was confused. Why were these people in his house?

Samuel went back to the table and sat down, putting his head into his hands. His elbows digging into his knees.

Clara was trying to figure out what was happening as she put her hand on her husband's back.

Before she could ask Samuel any questions, Richard came walking back into the kitchen followed by Wray and Anne.

Wray looked first at the boy sitting at his table and just as Richard had suspected in his quick recap upstairs, it was the boy he saw outside the hospital.

Lincoln looked into Wray's eyes as he looked to his dad to tell him this was the man who had his same eyes, he stopped short of saying anything.

Wray and Samuel were staring at each other. Neither of them seemed able to speak. Their eyes pooled with tears.

As Anne stepped around her husband, she saw Clara sitting at her table. She hadn't seen her in over 10 years but she would know her anywhere. Bursting into tears, Anne ran the few steps to Clara and wrapped her in a fierce hug.

Lincoln and Jacob watched the scene unfold and had no idea what was going on. Richard was smiling at the happy reunion.

*****

Back at the secret door deep in the woods, Chief Fletcher had his bomb squad set up the same explosives that the Yellow Zone had been about to detonate when they were caught. Not knowing who might be watching and waiting for the explosion, they wanted it to appear that the original bomb had in fact worked. They had gathered enough information with the dive team to continue their investigation at a more private location. When the bomb went off, the entrance to the cave was blown to bits and no one would ever have been able to locate it. The Chief knew he had some long days ahead if they were going to solve this crazy mystery of an underground town. He always knew the Yellow Zone had something to hide.

*****

Finally falling into a restless sleep after hours of tossing and turning, Simon was surprised to open his eyes and realize he had actually been sleeping. He rolled over on his cot to see if his dad was awake yet. It was still dark and the dim lights from the kitchen area didn't allow much visibility. But he could make out enough to see that his dad's cot was empty. Feeling panic surround him, he quickly got up and quietly started wandering through the sea of cots. No one was awake. Checking the bathrooms and the one large closet that housed supplies, he went back to his cot and covered himself with his blankets. Staring into space he started making a plan to get out of here and find out where his dad could be. Someone must have taken him. Simon didn't even know who to trust enough to ask for help. If all of the doors were locked then there must be an access somewhere else. Somewhere where no one would see or hear them entering or exiting. Kind of like in the cave. Trying to plan his escape, he sure

wished his friend Lincoln were here to help him. He wondered
where Lincoln was and if he was safe.

CHAPTER 15

Richard and the Chief had all of their manpower searching for the townspeople after getting full details from Samuel, Clara and Lincoln. They really didn't have much to go on other than it had to be space for hiding over 100 people.

At the same time the Blue Water Police Department searched for the townspeople, the Yellow Zone was interrogating Ron. He couldn't believe they had been able to get him out of the building without anyone seeing or hearing them. They were asking a lot of questions about his neighbor Samuel and about the friendship between Simon and Lincoln. Not knowing what was going to happen to him either way, he wouldn't answer any questions. He hoped that Samuel and his family had gotten out of the cave to safety and had indeed sent people looking for them. But they would only know to look in the cave. Now that they had been moved, would anyone be able to find them? He had never felt like a prisoner before. He felt the town had really stuck together after going through a tragedy in the beginning. Had they all been held as prisoners being made to feel like they had no other options this whole time? Obviously, some people knew there was still life outside the cave.

Sensing that he wasn't going to get any cooperation out of him, Commander Leclede walked behind Ron and put his hand on Ron's shoulder, roughly patting it. "That's ok. If you won't tell us anything, I'm sure we can get your son in here to help us out."

Ron felt trapped but hoped that before they got to him, Simon had found someone to trust and they might be able to protect him.

*****

It had been a quick night after cleaning up, treating Clara's leg, answering Richard's questions and finally getting some much-needed sleep. Everyone had agreed to catch up and discuss the overwhelming discoveries over breakfast.

The smell of coffee and bacon brought everyone quickly to the table. Each one was eager to learn more about the incredible discoveries of the previous night. Clara and Anne could hardly control their chatter as they set the food on the table.

Wray and Samuel were talking about possible leads to finding Samuel's captured neighbors.

Lincoln was listening closely to the unfamiliar stories of baseball teams and fishing. He felt like he had a lot of catching up to do but with Jacob's help, he knew he would get there quickly. They talked like old friends.

Jacob's sister, Jillian, stumbled into the kitchen still half asleep and looked around in confusion at all of the people gathered at the table. Clara's hand went up to cover her mouth as her eyes filled with tears and she glanced at Anne and whispered, "Is this your daughter?"

Anne nodded her head. "Yes. This is Jillian. The last time I saw you we were painting the nursery pink because we had just found out we were having a girl."

Clara let out a little laugh between her tears. Walking over to hug her niece, she replied, "Yes. And we were discussing names. Jillian was my first choice." As Clara embraced her, Jillian looked to her mom for answers.

"Jillian, this is your Aunt Clara." Motioning to the table she said, "And that's your Uncle Samuel and Cousin Lincoln."

Jillian looked even more confused. She looked from one face to another. "But I thought you were dead."

Jacob piped up, always ready to tell his sister what to do. "Grab a seat, sis, this is going to take a while."

Over a long breakfast followed by moving the conversation to the more comfortable living room, the past began to unfold.

*****

Samuel started telling of the night the main hospital administrator came to his house. "I had been working mainly night shifts at the ER but I was finally home for a few days. It was the middle of the night and he came pounding on our door. He told me that an unknown plague had attacked the town and most of the residents were dead. He said he knew of a safe place and we should gather a few belongings and go with him immediately. I had no reason not to trust him. Wondering if there wasn't something I could do for the town, he told me that I would have plenty of people to help at the safe zone we were heading to. He

102

explained the warning signs of the plague and what to watch for. If anyone started showing symptoms, I was to notify the mayor immediately." Samuel shook his head. "I never questioned him. We were devastated when they told us you all had been infected and died shortly after. We were put to work right away trying to put together this town of strangers all coming together in such a difficult situation. We made the best of it and we were grateful we had a safe place away from the danger of the plague. They said it was in the air and anyone who left the cave would die of exposure almost instantly."

Jacob began asking questions of what life was like in the cave.

They got caught up on the big events that had happened in the "real world" over the past years.

Wray asked, "What made you finally decide to try to leave?"

"Clara and I had been discussing it for quite some time. We just felt that there was a lot they weren't telling us. Imagine our surprise when I caught Lincoln sneaking back into town from the dark of the cave soaking wet with that huge cut on his face." He gestured toward Lincoln who could feel his face turning red.

Wray smiled at him. "He didn't have that cut on his face when he collided with me by the hospital."

Lincoln responded, "I was so scared. I don't know what I was thinking. I was looking for Jacob. After seeing him in the water, I knew there were people out here but I wasn't expecting all of this." He gestured out the front window.

*****

Simon was wandering around the building along the edge of the cots. He was feeling restless and worried about his missing dad. One of the neighbors, Mark, began to walk beside him and talking quietly told Simon that he had been awake during the night and saw three men in yellow uniforms come in and take his dad. He figured it was because they somehow knew he had been talking about an escape with other neighbors. He said from now on to be careful about who he talked to. The neighbors were making a plan on shifts of staying awake at night in case any of them came back. Simon felt relieved to know that they were trying to get everyone out of here. He would go find his dad as soon as he was able to.

*****

Until the investigation led to some answers, Lincoln and his family had to stay hidden. Wray had gone to work like any average day to avoid suspicion. Samuel was sitting at the kitchen table making notes and searching his memory for clues or ideas about where his neighbors could be. He had promised Ron that he would send help and he certainly planned to follow through with that promise. He would be meeting with Richard later in the day when he stopped by to update everyone on any new information.

Clara and Anne were giddy as children being together again. They had so much to tell each other. They were already making plans for upcoming holidays and celebrations beginning with the huge feast they planned to prepare to celebrate everyone from the cave being found. Hopefully that would be soon.

Lincoln and Jacob had been enjoying their time getting to know each other. They couldn't believe they were cousins. Jacob couldn't wait to get outside to play baseball with Lincoln. They had talked about their friends Mike and Simon and were planning a good game of 2 on 2 at the basketball court at the park. Jacob could tell how anxious Lincoln was about his friend and neighbors. Where could they be?

*****

The guards were visiting with each other as they went by to check their prisoner. He hadn't given up any information and they were discussing what they thought the next step would be. They looked into the cell and were shocked to see it empty. Ron had somehow escaped. They radioed to their supervisor as they ran back to headquarters to wait for further instructions.

*****

It was evening and Simon was getting ready for bed. Just like in the cave, it was hard to keep track of day and night. There were no windows to be able to see outside. Leaving the restroom where he had just brushed his teeth, Simon noticed that there was no one in the hallway for a change. Without thinking, he quickly opened the door to the storage room. Quietly closing the door behind him he felt around for the light switch. Deciding that it might show too much light under the door, he slid his hand along the countertop and began opening the drawers hoping to find a flashlight. It was difficult trying to figure out what he was feeling but he figured he would know if he came across the round coldness of a flashlight. Not finding anything helpful, he was ready to call it quits when he felt a small box that moved easily when he touched it. Picking it up and shaking it, he realized they were matches. He was just about to light one in hopes of being able to see for a few moments when the door abruptly opened. The light was turned on and glared brightly on his guilty face.

"What do you think you're doing? You can't be in here. You are trouble, just like your father." said a man in uniform. Reaching over, the man grabbed him by the arm and started pulling him toward the back of the storage room. He leaned behind one of the shelves and pushed a small button. An opening appeared between the shelves. Simon yelled for help as loud as he could. Luckily Mark had noticed that Simon had been gone for a while and had come looking for him. He was right outside the door when he heard Simon's pleading call. Running into the storage room, he caught the official by the back of his shirt. As they were fighting each other, several other neighbors came in and helped stop the attack.

Grabbing some duct tape from one of the shelves, they secured the official's hands and feet so he couldn't get away. It only took a few questions to know that they weren't going to get any information from their prisoner. Simon quickly explained what had happened and showed them the button behind the shelves.

Dividing up, the neighbors went to gather everyone together to make their escape. There was a sense of confused excitement as they opened the door to the outside world no one had seen in over 10 years. For the younger children, it was something they had never experienced. It was almost dark as Simon stepped foot on the grass outside the secret door. Turning to look at where they had been held for the past several days, he stepped aside to let others come through the passage. As the men and women, boys and girls took their first steps out in the new world their expressions were all similar. They were filled with awe and amazement. The moon allowed them to make out their surroundings. They could hear crickets chirping and the rustle of the trees blowing in the nice evening breeze.

Unsure which way to go, Mark began trailing through the woods with all of his neighbors following closely behind him. All of a sudden from every side there were officials wearing the same uniform as the person who had that tried to take Simon. It was chaos and the kids were screaming for their parents. The townspeople were more prepared this time and although they didn't have any weapons, they fought with everything they had. They were not going to be taken back and locked up again.

It seemed as though the Yellow Zone was about to take control of the townspeople when again chaos ripped through the crowd of people. In the semi-darkness, it was hard to see who was who or what was going on. Simon had gotten out of the grasp of an official and was crouched next to an area of bushes. As his eyes darted around looking for an escape, he saw a figure in the light of the moon across the creek bed. He couldn't see his face but he saw the figure put his hand on his shoulder, slide it down to his elbow and back up to his shoulder. Without even giving it another thought, Simon ran straight into the creek bed. He could feel his shoes filling up with water. His father met him part way and after a quick embrace, Ron grabbed his son's hand and started running back the way he had come. He knew his neighbors would be all right since Richard and his team had the whole area surrounded. Once they were out of the direct encounter between the Yellow Zone and Richard's team, they slowed down and stopped to rest. They both had a lot to tell the other about the past few hours.

*****

The following day, all of the townspeople along with the whole town of Blue Water, got the report directly from the police department that they had arrested the mayor and John. All of the Yellow Zone officials that were able to be captured were being questioned. They were quite certain they didn't have all of them. The residents of Blue Water had welcomed the new members of their town and were making plans on where all of the families could stay until more permanent arrangements were made. It was such a shock to so many people that they still had family alive and well. There were authorities meeting with each family to help them reunite with loved ones that still had to be located after moving from the area long ago.

Lincoln and Simon were sharing stories of the past several day's excitement. Simon couldn't believe that the boy Lincoln had seen under the water turned out to be his cousin. It was incredible to see the sun and feel the heat of it on their skin. They were all about to start a baseball game. Jacob was relieved this whole ordeal was behind him. To think that all of this started with him falling down a hill chasing after the dog. But something was bothering him. In the back of his mind Jacob wondered if there were other underground towns where people didn't know there was still life outside. Trying to shake the thoughts out of his head and enjoy the ball game, Jacob started jogging out to the field. Turning back after arriving at his center field position, he felt his pulse quicken and sweat bead on his forehead. Sitting in the bleachers staring at him was a man in dark sunglasses.

The

Discovered

Windows

Carol Shackleford

CHAPTER 1

It had been two weeks since Jacob saw the man in dark sunglasses watching him play baseball. Seeing him had taken all of the joy out of the big celebration honoring the citizens who had joined their town after escaping their underground prison. They had spent ten years being told it was not safe to go outside because of the deadly plague. They had finally learned the truth and were now adjusting to a new life on the outside.

Jacob and his cousin, Lincoln, were making up for lost time as their families were spending every possible minute together. Jacob had confided in his new friend about the mysterious man watching him. They were always on the lookout for the man in dark sunglasses as they went about their daily lives. After many long discussions deep into the night, the boys were convinced there might be more underground towns just waiting to be discovered. Jacob knew his Uncle Richie was working with a team of investigators to learn the answers to so many complicated questions. But Jacob and Lincoln couldn't help thinking maybe they could help move things along faster.

Sitting in Jacob's basement, Jacob and Lincoln along with their friend Simon were planning possible search areas.

Simon mentioned, "It's too bad we couldn't get our hands on the map of all the lakes in the state."

Lincoln and Simon agreed that other towns would probably also be by a lake. It was the only way for the people underground to get sunlight. It would have to come through a window like they had both experienced in their town.

Lincoln wondered out loud, "Do you think they would have two towns close together? What if there isn't another one for hundreds of miles? How would we ever find it?"

Jacob had an uneasy feeling in the pit of his stomach as he volunteered, "I bet my uncle has a copy of the map. I could try to find out where he keeps it."

The boys all looked at each other as slow smiles spread across their faces.

*****

"RJ, you need to get in here and wash up! Your supper is on the table. Please don't make me ask you again." Kristin hollered out the back door.

"Sorry! Be right there, mom." Yelled RJ from inside the tiny shed next to the house. He had been in there since getting home from school. He was, as usual, working on his project. He had spent months finding objects around town to work on what he called his "real town model". He tried to be content with his life but he never really felt like he belonged here. His mom had always told him stories about what life had been like for her before the plague had forced her into the cave. It was the only way of life he had ever known but he dreamed of something different. He had been born in this cave but every day he felt like the walls were closing in on him a little more.

It helped RJ to work on his model of what he imagined life would be like outside of these walls. Since he was the only person down here under the age of 30, he didn't have anyone to talk to about his discontent. He couldn't tell his mom. She tried her best to make it fun for him but she was so busy with work. Everyone depended on her. Their town had over 200 people and she was the only medical worker here. Most of the town members were over 60 years old and she had to take on the roll of doctor, nurse and pharmacist.

Kristin had told RJ stories of her days working at the hospital as an RN before coming here. What she missed most was seeing newborn babies and hearing their first cry out to the world. He could picture in his mind the hallways bustling with people wearing uniforms. There were machines beeping and loud voices that came through the air announcing codes. When they said "code blue" she told him it meant a big emergency that made everyone come running to help. She described the smell as clean and like medicine and the bleach they used on rare occasions to clean something in the cave. It was hard for him to imagine.

Letting his mind wander, he wasn't paying attention as he let the door slam behind him on his way in for supper. Quietly he whispered, "Oops!".

Kristin looked at him out of the corner of her eye as she bit the inside of her lip to keep from smiling. She had told him at least a thousand times not to let the door slam.

After washing his hands, RJ sat down at the table and perked up a bit when he saw his favorite meal of lasagna and French bread.

As they ate, RJ described the work he had completed on his model and Kristin told him about her day at work. The oldest member of their town, Ben, was under the weather again. It was the third time this year that he was struggling with his health. At 91, Kristin was afraid there wouldn't be much she could do to help him other than try to keep him comfortable. Her resources were limited.

After supper, they began their usual routine of cleaning up the dishes followed by going out to walk around the town. RJ didn't realize the convenience of it always being dry with an even temperature. He had never experienced rain or cold or hot.

Arriving at their nightly destination, they were both surprised at the number of people gathered around the window. Usually, the town members had already started turning in for the night. They were all talking at the same time and most of them were visibly upset.

"What's going on?" Kristin asked one of her favorite neighbors.

"There is talk from the mayor's office that they are going to cover up the window," answered Frankie.

RJ stared at the window and felt the space around him getting even smaller.

Kristin shook her head in disbelief. This would have a very negative impact on the town. They needed the window not only for the light but also as a connection to the life they had all left outside.

First thing in the morning, Kristin would have to go meet with the mayor and explain what a bad idea it would be. She didn't expect to get very far because he had always been a difficult person in her opinion.

*****

RJ waited until he knew his mom was sleeping before he quietly slipped out of the house. He entered the shed and stared in the mostly darkened room at his real town model. If there was a chance they were going to close off the window, he had to find a way out of this cave. He didn't know what was on the outside but he knew he couldn't stay in here for much longer.

Creeping through the neighborhood to the window, he crouched down beside a fake tree and stared out the window into total darkness. Nothing moved in the water. His mind was racing in the hope of coming up with a plan. He really didn't have any good ideas. Just as he was about to turn on his heels to stand up and head back home, he felt someone touch his back and lean down next to him. Sucking in his breath in a shocked gasp, he didn't know if he should be glad or terrified as he turned to see his mom looking at him with tears in her eyes.

*****

Richard and his team were following up on a lead about another possible secret town. They had sent a dive team down and one of the divers had indeed found a window under the water. After searching the area for several days, they had finally found the entrance. It was amazing to everyone how camouflaged the door was. It was time to discover what or who was inside.

The bomb squad set up their explosives to get the entrance opened. Everyone stood back while the door to another mystery was being cleared. With anticipation, Richard and his team headed forward. The last time they were in this situation, the cave had been filled with water. This one was dry and they were able to step inside and begin their journey in the direction of the window. The bright lights of their equipment lit up a clear path ahead.

∎∎

What had started as a slight foul odor kept getting worse the further in they went. All of the officers had to go back outside to get filtered masks before they could continue further. Glancing at each other as they walked back into the cave, they had a sense of dread concerning what they would find. There was no mistaking the smell of rotting flesh.

The officers slowed their pace as the lights bounced off of a large pile of something in front of them. Richard took the lead and walked over without saying a word. They all knew what they were about to find. Lifting a blanket that had been draped over the top of the pile, they discovered a heap consisting of not less than 100 people. They had all been placed in a straight line and each

117

wrapped in their own blanket. The pile of bodies was five individuals high.

Radioing in to headquarters, Richard requested the medical examiner. It appeared to him that the bodies had been here for quite a while but had not been deposited all at the same time. Some had been here longer than others.

With the need for some answers, Richard and his team continued toward the discovered underground town not knowing what horrors might await them.

CHAPTER 2

Lincoln and Jacob were trying to establish a plan to get the map Jacob was certain his uncle had possession of. Talking in hushed tones, their biggest concern was how to leave the house without anyone seeing them. Both of their moms were extra protective after finally being reunited. The phone's ringing stopped their quiet conversation. They could hear Jacob's mom, Anne, answer it.

"Hi Wray! I thought you were in the middle of your hospital rounds. Is everything ok?" After a short pause where they knew Jacob's dad was speaking, they heard Anne gasp loudly. "Oh no! Do they know how many?" Again, a short pause followed by, "Ok, I'll see you whenever you get home. Be careful."

"What's wrong?" asked Lincoln's mom, Clara.

Lowering her voice, Anne told Clara "Wray and Samuel have been called from work at the hospital to go to a cave where human remains have been found."

As Anne was explaining the few details she knew to Clara, the boys looked at each other with determination. Even with Anne lowering her voice, they were able to make out most of the conversation. They knew there might not be a better opportunity when everyone was busy and distracted with this new information. If they were going to find that map, it was going to have to be now.

*****

Samuel and Wray had made their way down to the cave to meet Richard and his team. While the medical examiner was inspecting the pile of blanket covered bodies, the rest of the group was continuing to investigate where the bodies had come from and if there were more anywhere else. Nobody was expecting to hear a young, weak voice coming from the edge of what appeared to be a small town.

"Hello? Is somebody there? Can you help us, please?" spoke a quiet, scared voice from the shadows.

Glancing at one another, Wray nodded his head and took the lead by himself. "Hello there. My name is Wray. Is it ok if I come closer?" He slowly walked toward the young boy leaning against a small tree. As he got closer, Wray noticed how thin and weak the boy appeared. He bent down next to him. "We are here to help. Can you tell me your name?"

"Joshua." He whispered.

"Hi Joshua. Can you tell me, are you the only one left?" Wray asked with compassion.

Lifting his head to look Wray right in the eyes, he tried to stand up. His voice got stronger as he said, "You have to go help Brian." With the words spoken, he collapsed into Wray's arms. Wray opened up his medical bag to start his exam on the boy as Richard, Samuel and the others quickly spread out to search the rest of the town calling out for Brian and hoping it wasn't too late.

*****

Jacob knew that his uncle wouldn't be home for hours if they were investigating another cave so he wasn't too worried about getting caught. However, his conscience was making it hard to follow through with the plan. The boys knew they couldn't all go together because it might cause suspicion. Jacob knew where everything was in his uncle's house so he went the final block by himself.

Going around the side of the front steps, he pulled at a loose brick on the bottom layer of bricks at the foundation of the house. Feeling around with his finger, he quickly found the house key and pulled it out. He hurried to the front door before he lost his nerve and fumbled with the key to fit it into the lock. Once inside the house, he made his way to his uncle's home office. The problem was going to be that he didn't know exactly where to look or what he was really looking for. Jacob knew his uncle would notice if anything was out of place so he was very careful not to move anything.

Searching through stacks of papers, he was starting to feel discouraged. It didn't appear that there was a map of any kind in the office. He started quietly walking toward the kitchen when he heard a noise from somewhere in the house. Surely his uncle wasn't home yet. They had just started the investigation and Jacob knew that would mean hours, if not days, away from home. He stood as still as possible. It seemed to him that his breathing was loud enough to be heard from a mile away. Just as he was about to take a step forward, Lincoln came quickly around the corner and ran right into him. Both of them yelled out in surprise.

"What are you doing here? You were supposed to be waiting with Simon." Jacob said impatiently and with a pounding heart.

Lincoln had his hand on his heart. "Man, you scared me half to death! What's taking you so long?"

"I can't find the map. I've looked everywhere."

Holding up a map with certain lakes circled, Lincoln said with a chuckle, "Well, apparently you didn't look on the kitchen table. Let's get out of here."

"Wait! He will notice right away that it's gone. Let's make a copy of it and leave that one here. I think he has a copier in his office." Jacob said as he tried to calm his nerves back to normal.

"Smart. It takes you twice as long to do stuff but you think twice as fast as anyone else."

They quickly made a copy of the map and Lincoln put the original one back on the table right from where he had taken it. At least he thought that's what he did.

CHAPTER 3

With Joshua in the care of Wray and Samuel, Richard and his team began the search for Brian. Having no knowledge of who Brian was, they spread out and began entering each house and looking in every corner. If Brian was as weak and sickly as Joshua, they knew he might not be able to answer their calling of his name.

Richard was entering the fourth house on his search. He had been noticing that everything was very neat and organized. He hadn't seen any indication that kids lived down here. There were no toys or smaller sized clothes hanging in closets. It was eerily quiet except for the occasional calling of "Brian!" from one of his officers in the distance and the tick of a wall clock.

Slowly, Richard pushed open a creaking door into the last room of the house. It was a dark bedroom. He reached toward the wall to turn the light switch on. As his hand touched the switch, he could hear shallow breathing close by. With light engulfing the room, he saw the body of a really thin boy on the ground.

Being careful not to move him in case he was injured, Richard knelt down beside him and checked his pulse. It was so weak he could hardly feel it. He radioed to the group, "I found him. I need immediate medical response. He's barely breathing. House number 38. Blue one fourth on the right"

One of his officers replied, "I have Dr. Lindstrom with me. One minute out."

Richard leaned over the young boy. "It's going to be ok. We are here now. You're going to be just fine, Brian."

Slowly scanning the room, his eyes finally rested on the boy. This boy was younger than his nephew Jacob. How did he get down here? It was obvious that he had not eaten in a long time. Shaking his head, he tried to stop the anger from taking over. What if they were too late?

He heard Samuel running through the front door.

"We're back here!" hollered Richard.

Samuel quickly started an assessment of Brian while Richard stood up. Looking over at his officer, he nodded his head indicating his departure. Walking out of the house, Richard clenched his hands into fists. Who was behind this terrible activity? He had to get answers and he had to get them now. There was no way to know how many other people were possibly going to die before he could save them. Picking up his pace, he grabbed the flashlight off of his belt and clicked it on to light the way as he started running to the entrance of the cave. He had work to do.

*****

Wray had been with Joshua since finding him in the cave. So far, he had not woken up. They had immediately started IV fluids to get him hydrated. The tests they had run were coming back normal. Hopefully with time, Joshua would wake up and be able to answer some of the many questions they had for him.

With the arrival of the other boy, Brian, coming any minute, Wray left Joshua's side to go make sure everything was ready. As he rounded the corner of the hospital, he saw one of his patients in the doorway of his room sitting in a wheelchair. Slowing down to speak quickly to him, Wray said, "Mr. Ellison, you need to go back in your room. There will be a lot of commotion out here in a minute."

"Will the boys be ok?" Asked Mr. Ellison.

"I don't know." Wray responded honestly as he hurried down the hallway. It briefly flashed through his mind to wonder how he knew about the boys. Just then, the doors swung open with Brian being wheeled on the ambulance stretcher into one of the emergency rooms. Wray followed the stretcher in while Samuel gave him a quick update on their newest patient.

*****

Lincoln spread the copy of the lake map on the floor in front of his friends. It took them a while to get the lay of the land. They all agreed to cross off the lakes that were too small or not close to heavily wooded areas. There had to be an entrance hidden in the woods or access to the cave would be impossible.

Jacob made a list of all the lakes that seemed like good possibilities. Suddenly he put his head in his hands and groaned.

"What's wrong?" asked Lincoln.

"It doesn't matter what we find. All of these lakes are too far away for us to go explore. How would we get there? We can't ride our bikes 60 miles." Jacob said with frustration. He was upset that they hadn't thought it through better before he had taken the chance of stealing the map.

"You're right." Replied Lincoln. "Plus, our moms are still hovering over us worse than usual. They would never let us be gone for that long before calling out the troops."

Feeling defeated, they sat quietly for a while. Breaking the silence, Lincoln asked his friend Simon, "Do you remember when we were looking for the door code in the mayor's office?"

Simon chuckled and said, "I sure do. I was so nervous we were going to get caught that I thought I would throw up."

Lincoln thought for a second. "I was looking in the file cabinet and all of the townspeople had a file. You said you had been born in Lancer. I didn't look at anybody else's files. That's where I was born too. Do you think that has anything to do with it? Maybe they broke the window to destroy evidence."

Slowly nodding their heads, the boys decided to ask around to see if any of the other people who had lived in the cave with Lincoln and Simon had a connection to Lancer. They weren't sure how to ask without raising suspicion but they had to start somewhere.

CHAPTER 4

RJ had followed Kristin home without any words spoken between them. It had been a restless night without much sleep. They both had a flood of emotions running through their thoughts. It was at these times that Kristin really missed her husband. He had been such a wonderful father to their first son that she believed that he would know exactly how to handle RJ. It broke her heart that RJ was so restless and unhappy in this life they were living. He had never known the outside world but she knew he would have thrived in it. She vowed to make sure the mayor didn't shut out the only glimpse of the world her son was missing.

RJ struggled with his feelings of restlessness. He felt bad that it made his mom sad knowing she couldn't do anything to change their circumstances. He didn't blame her for any of it. Wishing he could find a way out of the cave, he tried to put on a content face to ease his mom's anxiety.

Over a bowl of cereal, Kristin and RJ made small talk about their plans for the day. They didn't realize that they were both thinking the same thing. What is it going to take to get out of this cave?

*****

Richard was pacing the floor of his home office. After an uneasy night without proper sleep, he had just received word from the medical examiner that the people they had found in the cave had died from one of three reasons. The ones who had been there the longest had seemingly perished from natural causes. Somewhat recently that changed to the cause of death being from poisoning. But the most recent deaths had been from starvation and malnutrition. It made him sick to think about it.

He had checked with the hospital and the boys they found were still unconscious. The good news was that they seemed to be doing very well and were expected to make a full recovery. It was also expected to be a very long one.

After a discussion with the chief of police, he discovered that none of the Yellow Zone officials had spoken a word about what they knew. They would continue interviewing the prisoners in hopes of getting some information out of them but until then, Richard was going to have to keep digging to see if there were more innocent people being held with the awful misinformation that it was for their own good. What kind of terrible people were behind all of this?

Realizing that he hadn't eaten anything yet, he headed for the kitchen. As he walked past his table, he stopped dead in his tracks. He eyed the table closely. Something was not right.

••

Kristin made sure RJ had started his studies with the neighbor before she left to confront the mayor about the window. RJ was getting a good education from a former high school teacher from the outside. She enjoyed teaching RJ because she really missed all of her students from "back when". She loved telling him stories in between his lessons about "back when she was teaching". She was so good at story-telling that he could almost picture himself there with her class when one of her students was rowdy or being a class clown. RJ always wondered where he would have fit into a classroom. Would he have had a lot of friends? Kristin felt comfortable knowing the teacher would distract RJ at least temporarily. Now she just had to get through this meeting with the mayor.

Knocking on the mayor's door, Kristin's palms began to sweat. She didn't like confrontation and the mayor had never been especially friendly to her.

"Come in." A gruff voice mumbled from the other side of the door.

Rubbing her palms down her pants legs to dry them off, she tried to be as confident as possible when she opened the door and strode across the room to his desk. She reached over and shook his hand. "Mayor, I hope you have a minute. I have a matter of some urgency to discuss with you."

"Of course. Please have a seat." He said, gesturing to the chair across from his desk.

Kristin sat on the edge of the seat. "Mayor, I have heard rumors that you are thinking about closing the window. Boarding it up. May I just say, as a medical professional, that it would be extremely detrimental to everyone's health to take away the only connection they have to the outside world. It's the only source of natural light they have had in ten years."

Much to her surprise, the mayor didn't argue with her. He sat quietly for a long time. She began to wonder if it was some kind of a game and he was waiting for her to back down.

Leaning his elbows on the desk, he started rubbing his hands together. Then he started rubbing his temples. She could see just the slightest tremor in his hands. Leaning back in his chair, he looked her straight in the eye and announced, "Kristin, we have to get out of here."

*****

The medical staff had gotten Brian stabilized. There were still no answers as to why the boys had been down in the cave. After getting the results of the cause of death for every resident from the underground town, everyone agreed that it seemed odd that these two boys had been found alive and were the only two young people in the town. Everyone else was over the age of 80. Why were these boys with them? Why were they the only two survivors?

Neither of the boys had any trace of poison in their system. All of the evidence and symptoms pointed to starvation and malnutrition. It was no surprise when the investigation from the team of officers who continued the search of the cave resulted in finding no food anywhere. There was trace evidence that there had been a small amount recently but not enough to sustain two growing boys. It was lucky they were found when they were. Another day and they both would have joined their neighbors in death. It appeared that the only way to find out what had truly transpired in the cave would be if one of the boys would wake up and tell them the details.

. . . .

Lincoln and Jacob were working on a list of people who had been in the first cave and had been rescued. Many of them were already reunited with family and had moved to other locations but there were still several they thought of to start their inquiries. The first one on their list was Lincoln's friend Simon. They hadn't had a conversation about any of it since their full attention had been given to concentrating on finding the lake map.

Simon answered the knock on the door after the first rap. He wanted to do anything but pack. He and his dad were packing their few belongings and were going to leave town in a few days. They were going to live with Simon's grandparents for a while. Simon hadn't seen his grandparents in 10 years and he didn't know how to feel about the move. He liked living in Blue Water and had a lot of fun with Lincoln and Jacob. He worried that there wouldn't be anyone his age near his grandparent's house.

Opening the door, his face lit up at the sight of his friends. He opened the door wide to let them in.

"I'm so glad to see you. I am bored out of my mind and am really sick of packing." Simon said cheerfully.

"We are kind of here on a serious mission." Said Jacob with no smile on his face. Simon led them into the living room to sit down to talk.

Lincoln tried to lighten the mood by chuckling as he stated, "Jacob is always on a serious mission. We just wanted to talk to you about the cave before you move. Do you ever have questions about it? Like why we were there? Why they chose us?"

Jacob chimed in, "I want to know why they lied. And who all knew about it? All I ever remember was my parents talking about family that had died of the plague and now here they are. Alive after all this time. I had seen pictures of my aunt and ancle and cousin but they were never real to me. I didn't remember them. And now here they are." He gestured toward Lincoln. "I know the investigation is in full swing and I understand that we won't be the first to hear the answers, but it would help to know something so we can try to piece this together. Plus, we don't know how many other people are in the same boat." Jacob started wringing his hands together nervously.

Simon leaned back in his chair. "I don't have answers to any of those questions. Plus, I have a whole bunch of my own."

Lincoln looked at Simon for a moment before asking him the one thing he wanted to know the most right now. "Simon, we were neighbors and friends the whole time we lived in the cave. We never talked about life before we got there because I don't think either of us remembered it. Do you remember anything about Lancer? Do you remember anyone from there?"

Simon stared into the distance in deep thought for a minute. "I don't ever remember hearing anything specifically about Lancer but I could ask my dad. For some reason, the name does ring a bell but not because of where I was born."

"Simon, I don't want to upset you but you have never said anything about your mom. Why wasn't she in the cave with you and your dad?" Lincoln asked quietly with his eyes on the ground.

Looking up at the silence, Lincoln saw the color drain from Simon's face. Jacob got up from his seat and went over to kneel beside Simon who looked like he might pass out. After swallowing several times and breathing in long, slow breaths, Simon looked from Jacob to Lincoln. "They told us she had died from the plague. If they were lying about it....." He hesitated as he covered his mouth with his hands and his eyes grew wide and began to tear up. "If they were lying about it, maybe she is still alive." Jumping to his feet, he went to grab his shoes in order to walk out the door and find his dad.

"Simon." Lincoln asked as they followed behind him, "Do you remember your mom?"

Simon turned to look at his friends as he quietly recalled, "I remember she smelled like flowers. She would rub the tips of her fingers over my forehead to help me fall asleep. My dad said she was the best nurse, wife and mom in the world. Her name was Kristin." His friends followed him out the door to hunt for his dad hoping for more answers.

Kristin had a quick day at work following her meeting with the mayor. She could hardly focus on her patients. She was now looking out the kitchen window at the shed she knew RJ was working in.   He worked every day on that model of what he thought a real town was like. What if she could get her son to a real town? Her mind was racing at what the mayor had said and where they would go from here.

They had agreed that the whole town needed to know their current situation. Notice had been given door to door to ensure everyone was aware of the urgent town meeting this afternoon.

Going to the back door to holler out for RJ to come in for lunch, she was surprised when the door opened up before she got to it. RJ came in and saw his mom's face right when the door slammed behind him. "Oops. Sorry." He said out of habit. She tried to hide her grin from him but he saw it and a big smile spread across his face as he went to wash his hands. Glancing over his shoulder he could see his mom staring at him. "What?" He asked. He thought maybe his teacher had given her a bad report on him. He was having a terrible time concentrating on school lately.

"There is a town meeting soon. You usually stay home because you say they are boring but I think it's important you go tonight. There is something going on that you need to know about."

"What is it?" RJ asked.

"Well, if I tell you, there would be no need to go to the meeting." she answered jokingly. She was trying to keep the mood light but this meeting would be anything but light. The town needed to devise a plan to get out of the cave. Their days here were numbered. They had to keep the upper hand and stay one step ahead of the Yellow Zone. Learning about the Yellow Zone in her meeting today with the mayor made her feel sick to her stomach. If they lived to make it out of here, what would be waiting for them on the outside? More importantly, who might be there?

*****

Wray walked down the hall making his rounds at the hospital. He went in to room 203 to check on Mr. Ellison. He had been declining and wasn't expected to make it much longer. Walking into the room with a cheerful "Good afternoon!", Wray was surprised to find the room empty. Checking the bathroom before he left the room, he looked down the hallways in each direction. Mr. Ellison was hardly functioning. It didn't make sense that he could leave on his own. Where could he be? He started toward the nurse's station but stopped abruptly when he heard muted crying.

He followed the noise into Brian's room. There by the side of the bed sat Mr. Ellison in his wheelchair with his head down and tears streaming from his eyes. He was holding Brian's hand between both of his worn, wrinkled, frail hands. He was sobbing almost uncontrollably.

Wray walked slowly and quietly over to Mr. Ellison and placed a gentle hand on his shoulder. Squatting down to look him in the eyes, Wray asked, "Mr. Ellison, do you know this boy?"

Mr. Ellison let go of Brian's hand and reached over to grab Wray's hand. "I'm sorry." He gasped out right before he fell forward in his wheelchair and quit breathing.

Wray hollered out, "Code Blue! Bring the paddles." He carefully lifted Mr. Ellison to the empty bed next to Brian as the medical team brought in the equipment meant to keep Mr. Ellison alive. As Wray glanced over to the next bed, he was surprised to see Brian's eyes open and staring at Mr. Ellison.

∙∙

Lincoln, Jacob and Simon were on their way to find Simon's dad. Simon didn't know where he was other than "wrapping some things up" before they moved. They had been to his dad's work but the secretary told the boys that Ron had left after lunch. They were walking out of the office building deep in conversation about where to look next when they rounded the corner and saw a large man with his arms crossed over his chest at the end of the sidewalk.

Jacob recognized even from a distance that it was his Uncle Richie and he began to break out in a sweat. He knew before the confrontation that his uncle had discovered they had been in his house. He didn't know how he knew. But his uncle always seemed to know everything.

Richard waited until the boys had finished walking to him. He dropped his hands to his sides and said sternly, "Come with me." He led them to an outdoor table and luckily – or not very lucky for the boys – there weren't any other people around.

Richard tried to make eye contact with each of the boys but they were too busy looking at the ground, at each other and everywhere except looking back at Richard. He loudly cleared his throat and he could see all three of the boys jump a little in their seats. "Do any of you have something to tell me?"

There was total silence.

"It's funny," Richard began, "I always leave things a certain way. You know, just to make sure it's right where I left it when I come back later. Maybe it's my police training. Maybe I'm paranoid." He was quiet for a long time. "Jacob, do you think I'm paranoid?" Richard asked.

Shaking his head fiercely, Jacob answered, "No." He shot Lincoln a look of anger. Lincoln had been so sure he put the lake map right back exactly where he got it.

"Lincoln. Simon. Do either of you have anything you would like to tell me?" Richard asked crossing his arms and leaning over to rest his arms and elbows on the table. He strummed the fingers of his right hand on the top of his left bicep.

They both shook their heads slightly. The maps hadn't been very helpful so maybe they should just go ahead and tell him that they made a copy of it. They had entered his house without permission and had taken police property and made a copy of it. Looking back, that was probably not a very smart thing to do.

"I don't need to tell you that…" Richard's radio interrupted his sentence. "Wait here." He said as he went out of earshot to make a phone call.

He hollered to the boys while waving them over. "Come on. We have somewhere to go."

The boys got up slowly thinking he was going to take them to the station. They hadn't even talked out a plan of what to say if they got caught. With a feeling of dread, they got into the squad car and started sweating as they neared the police station.

CHAPTER 6

Lincoln elbowed Jacob in the ribs. Jacob looked over at him in disgust. It was his fault they were in this mess to begin with. Lincoln motioned out the window. They had just driven past the police station. Where was Uncle Richie taking them? He looked back at Lincoln and Lincoln nodded his head toward his uncle. Jacob agreed but needed to build up a bit of nerve first. "Uncle Richie?" He asked nervously. "Where are we going?"

"We are going to the hospital. One of the boys we found in the cave is awake but he won't talk to anyone. We are hoping maybe he will talk to one of you." Richard drove in silence for another minute before continuing. "Listen. This is really important. He may have a lot of information that will help us. He is bound to be really scared after what he has been through. We have a lot of questions but first we need him to feel comfortable with us and be able to trust us. I think it's best if just one of you go in to start with."

"Who decides which one of us will be going in?" asked Jacob.

"I think it should be Simon. He lived in one of the caves so he will be understanding and no offense to you Lincoln but Simon is a bit calmer and quieter than you are. You might intimidate him." Richard half chuckled. He hadn't known Lincoln long but he had quite a big personality. After all, he had taken it upon himself to escape from his underground town but had still returned to it with the information he had gathered. "What do you think, Simon? Are you up for it?"

"I think so." Simon replied.

"Just talk to him and see if he opens up. We'll go from there."

Simon nodded his head. He wasn't sure he wanted all of this pressure but if it could help them get answers maybe it would be a step closer to knowing more about his mom.

....

Simon's dad, Ron, had also been looking for more information. He was wanting details about what had actually happened to his wife. When Ron and Simon had been taken to the cave over 10 years ago, they had been told a plague had taken her life along with most others.

He had left his office several hours ago and had driven over to a town called Lancer to make some inquiries at the hospital where his wife, Kristin, had worked when the so-called plague had changed everything.

His mind wandered to memories of his wife. She had been an amazing person. She was the sweetest, hardest working, most dedicated person he had ever known. They had been best friends. His life hadn't been the same since she left it. He could still hear her telling wonderful stories about her days at work. The people she helped all loved her. They were overjoyed the day Simon had entered their lives. She had loved her son with everything she had.

As Ron's thoughts started turning toward their time together being cut short, he arrived in Lancer. He hadn't seen the town in over a decade. It had changed a lot. They had enjoyed living here. He drove past the tiny house they bought right after getting married. There was new vinyl siding replacing the old peeled paint. They had removed the window boxes where they had planted new flowers every year. It looked even smaller than he remembered. As he slowed down to take a closer look, he noticed a car behind him. He didn't want to hold up what little traffic was on the street so he pulled over in front of the house.

The car behind him slowed down almost to a stop before speeding up and turning at the next corner. He didn't pay any attention to it as he sat staring at his old house as more memories came rushing back.

• •

Walking across the parking lot of the hospital, everyone was silent. Richard was walking next to his nephew, Jacob. He knew Jacob was upset at disappointing him with going into his house without permission and looking at private and confidential information. Jacob was a good kid and he didn't want him making himself sick with worry over it. He reached out and tousled his hair. Jacob looked up at him and Richard patted him on the shoulder. He could feel the tension drain from Jacob as a half-smile crossed his face. Jacob leaned in slightly, feeling the comfort of his uncle's strength and forgiveness.

As they entered the section of the hospital where Brian was a patient, Wray met them and led them into a conference room. They discussed what Simon should talk to Brian about and agreed that they would all meet in an hour in the cafeteria for a drink. Wray told Richard he wanted to discuss something with him in private. They left to take Simon to Brian's room and then have their discussion. This left Lincoln and Jacob alone in the conference room. After talking for a while, Jacob decided to go outside and get some fresh air but Lincoln wanted to check to see if his dad was working in his office. He would stop in to say hi if he was there but if he was on rounds, he would just check back later. Jacob headed outside to enjoy the warm weather and try to clear his head.

Lincoln was walking down the hall to his dad's office when he walked by room 203. He had been scanning the rooms wondering which one Brian was in. As he walked by, he saw an elderly man lying in the bed staring out the window. He was several feet past the room when he realized that he recognized the man from the night of the storm when he had escaped from the cave. He had waved to him through the window of the nursing home side of the hospital. Even though he knew better than to bother patients in the hospital, he took the few steps back to the doorway. He leaned his head inside and quietly called out, "Hello! I remember you."

Mr. Ellison shifted his gaze from the window to Lincoln. His face looked a little brighter. He smiled at him and Lincoln walked part way to the bed. Mr. Ellison was hooked to all kinds of monitors and tubes. He didn't look good at all.

Walking the rest of the way to the bed, Lincoln moved the chair from the corner and pulled it up close so Mr. Ellison didn't have to look up at him. He sat down with a smile on his face but inside he felt sad. Obviously, this man wasn't going to live much longer but no one was here with him. Lincoln could see the deep lines of age on his face and wondered what kind of stories he could tell. Now that he was sitting here, Lincoln didn't really know what to say.

"How are you doing?" Lincoln asked as a way to break the ice.

Mr. Ellison slightly lifted his shoulders as if to reply that he wasn't sure. His voice was so quiet that Lincoln had to lean right down next to him to hear what he had to say. The raspy, hoarse words he was able to speak were only, "The boys."

Lincoln leaned back in his chair and looked at Mr. Ellison for a minute. How did he know about the boys from the cave? He supposed it was from overhearing some of the staff discussing them. He didn't think it would hurt to talk about them. The news would be all over town soon if it wasn't already anyway. "I don't know much except they found them in a cave. One of them just woke up so they are trying to figure out what happened down there."

Mr. Ellison looked like he was about to speak so Lincoln again leaned over close again to hear. "What about the others?"

It didn't occur to Lincoln that no one other than the police and the hospital staff had information that there had been others found in the cave. "Well, just between you and me, I overheard my aunt on the phone. I don't know how many people there were but other than the two boys, everyone else was dead."

Mr. Ellison gasped and his eyes closed with his brow creasing in pain. Several of his monitors started beeping and a nurse ran in the door. Lincoln jumped up from his chair afraid maybe he had caused it. He backed out of the way and stood against the wall afraid to stay but afraid to leave. His Uncle Wray came rushing into the room and was surprised to see Lincoln in there. "Doctor, his blood pressure is through the roof." The nurse calmly stated.

Wray nodded as he looked over at Lincoln and said, "Lincoln, can you step outside please?"

As Lincoln left the room, he wondered if the old man would live another day.

CHAPTER 7

RJ usually had a hard time sitting still but he sat quiet as a mouse as the town meeting started. He could feel a tension in the air. Something was going on and he could tell people were nervous.

"Is this about closing up the window?" Someone asked from behind him.

"You can't do that. It's all we have." Another raised voice called out.

Pretty soon everyone was talking at the same time and people were yelling at the mayor for answers.

Kristin got up from her seat next to RJ and walked up to the front. She stood next to the mayor and asked if everyone would please take a seat and listen.

The mayor stood up next to Kristin and the townspeople stayed quiet in anticipation of his response. "I know you think this meeting is about the window. It is not. We have a problem a lot bigger than a window to the outside." Holding up his hand expecting a lot of interruptions and hoping he could finish his statement before the flood of demanding questions, he ran his hand across his forehead and took a deep breath. "Friends and neighbors, we are in immediate danger and we have to work together to figure out a plan to get out of this cave." As expected, everyone started talking at once.

Kristin spoke up. She was well respected by everyone in town and she knew they would listen to her. "Please stay calm. We have to work as a team. We need each other to survive. Please listen to the rest of what the mayor has to say and he will take questions at the end." Sitting back down she looked over at RJ and she couldn't tell if the expression on his face was fear or excitement.

RJ looked at his mom and she gave him a reassuring smile. He knew she would take care of him. His heart pounded. He couldn't believe his ears. He was getting out of this cave!

The mayor continued, "I wish I had more details to give you but here is what I do know at this time. You were brought here by a group called the Yellow Zone. They are the ones who continue to keep us alive by bringing us supplies and food. I believe that there are other towns like ours. More towns in underground locations. One of these locations has been found by the outside. The outside is not what we were led to believe. It is not dangerous. It is not contaminated anymore. I'm not sure why we are here but I do know that as of yesterday, we have been shut off from all supplies and food. We have to get out of here while we are still strong enough to do so."

Instead of questions and demands being yelled across the room, the mayor was surprised at the loud silence. Everyone was in shock as what they just heard was starting to sink in. They had to work together and make a plan or they would all watch each other die.

Kristin and the mayor had set up groups of town members to complete certain tasks. One group, headed by the mayor, was about to leave on a mission to find the entrance to the cave. If they found it, they were going to try to come up with a plan of how to get it open. Kristin had been surprised to learn that the mayor had never questioned how to leave in case of emergency.

Meanwhile, several of the neighbors were gathering all of the food they could find so they could begin rationing. It was possible that they were still going to be here for a while and with no food coming in, they would soon run short.

Since many in the town were advanced in age, Kristin worried about their health. This was a very stressful situation along with a huge shock to learn of their circumstances. Some of them would most likely not be able to walk the distance needed to get out of the cave. And what would happen when they got out? Who knew how far away they were from anything? They might have to send some friends ahead and leave some here temporarily. But would they be safe?

Everyone had been told to gather their belongings. They would not take their things initially but with any luck, they would get out of here and someone would be sent back to collect all of their items.

RJ stood looking out the window. He didn't understand why he wasn't allowed to go with the group that was exploring to find the entrance. He was trying to imagine in his mind what it would be like to finally get outside. One thing he knew for sure. When he got out of here, he definitely wanted a dog. He had heard stories about people's pets. While gazing out at the water, he tried to think of a good name for his new dog.

• •

Simon had been sitting patiently watching Brian sleep. He wondered how long he should stay here before giving up. He had counted the number of floor tiles that were visible three times already. He watched the monitor's lights and numbers and tried to figure out what they all meant. He tried to listen to the activity in the hallway to hear what was going on. Other than the lady in the next room needing help to go to the bathroom and someone in the room next to hers complaining loudly about wanting more medication, he didn't hear anything interesting.

He was about to get up to at least walk around a little when Brian started to stir. Simon was still shocked to see someone so skinny. It barely looked like anyone was under the covers.

Brian opened his eyes and saw Simon looking at him. His eyes started darting around the room. They were large eyes sunken into his skull with dark circles underneath and they had a look of fear in them. Simon smiled nervously at him. "It's ok. I'm here as your friend. You are in the hospital in Blue Water."

Brian looked him over for a minute. "How did I get here?" He whispered as he licked his lips.

"Do you want something to drink? I can get you water or I bet they have something better." Simon had only been with him for a minute but he felt somewhat protective of him already. He had always wanted a brother.

Starting to look a little more relaxed, Brian nodded and said, "Water is ok."

Simon took the large cup that was on the rolling table by the bed and went to the sink to fill it up.

Brian took a few long sips of the water as Simon helped him hold the cup. Setting it back on the table, Simon turned to him and asked, "So, how long were you down in the cave?"

Brian looked at him blankly. "What cave?" He asked with confusion.

• •

Lincoln had walked outside to get some fresh air. It troubled him to see that nice man having so much trouble. He wondered if he had any family and if so, why were they not here with him?

Walking along the tree lined path on the side of the hospital he noticed Jacob up ahead. He was standing on the sidewalk looking at the ducks in the pond. Sitting behind him on a bench was a man who looked out of place in the setting. He was wearing a nice-looking suit and large dark sunglasses. But what seemed odd was that he appeared to be focused on Jacob. Maybe he had underestimated Jacob's fear of the man he was always on the

149

lookout for. As he was wondering about it, the man got up from the bench and started to walk up behind Jacob. With his heart pounding, Lincoln began running as he shouted, "Jacob!"

Jacob turned to see Lincoln running toward him and smiled before he saw the look on Lincoln's face. It was fear. Jacob turned to see what Lincoln was looking at and saw the back of a man walking quickly to the parking lot.

Lincoln reached him in only a few seconds and just slightly out of breath asked, "Are you ok? Did you know who that was?"

"Who "who" was? I didn't see anyone."

"The man in the suit with dark sunglasses. He was sitting right there watching you." Lincoln answered.

The color drained from Jacob's face. He hadn't seen anyone like that since the baseball game several weeks ago. "We better go tell my uncle. Did you see where he went?"

Lincoln shook his head. "No, he just went between the cars in the parking lot."

Jacob hoped it was just a coincidence because he didn't want to start looking over his shoulder all the time again. He had just started being able to finally relax.

• •

Ron made his way to Lancer Memorial Hospital. It was much larger than when his wife worked there so many years ago. It looked like they had added several wings to the building and even a parking garage off to one side. Unsure of how to proceed,

Ron parked his car and walked into the hospital's main entrance. He walked with purpose up to the information desk. Waiting patiently while the lady in front of him inquired about what room her sister was in after suffering a burn from a dropped pan of hot oil, he slowly scanned the entrance area. Everyone seemed to be in a hurry whether rushing in or out. His gaze landed on a man sitting in a chair by the door. He had been looking at Ron when he first glanced over but now held a newspaper awkwardly up in front of his face. He certainly didn't know anyone who would be in Lancer so that seemed odd. Before he had a chance to think more about it, the volunteer behind the counter asked how she could help.

"Hi. I was wondering how I would go about finding information about any records regarding my wife who used to work here about 10 years ago." Ron said in a friendly tone.

"Sir, I don't think that's the kind of information we would be able to freely give you. But you are more than welcome to go up to the second floor. Room 211 is our Human Resources Department."

"Thank you so much. I appreciate it." Ron said as he turned to find a staircase or an elevator. He glanced back toward the door where he had noticed the man with the newspaper. The newspaper lay in a crumpled heap on the empty chair. Thinking it must have just been someone waiting for a ride that had arrived, he never gave it a second thought as he headed up to Human

151

Resources to hopefully get answers to some never before asked questions.

Simon smiled reassuringly at Brian who looked confused and scared after being asked about the cave. He had to go get someone to find out what he was supposed to do now. He certainly didn't want to make the situation worse. Standing up, Simon asked, "Can I get you something to eat? I can go hunt something down. How about some ice cream?"

Brian's eyes bulged. "Ice cream? Really? You could get that for me? I have only had it a few times and I love it!"

Simon was happy to see the excitement replace the fear. "I sure can. I'll see what kinds they have. Do you like chocolate or vanilla better?"

Brian's eyes bulged again. "Ice cream can be chocolate? Oh, I think I would really like to try that if you can find some."

Smiling so big he could feel it reach to crinkle the corners of his eyes, Simon replied, "I can guarantee that one way or another, when I come back, I will have some chocolate ice cream for you."

Brian's eyes started to dart around nervously again. "Do you promise you will come back? You won't be gone long, will you?"

With a strong feeling of protection toward this new friend of his, Simon looked him right in the eye as he gently squeezed Brian's frail shoulder. "I absolutely promise I will come back. And I won't be gone long. You have my word."

With a look of relief, Brian relaxed into the bed and watched the one person he trusted as he headed for the door. "Wait!" He called quickly.

Simon turned toward the bed as Brian smiled and said, "What's your name?"

"Simon. My name is Simon. I'll be right back with that ice cream. Try to rest a little if you can." Simon raised up his hand with a quick wave and walked out the door. He was two steps out the door when he picked up his pace and hurried to find Richard. He had to tell him what he had found out in his talk with the mysterious boy who had no memories.

· ·

Kristin was at her desk in the tiny medical office trying to decide what to do with all of the paperwork she had accumulated over the past decade on each of the town members. When they had arrived in the cave, she had nothing about anyone's history so she started from scratch with a folder for each person. If it was true that there had been no plague, then what was the reason they were here? She leaned back in her chair and stared at the ceiling. She had stared at that spot on the ceiling so often over the years. It was her concentration spot. If she focused on that one spot, she was able to block out distractions and think strictly of the problem she was trying to figure out.

Now she was staring at the ceiling spot and wondering how everyone in the cave was connected? If they weren't down here to save their lives from the awful death on the outside, why were they the ones chosen?

Her thoughts were interrupted by RJ barging not very gracefully through her office door. "Mom, the mayor sent me to get you. They are back from the entrance and everyone is gathered to discuss what they found."

"RJ, if I didn't know better, I would think you are busting at the seams with the thought of getting out of here." Kristin said jokingly to her son. She could only imagine how excited he must be at the thought of it. Her biggest concern was that whoever had decided to quit sending food and supplies down to them made that choice because they wanted the townspeople dead. Whether they were in the cave or on the outside, wouldn't those people still want them all dead?

RJ grinned widely and exclaimed, "I get to see how much the outside really looks like my real town model! And mom, I've been thinking," he bit his bottom lip for a second. "If we could get a dog, I would like to name him Alaska. Because in books, Alaska looks and sounds like a really cool place!".

Getting up from her desk, she put her arm around RJ's shoulder as they walked out the door and started heading to the meeting. Squeezing him a little closer, she said, "Bud, when we get out of here, you can get a dog and name him whatever you like."

*****

Jacob and Lincoln rushed into the hospital to find Richard. As they rounded the corner, they almost collided with Simon who was rushing down the hallway. All three boys started talking at once and several people walking by shushed them. Remembering they were in a hospital, Jacob motioned the others to a nearby waiting room that appeared to be empty. They were almost to the door when they saw Richard and Wray deep in conversation coming from the other direction.

Jacob rushed toward them and said in a whispered plea, "We have to talk to you!"

Richard closed the door behind him as everyone took a seat in the quiet waiting room. All three of the boys started talking over each other.

Holding up his hand to quiet each of the boys, Wray turned his attention to Simon first. "Simon, were you able to get Brian to talk to you?"

"I did. But he doesn't remember anything about being in the cave. And he didn't even know what chocolate ice cream is. He said he only had ice cream a few times. We had it quite often, right Lincoln? So, I wonder if he can't remember anything at all? He's really scared."

Wray nodded his head with approval. "I'm glad you were able to get him to open up. I'll ask him some questions to see if his memory loss is from trauma which should be temporary. I would like you to keep spending time with him if you can. He needs to feel like he has someone to trust."

"Oh, I will for sure but my dad and I are moving in a few days so I don't know what will happen after that. "

"We'll slowly introduce Lincoln and Jacob so he can have someone closer to his own age to continue talking with."

Jacob spoke up. "What about the other kid that was with him? Is he ok?"

Wray was solemn, "Medically, Joshua is doing better but he is still in a coma. They went an awful long time without any food."

Richard turned his attention to Lincoln and Jacob. "Now what were you two going on about?"

Lincoln piped up, "A man in dark glasses was watching Jacob and I think he would have gone after him if I hadn't come along."

"What? Where did this happen?" Richard said. He could feel his blood pressure rising.

Wray looked concerned. "Did you see his face, Jacob?"

"No. Lincoln chased him off. I've been watching for him though and it's the first time in weeks that he's shown up. At least that I know of." Jacob stated as he smacked Lincoln on the back. He thought Lincoln might have saved his life.

In response to Richard's question, Lincoln replied, "He was over by the pond sitting on the bench. He went into the parking lot."

Richard stood up and said, "I'm going to request footage of the cameras in the area and then Simon, you and I are going in to talk a little more to Brian. Are you good with that?"

Simon jumped up. "Yep! As soon as I find some chocolate ice cream."

Wray took out his wallet and handed some money to Simon. "Why don't the three of you go down to the cafeteria. I know they have ice cream down there. Get yourselves a snack. You must be hungry after such an interesting day."

As the boys headed down to the cafeteria, Richard radioed in to have an investigator follow the boys to make sure they stayed safe.

CHAPTER 9

Ron found his way to the Human Resources office. He waited for several other people to be helped first. When he finally got up to the counter, he explained what he was looking for.

"Sir," the woman began, "that is probably not something we can give you."

"Well, I will wait here until you find out where I can get that information. I'm not leaving without something to help me." Ron was tired of being patient.

The woman huffed and went into the office down a short hallway. He could hear two people exchanging words although he couldn't make out what they were saying.

Walking back toward Ron, she sat at her computer as she said, "I will print out a request form."

"That's fine. How long have you worked here?" He asked.

"Three years." She replied defensively.

"Do you know anyone who has worked here for over ten years?" Ron asked quietly. "I would like to talk to someone who maybe worked with my wife."

Realizing she had maybe been hasty in her judgment of this man and his request, she answered, "Most people I know have been here less than 5 years. But Sue down in accounting has been here probably since the place opened." She handed him the paper. "If you fill this out right now, I will process it immediately and can get that information to you in 30 minutes. You can go see if she is around and I will have it for you as soon as I can."

Smiling at her with renewed energy, Ron thanked her and started on his way down the hall to the accounting department. He felt like he was finally getting somewhere. He was interested to hear a few stories about his wife along with finding out what the paperwork showed as her last date of employment and the reason for leaving.

∙∙∙

Kristin and RJ arrived just as the meeting was about to start. Everyone had been anxiously waiting for the return of the group who had some information about their discoveries at the entrance. Everyone was somewhat surprised that they were back so soon. They didn't know if that was a good sign or a bad one.

"Well, what did you learn?" asked Frankie. No one was surprised that she was the one to start the conversation. She liked things done in a timely manner and in a no-nonsense sort of way.

The group signaled they wanted the mayor to speak for all of them. "Ok. Well folks, it didn't take us too long to find the door to the outside." There were murmurs throughout the town members at the information. "There is a key pad next to the door but we could spend weeks trying every combination we could think of. We believe if we gather any type of tool, wood, metal bar, some type of explosive material, anything we think might break that door, and we send a group of strong, healthy neighbors, we

160

have a chance of getting through. It won't be easy. It's a solid structure. But we sure have to give it a try. Now, the next step is gathering the supplies. And you will need to decide who will go and who will stay."

RJ felt like he had been holding his breath through everything the mayor said. Had he heard correctly? Could it be that easy? He wondered if he would be allowed to go along when they were trying to open the door.

The mayor continued, "It is early summer and depending on where we are, the weather should be favorable. We don't know how long we will be out there looking for help. We don't know what kind of terrain we will encounter. We have to be prepared for heat, storms, animals, water and food shortages and there is always a question of who might be looking for us if they realize we aren't here anymore."

Ben, the 91-year-old resident, stated with confidence, "I know you will be successful. But as you all know, I will not be able to take this journey with you. Some of us have been talking and we just aren't going to physically be capable to go. Now, that being said, we will remain here and be prepared to defend each other against anyone with bad intentions."

Several people nodded and there was some applause. Kristin sat with her head down so no one would see her tears. RJ noticed and swallowed the lump in his throat.

Kristin didn't know how she would choose whether to go to help search for freedom or to stay and help the most fragile in their community. It was going to be a hard decision.

Frankie stood up and said, "All right then. Let's gather what we think can open that door and meet back here in one hour. I would recommend we all start getting together any sort of portable drinking containers for those who will be going out into unknown elements. They need good drinking water. Also, whatever we can put together for waterproof shelters. Gather all of your items that you think might be used for hunting or fishing. We obviously haven't had to use that sort of thing down here so be creative. Whether we stay or go, we are in this together."

∎∎

Richard had some of his team working on watching the video of what had taken place outside with Jacob. He said to watch to see where the guy had come from and if they could get a license plate or vehicle description of what he left in.

As he was leaving the surveillance room, he saw Wray up ahead in the hallway. Jogging slightly to catch up to him, he asked about the condition of the boys.

"We are feeling good about Brian's progress. It's not uncommon for some memory loss and his physical concerns are quickly improving. I think it will help a lot for him to have a buddy to talk to. Even just to have someone his own age to relate with will continue to positively affect his progress."

162

"That's great. I'm going to go in to visit him with Simon soon. I want to talk with him and see if we can start building a relationship so he feels comfortable with me. What about Joshua?" Richard asked with concern.

"No news to report, unfortunately. It's kind of a waiting game. His vitals show he is gaining strength but he shows no signs of waking up anytime soon. His body has been through a terrible trauma." Wray shook his head. "I can't imagine what those boys witnessed if they were there for all of those deaths. They were their friends and neighbors. However, reports from the coroner show that the boys are not related to any of the people they identified down there. I just don't understand how they got there."

Richard replied with frustration, "I hope we are able to find some answers. We still have a team looking for more towns but it would help to have something to go on."

"I agree. Good luck to you. I've got to go meet with some patients. We'll touch base later."

Richard continued down the hallway and hopped onto the elevator to head to the cafeteria.

• •

Arriving at the Accounting Department, Ron asked to speak to Sue.

"May I tell her what this is regarding?" asked the front desk attendant.

"I would like to ask her about my wife who used to work here."

Looking confused, she asked, "Her name?"

"Kristin Claye." He said proudly.

"Ok. Give me a minute." Getting up from her desk, she walked down to the second door and stuck her head in. Ron heard them speaking before they both walked back up to the desk.

"Can I help you?" asked Sue in a clipped tone.

Ron smiled and replied, "Hi Sue. I was told you used to work with my wife. Kristin Claye. She worked in labor and delivery. It would have been just over 10 years ago."

Not returning his smile, she answered curtly, "That name doesn't ring a bell."

He pulled his wallet out of his back pocket and took out the worn picture he had memorized. Handing it to her he said, "See. This is from right around that time. She was an RN in labor and delivery. She worked here for several years."

Not even glancing at the picture she shook her head. "I don't know who that is. I'm sorry, I have a lot of work to do." She turned on her heel and walked back to her office closing the door behind her.

"Please." Ron called out. "I need to talk to someone who knew her. Will you just look at the picture?"

Looking apologetic, the front desk attendant watched as Ron quietly walked out of the accounting office.

With trembling hands, Sue dug her cell phone out of her purse. As she waited for an answer on the other end, she paced the room. After several rings, her call went to voice mail. She stopped pacing and in a hushed, annoyed voice she left her message. "Winston, call me back as soon as you get this. Ron Claye was just here asking about his wife."

• •

After wandering around the hospital for a while, Ron went to the labor and delivery floor but the ward was not accessible for visitors. There was not one area he walked by where he recognized anything. Everything had changed. Ten years was a long time but it seemed like an eternity as he looked for memories which were nowhere to be found in this building.

Not feeling very optimistic, he headed back to the Human Resources department. The woman who had helped him met him in the doorway.

"Mr. Claye, I have the results of your request. I'm sorry but we don't show that there was ever anyone by your wife's name that has worked here." She gave him the news that he didn't want but that was not a surprise. Something was definitely not right. Nothing was making sense.

"Thank you for your time. I do appreciate it." Ron said as he turned to leave.

Knowing it was a bad idea, she stopped him. "Mr. Claye, why don't you leave your phone number with me. I can ask around to see who worked here ten years ago and ask if they remember her. I will call you if I find anything out."

Perking up a little, he followed her back to her desk to write down his information. Smiling as he left, he felt just a little better knowing someone around here might be on his side.

• •

Kristin and RJ stopped for a few minutes at the window as they walked back to their house. Staring out into the deep, dark water, both were silent at first.

Breaking the silence, RJ spoke first. "Mom, are you nervous about seeing what it's like out there? What if it's changed too much since you were there last? Maybe you won't recognize it."

"Well, I think I'm anxious more than nervous. I'm excited for you to see trees and grass and buildings and animals and….so many things. Wait until you feel a cool breeze – or a warm breeze on your face! And there are so many smells. Most of them are nice. Like the air after it rains. Some are not so pleasant but you can usually stay away from those!" Kristin laughed lightly.

Looking out into the water another minute to figure out how to ask her an important question, he put his hands into his pockets. He rocked back and forth from his heels to his toes a few times. "Mom," RJ turned to look her in the eyes. "Are we going to go with them when they first leave or stay here until they come back to get us?"

166

Seeing the sadness in her eyes, he was sorry he had asked. She shrugged her shoulders. "I'm not really sure quite yet. It will be a hard decision. I hope I can count on your support no matter which way I choose."

Slowly nodding his head but feeling a sense of defeat, he replied, "Yea. Sure. Whatever you think is best, mom." They both turned and headed for home. Regardless of what decision they made, they had a lot of work to do.

As they were about to walk through the front door, the neighbor, Frankie hollered to Kristin from the edge of the yard.

"You go on in and start looking for items for the journey. I'll be right in to help you." Kristin hurried over to see what Frankie had called to her about.

"Hi Frankie! How are you feeling after that meeting?"

Frankie gave Kristin a knowing look. "Now you look here." Frankie started. It took all of Kristin's willpower not to smile at her. Their relationship had started a little rocky because Kristin had felt intimidated by Frankie's strong personality. She had grown to love her like a mix between a grandma, mom and best friend. When a sentence began with "Now you look here", she knew she was in for a lecture. Frankie continued, "I know what you're thinking. And you can just stop right now. I will not allow you to stay here with us old folks because you don't think we can take care of ourselves. We will be just fine. Don't you even think another second about it. You go in that house and get your stuff packed and get that boy out of this place. He needs you and the

167

ones going will need you. Now go on with you. You send that boy over in a bit. He can get what I put together to send along on your trip. I will see you before you leave." She turned and because of her bad hips and knees, slowly began the agonizing short walk back to her own house.

Kristin watched her with tears in her eyes and an aching heart. She would go with the group as they left for the unknown outside but a big part of her heart would stay here with her beloved friends and neighbors.

Walking into the house, she found RJ in his bedroom searching the shallow depth of his small closet for possible treasures to take along. She sat on the edge of his bed and with a big sigh, she fell back onto the bed wishing she could sleep through the next several days.

RJ turned around and looked at her. She peeked an eye open and looked at him. "We're going." She spoke.

With eyes wide open and a grin from ear to ear, he laughed and flopped onto the bed right next to her practically flipping her right off onto the floor. She laughed with him. "Let's get packing!"

CHAPTER 10

Richard and Simon quietly entered Brian's hospital room. He was laying so still they thought he might be sleeping. They looked at each other and were about to sneak back out to let him continue resting. Brian turned his head and smiled when he saw Simon. Glad to see him smile, Simon quickly held up the cup of chocolate ice cream and was rewarded with an even bigger smile.

Struggling to sit up in the bed, Richard went over and hit the button for the head of the bed to rise to a sitting position. Taking the cup from Simon, Brian just stared at it for few seconds. He leaned his face over it and took a deep breath through his nose to savor the sweet smell of the chocolate. Surprising Simon and Richard, he took very small bites to savor each taste of it. Simon chuckled and said, "I usually eat my ice cream in about three bites. Next time I will stop and remember to enjoy it a little."

Simon introduced Richard to Brian. Richard had taken a seat next to the bed so Brian didn't feel like he was towering over him. "How are you feeling?" Richard asked Brian in between his bites.

Brian nodded his head as he replied, "A lot better."

Richard continued, "Do you mind if I ask you a few questions?"

Seeing Brian's eyebrows wrinkle with worry, Simon tried to help his new friend relax. "It's ok. He's a good guy. He is with the police and he wants to help you."

"Will you stay in here with me?" Brian asked Simon.

"He sure can." Richard answered for Simon.

Taking his last bite of ice cream, he put the empty cup on the bedside table. He leaned back against his pillow. Closing his eyes for a minute, Brian popped them back open and looked at Richard. "Are you the one who found me?" He asked slowly.

"Yes, I am."

"I kind of think I remember your voice." Brian said trying to concentrate on his memory.

Trying to make him feel at ease, Richard joked with him. "I do have a memorable voice. It can be a bit booming at times."

Brian smiled. "Where was I?" He asked.

"You were in an underground town. In a cave. Do you remember anything about a cave?" He asked.

Brian tried to think. "I don't think so."

Richard tried again. "Do you remember someone named Joshua?"

"Joshua?" Brian said the name several times quietly to himself. "Joshua. Not that I can think of."

"Do you remember being hungry?"

Brian looked at his empty ice cream cup and then looked up at the bag of fluids going into his arm. Tilting his head to one side in concentration he closed his eyes. Opening again, he looked at Richard. "I remember kids. A lot of them."

"Kids?" Richard nodded.. "Ok." That didn't make any sense. He was found in a cave with only elderly people except for him and Joshua. "Little kids or older kids?" He asked.

"Like my age and a little older. No one old like you." He said motioning at Richard.

Richard smiled at him chuckling a little. "Kids like you and Joshua. Do you remember where you lived?"

Gesturing with his head to indicate to the negative, he leaned back into the bed. Richard could tell he was getting worn out from the questions. He decided to quit and let him rest. "Is it ok if I come back to see you again?" He asked Brian.

"Yes." Turning to Simon, he asked, "Can you stay with me?"

Simon looked at Richard. "Do you think I could stay with him tonight? I can sleep in the chair. I'll call my dad and let him know."

Richard got up from his seat and headed to the door. "I'll ask the nurse if that's ok and maybe she can get a roll away bed in here for you. I'll call your dad because I have to talk to him anyway. I'll see you two tomorrow." As he was walking out of the room, he heard Brian asking what the box on the wall was for. He knew Simon would love to show him the different things on tv. They were in for a fun night!

Wray caught up to Richard in the hallway. "How did it go in there?" Wray asked.

Shaking his head with a troubled look on his face he replied, "Nothing. He doesn't remember being in the cave but he remembers kids his age. I'm not really sure what that means."

Interrupting their conversation, the lead investigator that had been watching the surveillance videos asked to speak to them. Following him back to the surveillance room, they followed him over to the video equipment. The investigator showed them the footage of the man who went up behind Jacob on the path near the parking lot. It appeared obvious that Jacob was his target and that Lincoln had thankfully scared him away.

Richard asked, "Were you able to trace him to a vehicle and get a plate number?"

"No." The investigator answered. "But I do have something else to show you." He showed them several video clips from different areas of the hospital. "This is the part that is most interesting." He slowed the screen to show the man as he was coming out of a hospital room. "This was about an hour before Jacob's incident at the pond."

Richard demanded, "What room number is that?"

Both the investigator and Wray spoke at the same time. "Two Oh Three"

Wray looked confused as he rubbed his fingertips across his forehead. "Why was he in Mr. Ellison's room?"

Richard pulled open the door so hard it slammed into the wall. "That's what we are about to find out!" With quick, purposeful steps, he started heading to room 203. Following close behind him, Wray entered the room on his heels.

"What's going on here?" Asked Wray as they stopped in their tracks.

The nurse was pulling a sheet over the body. "I'm sorry Dr. Lindstom. Mr. Ellison just went into cardiac arrest and we couldn't save him. Time of death was 8:32."

Richard radioed to the investigator they had left in the surveillance room. "Get me a close up of the man entering this room and trying to contact Jacob. We need to get his picture out there and find him now!"

"We have a car watching the boys, but I will go over to check on them and show them the photo to see if either of them recognizes him." Richard said.

Wray nodded and asked, "Do you think we should have an officer on the boys here too?"

"Already done. Plain clothes officers so you shouldn't even notice them. They will get the update and know to be on high alert."

"What are we dealing with here, Richard?"

"I wish I knew. I think this is much bigger than anyone anticipated. I'll keep you posted." Reaching out to shake hands with his brother-in-law, Richard hoped the next time he saw him it would be with some answers.

CHAPTER 11

Ron had gotten the message about Simon staying at the hospital. He decided to stop by to check on him before going home. Wray had seen him walking toward Brian's room and met him before he got ambushed by the undercover officers covering the room. Wray explained the situation and walked with him to the room. Opening the door, they looked inside to find Brian sound asleep and Simon laying on a roll away bed watching a baseball game. The volume could hardly be heard and the tv screen sent shadows of light around the room.

Simon smiled at the sight of his dad. Ron walked over and sat in the chair next to him. Bending down close to him so he didn't wake up Brian, Ron asked him questions about his day. Knowing he was in good hands staying here with police protection, Ron was about to leave for the night. He felt there were so many unanswered questions about their old town, the events leading up to being there and the dead end trying to find information about his wife that he was overwhelmed. Simon really seemed happy when he was telling him about his day. It helped Ron feel more relaxed.

"Simon?" Ron started. He took a deep breath and slowly exhaled. "There is a lot going on right now. What would you think about staying around here for a while and we could get Grandpa and Grandma to just come for a visit instead?"

"Really?" Simon responded with enthusiasm. It made Ron feel better about his decision. "That would be great! Brian needs me. Lincoln and Jacob are coming back in the morning to hang out. And I don't have to keep packing! Hey, I tried to find you today but you had left your office. The guys and I wanted to ask you some questions. Where were you?"

Ron preferred to keep his search for information about Kristin to himself for now. "Just trying to tie up some loose ends. How about if you ask me those questions tomorrow?"

"Sounds good. Have a good night." Simon replied with a yawn. He was asleep before Ron made it out to his car. It had been a long day for everyone.

• •

Kristin and RJ had searched the house from top to bottom. They had a pile of items on the table along with two backpacks and some of Kristin's medical supplies in a small duffle bag.

RJ was going to go out to the shed to hunt for more items for their travels while Kristin went to the clinic to get things in order for her patients. It was going to be tough because they now had a limited supply of medication. Someone had been supplying them with what they needed up until a few days ago. She didn't know how long her dear neighbors would be down here before someone came for them. She would have to spread out the limited supply and make sure everyone knew what to do when she left.

Sitting at her desk she leaned back and stared at her spot on the ceiling. Realizing she may never sit here again, she tried to make a picture in her mind of her surroundings. This was the place she spent the most time thinking. Thinking about the past. She tried to put on a brave, happy face for RJ and her patients and neighbors. But the truth was she had been broken since coming down here. She had never been the same after finding out her husband and first-born son had died. She didn't know what to expect when she got back outside. The mayor said it was not contaminated any more. But did it look the same? Would they have access to what they needed? How long would it take for them to find help? No one down here even knew where they were. Talking to herself, Kristin said aloud, "Well, staring at the ceiling isn't going to get us anywhere so here we go!" Pushing herself out of her chair for the last time, she walked back home to see if RJ had found any useful items for their adventure.

• •

All of the town members gathered at the meeting center. The mayor called everyone's attention. "First of all, has everyone decided if they will leave or stay?" There were a lot of affirmative answers. "To those who are staying, please know that everything here is at your disposal. If you run out of something, go to a neighbor's house and get it from there. Check on each other every day. Don't give up on us. We will find our way to help and will send it to you as soon as we possibly can. Get your group together and set up teams to keep watch for anyone entering the cave that may be unwelcome. Have a plan." He pointed at Kristin and she stood up to continue the conversation.

"Whether you are staying or going, if you are taking any medication, please go to the pharmacy area of the clinic as soon as the meeting is over. You will be responsible for your own meds starting tonight. I will disburse all I have. Hopefully we will have access to what we need on the outside before anyone runs short. You know what to do. Please be responsible." Kristin made eye contact with her neighbor Ben who was constantly needing to be reminded to take his pills. She didn't know if it was because he really forgot or he just liked to visit with her every day when she checked in on him. He smiled broadly at her and held up his index and middle fingers like a pledge promising to remember. Sitting back down, she started preparing a list in her head of all the things she still needed to do before they left.

The mayor walked over to the tables where the town's people had dropped off the supplies that they thought might be useful for their journey. "I have a group of ten people that will start out at six o'clock tomorrow morning. They will gather what they think might be helpful getting the entrance open. The rest of the group that will be leaving will depart at eight o'clock. Meet here and we will divide up the items to pack out with us. Have all of your personal supplies with you. Once we leave, only a few will be coming back to get the others after we find help. Bring only what you absolutely need or feel will help us on our travels. It may be a long walk and we don't want to burden ourselves with a bunch of unnecessary items. Does anyone have any questions?" He turned and looked into the faces of the individuals who had been his neighbors for over a decade. He couldn't help but wonder if anyone blamed him for their circumstances. He certainly blamed himself. Looking back, it didn't make sense that he never questioned what was going on. Well, from here on out, he was going to do everything in his power to take care of these good people and make sure they got to safety. He just hoped they could do it without encountering too many obstacles.

With no questions being raised, the meeting was adjourned. No one was in a hurry to leave because they didn't know if they would ever see everyone together again. There were a lot of tears and hugs as friends and neighbors said good bye to each other.

CHAPTER 12

Richard woke to the loud ring of his phone. Answering on the second ring he was surprised to hear from Wray so early in the morning.

"I'm guessing you have some news?" Richard asked as rolled out of bed and headed to the kitchen to start a pot of coffee. He knew it would be another long day ahead.

"Yes and no." Wray answered. "We haven't received an official cause of death for Mr. Ellison yet but it's entirely possible he died of natural causes. There didn't appear to be any visible trauma. Maybe the mystery guy we saw on the camera didn't harm him. But here is the reason I called. Looking back in his chart, I noticed something interesting. I did a little research and guess where he used to work?"

"I have no idea." Richard said as he pulled the container of coffee off the pantry shelf.

"He was the Head of Research at the hospital in Lancer."

Almost dropping the container, Richard set it on the countertop and sat down at the table. "That's where Lincoln was born and where Ron's son was born as well as where his wife worked." Rubbing his hand several times over his forehead, his mind was going a hundred different directions. "I will check with the team and see if we have any other connections with people who were found in the cave. Let me know if you hear anything else. Thanks so much for the heads up."

"You bet. I'll stay in touch. I'm headed in to check on Joshua and Brian soon. Maybe we can get a few answers there. Have an extra cup of coffee. I think you'll need it!" Wray said.

· ·

When Simon rolled over on the squeaky roll away bed, his eyes popped open and for a brief moment he didn't remember where he was. His eyes scanned the hospital room and finally settled on a grinning Brian.

"I didn't know if you would still be here when I woke up." Brian said with obvious relief that Simon was indeed still in the room.

Yawning and stretching, Simon felt a sense of satisfaction that he had been able to do something to help his new friend. Reaching up to scratch his head in an effort to completely wake up, he was surprised to hear voices he recognized right outside the door. Entering the room full of energy and chatter, Lincoln and Jacob made themselves right at home. Jacob sat on the chair by the bed and Lincoln shoved Simon's legs off the small portable bed and dropped down on the edge. He looked from Simon to Brian. "Did you guys just wake up?"

Simon shrugged his shoulders. "I guess so. I must have been tired. What about you, Brian? Have you been up for long?"

Brian felt a little overwhelmed with all of the commotion. He shook his head and replied, "The nurse was in to check on me a few hours ago but I must have fallen asleep again after that. I've been awake for just a few minutes."

Jacob rubbed his hands together and excitedly shared some news. "My dad," he started then gestured toward Brian before continuing, "your doctor - said if you were feeling up to it, we could take you out in the wheelchair to get some fresh air. It's a perfect day outside. We have to stay in the courtyard but that's ok. If you just woke up, you guys probably haven't eaten breakfast yet. Maybe we can eat outside."

Simon was happy to see his friends and although he could see some hesitation in Brian's face, he really wanted to go. He had been cooped up in the hospital for too long. Watching Brian's eyes dart to the window, he immediately felt bad that the thought hadn't occurred to him before. "Brian, when is the last time you were outside...in the fresh air?"

Brian looked into the eyes of his friend then to Jacob and Lincoln. He shook his head, "I don't think I have ever been outside." Lincoln and Simon knew how he was feeling. They too had been in a cave for most of their life. The boys all gave Brian a minute to think about it. Slowly a big smile spread across his face. Out of nowhere a loud laugh rang through the room as Brian beamed and said, "Let's go!"

As they were getting ready to leave, Jacob's mom, Anne came through the door. "Hi fellas." She held up a large bag with a grin on her face. "I thought I would bring some breakfast."

With exclamations of appreciation, the boys gathered what they needed and Lincoln left the room to hunt down a wheelchair. Anne sat down on the edge of Brian's hospital bed. Her heart was heavy wondering what his young life had been like. "How are you feeling today, Brian?" She asked quietly.

Something about the look in her eyes almost made Brian feel sad. He wondered if anyone had ever asked him that question outside of this hospital? He managed a small smile and nodded his head as he replied, "I'm good. I'm about to go see the sun."

She patted his hand and gently squeezed it. "It's been waiting for you."

Getting up from the bed, she looked around the room and could almost feel their excitement. She chuckled. "You boys have fun!" she said as she walked out the door.

Walking out of the room, she noticed a plain clothes officer sitting in the room across the hall. She knew most of the officers in town through her brother, Richard. He made a small affirmative gesture with his head to acknowledge her. Even though she knew the police would have eyes on the boys at all times, she couldn't help but be a little worried.

*****

The Human Resources office was quiet at the moment. Betty sat at the front desk staring off into space. She couldn't get Mr. Claye out of her mind. It didn't make sense. She could tell he was sincerely distraught after hearing the information that his wife hadn't been on file for ever having worked here. After thinking about it for most of the night, she had made up her mind. Her fingers flew over the keyboard searching for the name of anyone who had worked in labor and delivery ten years ago. She discovered two names. She wrote the information down and slipped the note into her purse. Something about the whole situation made her want to keep it a secret that she was doing her own little investigation.

• •

Richard had set a meeting at the station with Ron, Samuel and Clara. They had all been in the originally discovered cave together. They had been questioned individually upon their discovery but had never been in a discussion with an investigator together. Richard wondered how they would react to the news about Lancer and Mr. Ellison. It felt like they were getting close to some answers.

Walking into the room and closing the door behind him, he could sense some tension in the air. Taking a seat next to Ron at the table, he placed several file folders in front of him.

Samuel was the first to speak. "Is this about our cave or the new one? Do you have any new information?"

Richard didn't know where to start. He let out a long breath. "We obviously feel that the caves are related. Our investigators came across some information that you may find important. We are full steam ahead on this because we think there may be more caves and the people behind this scheme may be feeling the pressure. We are in a time crunch if they are abandoning more caves with no food."

It had been a shock to everyone when a second cave had been found. Ron jumped into the conversation. "We are here for whatever you need. What can we do?"

Richard tapped his finger on the top file folder in front of him. "Clara, do you remember who delivered your baby?"

Clara gasped. He had taken her by surprise. "Who delivered Lincoln?" she asked with confusion.

"Yes."

"Well, let me think." She couldn't get her thoughts together. It took a minute. "I don't really remember. There was one really sweet younger lady but I don't remember her name. She was my favorite. Then if I remember right, there was another nurse named...." She hesitated. It had been so long. "Kylie. Kelly. Something like that. Of course, Samuel was in there and the doctor showed up right before I delivered." She looked to her husband. "Samuel, do you remember his name? Doctor Olingham?

Samuel nodded in recognition. "Yes. That was it."

Richard opened up his notebook and wrote the names down. "Ron. What about you? Were you in the delivery room when Simon was born?"

Looking very confused, Ron answered, "Well, yes. But I was so nervous that I don't remember a thing. Certainly not who delivered him. Can I ask why?"

"Lincoln and Simon were both born at Lancer Memorial, correct?" Richard asked the group.

Taken aback, Samuel looked at Ron. "I didn't know Simon was born there too."

Ron nodded his head. "I knew the boys were about the same age but I never thought any more about it than that."

Richard quickly asked, "What date?"

Ron replied, "March 3rd."

Clara answered, "February 16th."

Jotting it down he then pulled out a picture from the folder. He set it on the table. "Do you recognize this man?" Samuel and Clara leaned over it and both shook their heads. Ron pulled it to his side of the table. He also shook his head no. Richard took the photo back and pulled out another one handing it to Ron. He held it for just a moment and not recognizing the individual, he handed it across the table.

Examining the picture from a surveillance camera of a man standing next to a bench by a pond, Clara dismissed it almost right away. "He doesn't look familiar." She said with some disappointment. She had hoped she could be helpful.

Samuel was still looking at it. He pulled it closer. Richard slid another picture from his folder of the same man coming out of a hospital room. Samuel pointed his finger at the picture. He was nodding his head as he looked into the distance trying to draw a memory from his mind. After several minutes, he looked back at

Richard and said, "I do recognize him but I can't remember from where."

There was a knock on the door and an officer opened it up. "Sir. We found something."

Richard quickly got up from his seat and grabbed his paperwork off the table. "Thank you for your time. I will be in touch."

Leaving Ron, Samuel and Clara with a lot of unanswered questions, he followed the officer into another room. The lead investigator looked troubled. "What did you find?" Richard questioned.

The investigator handed Richard the information he had requested. "It appears that there were three other babies born at Lancer Memorial Hospital during that time period. All three of them reportedly died from the virus. We are tracking down the parents at this time. None of them stayed in the area."

Richard had to sit down. He felt sick to his stomach. What are the odds that all five babies born in that hospital at that time ceased to exist? If two of them were in the first cave, were the other three in another one?

CHAPTER 13

Wheeling down the hallway at a much faster pace than was necessary, the boys could hardly contain their excitement. They got to the back door of the hospital that led out to an enclosed courtyard. Simon held the door open and they all watched Brian's face as he took a deep breath of the air coming in the door. The light breeze ran through his hair and he sat up taller in the wheelchair. With a glance up at the clear blue sky, he beamed with joy as they pushed the chair past the doorway and out into the open area.

He had seen things from the window of his hospital room but it did not prepare him for the overwhelming feelings he was having. The sights and sounds and smells. He watched a robin pull a worm out of the grass and fly away. Several kinds of trees swayed their branches as if to say hello. Flowers were blooming and each color seemed more vivid than the last. At the center of the courtyard was a round water fountain surrounded by benches and tables. Simon slid the chair up to a table as Jacob plopped down the bag of goodies his mom had brought for them.

Lincoln was cautious. "Take it from me. You don't want to eat too much too fast. It will make you feel sick. Right Simon?"

Simon agreed but was eager for his friend to try something new. "Have you ever had a donut?" He asked as he pulled a gooey maple fried donut from a box that had been inside the bag Jacob set down.

Brian leaned toward the sweet smell of the donut. His hand reached over for it and it was like a dream to take that first delicious bite. "This is even better than chocolate ice cream!" He exclaimed.

He looked over at the table with all sorts of different things to try. He had seen and even eaten some of them before. He passed on the apples and bananas. There were little covered bowls of cereal but none he had ever seen. Just as he was debating his choice of milk or apple juice or orange juice, a small bird flew down just feet from them and started hopping around. Lincoln quietly said, "Tear off a small piece of that donut and throw it toward him."

He did as Lincoln requested and was rewarded by the bird grabbing it and eating it right there in front of him. The bird hopped a few steps closer to the boys and Brian laughed with such delight that the sound startled the bird and it flew off.

"I know you can't get out of your wheelchair because of the tubes and stuff but can you move your arms enough to throw the football?" Jacob answered. His mom had thought of everything, including a junior size squishy football.

"I will sure try!" Brian said with excitement. They finished eating assorted breakfast items before they moved away from the tables and spread out to toss the football to each other. "Did you guys have a football in the cave you lived in?" He asked Lincoln and Simon.

Simon answered, "We did. And a baseball and baseball gloves. There wasn't a whole lot of room to throw though. We were always afraid we would break something. You seem to know how to throw it. Do you think you had a football?"

Brian thought about it for a minute. "Well, I don't really remember but it does seem familiar to me so I guess I must have. I wonder who threw it to me?"

Simon hoped that he had indeed had a friend to throw the ball to. Maybe Joshua. He didn't want to bring that up in case it might make him feel bad.

∎∎∎

On her lunch break, Betty walked down to labor and delivery.

"Hi Betty! What brings you down here?" asked the nurse who was sitting at her computer charting the morning's activities.

"Hi. I was wondering if Kelsey is working today?" Betty asked somewhat nervously. She didn't really feel right about digging around but she really wanted to get some answers so she could help Mr. Claye.

"No. She's not in until Saturday night. Anything I can help you with?" She asked politely.

"No. Thank you though." She turned to leave but stopped and before she lost her nerve, turned back and quickly asked, "How long have you worked here?"

"Going on 7 years in August."

Betty bit her lip and plowed ahead. "Did you ever hear of a nurse here by the name of Kristin Claye? She would have been here several years before you started."

"Kristin Claye. Kristin Claye. I do remember hearing about a Kristin that was a fantastic nurse. She was one of those types that everyone just loved working with because she was so good at her job and very sweet. I don't know if I ever heard what her last name was."

"Do you know why she left?" Betty asked with hope.

"If I remember right, now it's been a long time and my memory might not be perfect, but I think she moved away to take a job somewhere else. It's too bad. We could use more nurses like her."

Betty felt defeated but she had to start somewhere and answers that weren't helpful were still answers. "Thank you so much. Have a great rest of your shift."

• •

Ron, Samuel and Clara were still sitting at the table where they had talked to Richard. It had been silent in the room for several minutes. Ron cleared his throat and began trying to clear up the questions he had running through his mind. "I guess I never knew that the boys were born at the same hospital."

Clara gestured her agreement. "I don't suppose it ever came up in conversation. That is really strange."

Ron struggled to ask his next thought. He swallowed several times and tried to calm his nerves. "Do you know if my wife helped deliver Lincoln?"

The shock registered on Samuel's face. "Your wife worked at Lancer Memorial?"

Looking down at the table but not before they could see the sorrow in his face, he said, "Yes. For many years. She loved it there." He leaned forward and pulled his wallet from his back pocket. He pulled the picture of Kristin from inside and gazed at it for a second before handing it across the table. "This is her a few months before the plague."

Clara put her hand over her mouth as tears came to her eyes and memories came flooding back. "Of course I remember her. She was so pregnant! I wondered how she could be on her feet taking care of me for so long. She had Simon shortly after that then, didn't she?"

Ron felt a strange mixture of the constant sadness of losing her and elation to have met someone who remembered her too. "Yes. I guess it would have just been a few weeks."

Clara reached over and put her hand over Ron's in a comforting way. "Oh Ron. She was an angel. So patient and kind. She wasn't the main nurse in my room but she was the one I always looked to for comfort. Well, you know, now that I think about it, I do see a resemblance of her in Simon. He has her gentle eyes."

Ron sucked in his breath to keep his emotions in check. "Yes. He sure does. I see her every day when I look at him."

Samuel interrupted their conversation. "Why do you suppose Richard was asking who delivered Lincoln and what date they were born?"

"That's a really good question." Ron's eyebrow furrowed in confusion. "I have been asking around at the hospital and there is no record of Kristin ever working there. Something isn't adding up."

"I'll ask Richard if I can accompany him to Lancer later today or tomorrow. We'll get to the bottom of this." Samuel hoped that with his medical degree or his ex-military status maybe he could make some headway. Whichever way it needed to happen.

CHAPTER 14

RJ and Kristin had enjoyed one final big breakfast with Frankie before beginning their journey into the unknown. As they got up to leave her house, Frankie hugged Kristin then turned to RJ and surprised him by pulling him into a hug and whispering into his ear, "Take care of your mom, RJ." She then kissed him on the cheek. RJ had never seen Frankie being affectionate so it made him wonder if she thought she would never see them again.

Knowing her emotions were about to take over, she gruffly waved her hand in the air. "Now go on with you two."

Kristin smiled through her tears as she reassuringly told Frankie "See you soon." She hoped with her whole heart that those words would come true.

As they walked from the only town RJ had ever lived in, he felt a touch of sadness but mostly just elation. He was finally going to get out from these walls that had been closing in on him for years. Kristin stopped at the edge of town before it became dark as night in the cave. Turning for one last wave good bye to her dear neighbors, she couldn't help but wonder if she would ever see them again.

Kristin's mind was racing trying to make sure she had given everyone who was staying what they needed to get by. She wished she could stay to protect them and take care of them. But she knew she was needed for the unexpected conditions on the outside.

The town's people who were leaving the cave walked by flashlight to the door in total silence. No one knew what to expect in the next several hours. Hopefully they had all the tools and equipment necessary to get them to safety and find help to send back for the rest of the friends before they ran out of food and medication.

Only the leader of the group with the shining light knew which direction to go. Kristin didn't know how far they had gone when a loud blast sounded in the distance. It felt like it shook the ground underneath her feet. The leader yelled to the group. "We're close. Let's pick up the pace and see if they got it open."

RJ wanted to run towards the sound. This seemed like it was taking entirely too long. He had to stay with the group because it was still too dark to see anything. After several minutes, they heard voices and saw a small sliver of light.

Arriving at the small group of people who had left early to get the door open, the leader of Kristin's group called out, "Was anyone hurt?"

Much to everyone's relief, the reply was negative.

They gathered around and stood in awe looking out a crack in the side of the door. The bright sliver of light gave them the knowledge that their hopes of getting outside were within reach.

"We're almost there. It didn't work quite as well as we had hoped but we are close."

A small group of the strongest folks pulled on the door as hard as they could. They were grunting and straining and slowly

194

the door started to give way. The sliver of light got bigger and bigger until there was enough room for people to slide out the opening.

RJ was about to bolt out the door when his mom restrained him by the arm. "RJ. You need to stay by my side every minute. Do you hear me? Please. I need to know where you are at all times."

"Ok." He understood even though it felt like it was suffocating him.

She grabbed his hand and ran to the front of the line. Everyone was more than happy to let them be one of the first ones out. They knew RJ had waited his whole life for this moment.

They squeezed through the opening and into light that was so bright they had to close their eyes for a minute. Opening their eyes slowly they looked around and RJ began scanning the horizon at what he had been missing all these years. He could see forever. There were no walls to interrupt his view. He took a deep breath and turned his face to the sun which was filtering through the trees. It was so warm. There were trees everywhere and so many noises. He turned to his mom and threw his arms around her. He had never been this happy in his whole life. He couldn't wait for this new adventure to begin!

The boys were outside for the second day in a row playing catch with the football when Wray came out to check on Brian. He could tell from a distance that Brian looked happy but worn out.

Wray called out to the boys as he walked toward them. "Hello! Looks like another nice day to be outside." Squatting down at the wheelchair he made a quick visual assessment of Brian. "How are you doing with all this fresh air and activity?"

Brian smiled. "Great! Can we stay outside a little longer Dr. Lindstrom? I feel fine. Honest."

Wray hated to break up their good time but he was worried about Brian overexerting himself and the sun was just about to reach the point in the sky that the boys wouldn't be shaded anymore. Brian would burn in no time. "Sorry guys. It's time to go inside now but maybe you can come out again tonight."

"Ok." They were disappointed but didn't argue.

Wray pulled Jacob aside for one moment to say, "Meet me in my office in five minutes."

Jacob nodded his understanding.

After gathering up the items that they brought outside with them, they all slowly headed back toward Brian's room. Jacob excused himself from the group and said he would meet up with them shortly.

Unsure what his dad wanted to talk to him about, Jacob's mind started wandering and he worried that maybe he had done something wrong. Entering the office, he was surprised to see his mom sitting in one of the chairs across the desk from his dad. She looked up as he entered and tilted her head toward the vacant chair next to her. "Have a seat." She said with a smile.

Jacob sat down and looked to his dad with a question in his eyes.

Wray chuckled and said, "Jacob, why do you look so nervous? Have you done something you think you should be in trouble for?"

With quick wit, Jacob replied, "I prefer not to answer that question so I don't incriminate myself."

Exchanging a humorous glance with his wife, Wray leaned back in his chair in a way that Jacob recognized as a serious conversation lean. "Your mom and I have been talking and we want to discuss something with you before we make a final decision. What would your thoughts be about having Brian come and stay with us for a while?"

The question took Jacob by surprise. "Really?"

Wray continued, "He is getting better and I think he would thrive outside of these walls. I could still keep an eye on him and your mom is there to be with him when I'm not home. We don't know if he has any family. If he does, we still have to locate them. It would give him time to finish healing and start getting used to being outside the cave. You would have to understand that it does not mean that you guys will be able to wander around and do whatever you want. There is still a very active investigation going on and as they get closer to some answers..." Wray hesitated.

"Well, let's just say some people may not want answers to be found. We have to be very watchful."

Jacob swallowed the lump in his throat. He had just started to relax a little before the man in dark glasses appeared again. He knew there were threats out there. But the opportunity of having Brian stay and getting to watch him experience new things for the first time was very exciting.

"There is enough room in the basement for you two to stay together and even have Lincoln and Simon join you if they want. What do you think?" Anne was hoping his answer would be positive because that way all of the boys would be together and there would be an officer keeping watch over them every minute. She had been a bundle of nerves ever since Jacob had fallen into the lake. There were just so many loose ends and dangerous possibilities. Whoever was behind this had to know that Brian and Joshua had been saved from the second cave. They weren't going to want Brian to start remembering anything.

"I think it's a great idea! I can't wait to tell everyone. When is he coming home with us?" Jacob was eager to get back to his friends and share the news.

Wray said, "I think one more night of observation would do the trick. First thing tomorrow morning he should be able to be discharged."

Jacob jumped from his chair almost knocking it into the wall behind him. "Oops. Sorry. Can I go now?"

Wray and Anne both spoke at the same time with cheerful tones, "Go!"

Jacob took off down the hall to spread the news.

•••

Richard was pacing the floor in his office at the police station. Ron had been in to talk to him about Kristin. Richard wondered if Kristin had known Mr. Ellison. His team had found that no other staff members from Lancer Memorial had disappeared like she had. There had never been any information found that she had supposedly perished in the plague. It was just like she had ceased to exist. However, the labor and delivery doctor, Doctor Olingham, had given his notice shortly after the babies were born and no one seemed to be able to track him down. He wished he would have been able to question Mr. Ellison before he had passed away. He would have had a lot of answers. The search continued for the man that tried to confront Jacob outside the hospital and who was also one of the last people to see Mr. Ellison alive.

There was something else bugging him. He couldn't get it off his mind. Brian stated that he had only tasted ice cream a few times. Lincoln and Simon said they had it quite often. That could mean that the cave that Brian was in must have been a lot further out. Too far out to drag unnecessary frozen items. He pulled out his lake maps again and spread them across his desk. They had started their search close and were slowly spreading further out. Maybe they had to start looking farther away.

After analyzing the map and narrowing down the options, he called up his good friend who happened to be a great woodsman and tracker.

Richard waited somewhat impatiently as the phone connected and rang.

"Hello?"

"Randy? It's Richard. I need your help with an investigation." He quickly explained the reasons behind his narrowed lake search. The woods were necessary to keep the cave hidden. It would be hidden well and someone with Randy's experience would make the search go much faster. Time might be running out for anyone still being held in a cave.

"You betcha! I'll gather my gear and head your direction. Expect me first thing in the morning."

CHAPTER 15

It had been an interesting first few hours outside the cave. RJ and Kristin sat on a fallen tree to take a breather and get a drink. Their group had been traveling at a steady pace and were stopping to rest and make sure they were still on their planned course. It had been amazing to step into a clearing in the woods at the top of a steep hill and get their first glimpse at the lake that they had only seen from underwater through a window. It had been their only connection to the outside world for ten years. It was so much bigger than anyone had anticipated. It was a beautiful sight but they hadn't stayed long to enjoy the view. They figured they had a lot of ground to cover.

Kristin was closely watching her son's reaction to everything he was seeing and hearing and smelling. He had a constant smile on his face and she could see him regularly taking deep breaths to enjoy the smells of nature.

No one was used to getting this much exercise and it was much hotter than they were used to. She had insisted that everyone stop to rest and to constantly drink water to stay hydrated.

All of a sudden RJ jumped and smacked himself on the arm. He had a startled look on his face as he watched a small red lump start appearing on his arm.

Kristin and several of the townspeople burst out laughing. The mayor walked by and patted him on the back. "Welcome to your first mosquito bite." He said with a smile in his voice.

RJ grinned as he started scratching the fresh bite.

"Try to leave it alone." Kristin encouraged.

The group had been resting for long enough and everyone was anxious to continue their journey. They had limited sunlight and wanted plenty of time to set up a camp before dark.

■■■

Richard was getting an update on the Yellow Zone officials they had captured and arrested after locating the residents of the first cave. So far none of them had spoken a word but just moments ago, one of them decided to be questioned in hopes of getting a more lenient sentence.

The investigators didn't get much new information from the official. It appeared that the officials were just doing their job. They had been told that they were guarding the cave because the people inside had been quarantined and were an escape risk that could put everyone in harm's way if they got back out into the population. They were under strict confidentiality agreements and everyone pretty much kept to themselves.

The Yellow Zone official that had chosen to talk to an investigator said he was afraid that whoever was in charge might hurt his family if he said too much. He claimed to have no knowledge about the location of any other caves or how many people were presumed to be considered under quarantine.

He did not even know his location because his group had been flown in and no one knew who in the group was reporting back to the main boss. They got paid a lot of money but there was no leniency. One person started asking questions and later that day he disappeared and no one ever saw him again.

Richard felt frustrated. Not only did this not help his investigation, it added so much more complexity to it. Somebody must have had a lot of money and position to pull this off. And so far, it didn't seem like there was any reasonable explanation for any of it. Still unsure of how many more caves not to mention how many more lives were involved, Richard knew his work was about to get more intense.

∙∙

As the members of the cave who chose to stay put and wait for help to arrive decided to turn in for the night, Frankie checked to make sure the four neighbors who were to keep watch through the night had everything they needed.

It had been a long day and everyone was exhausted. They had spent the whole day in the gathering area located by the window. Frankie had no way of knowing that at the same time she had been staring out the window into the deep blue water, Kristin had been up on a hilltop staring down into the water wondering just where the location of the window might be. The group of townsfolk had made good progress on plans of keeping watch and making buddy systems to keep an eye on each other. Frankie chose to be a buddy with Ben. She knew Kristin would want to be sure someone responsible would make sure he was taking his medication.

She walked slowly back with Ben to his house. Luckily, they didn't have far to walk because between the both of them, none of their bones, joints or muscles wanted to make much of a journey. She helped him get his walker through the front door then using her cane she hobbled over to his kitchen sink. "Where do you keep your pills, Ben?" She asked as she started opening cupboards looking for a glass for water.

"What?" He asked loudly as he pulled out the chair and took a seat at the kitchen table.

"Well, you can't hear a thing, can you?" Frankie replied. Talking louder and making sure he could see her face so he could maybe read her lips, she asked again loudly and slowly, "Where do you keep your pills?"

Ben mumbled under his breath. He much preferred the help of Kristin. He already missed her and knew he would worry about her until he found out she was safe. He grumbled, "They are in the drawer left of the sink."

"Well, now who needs to speak up? Quit your grumbling." She opened the drawer and pulled out his pills. Kristin had seen to it that they were all neatly in order in a container with the days clearly marked. She poured the day's pills out into her hand and grabbed the glass of water. Setting them down on the table in front of him, she took the seat next to him to make sure he actually took them.

"You don't have to watch over me like a child. I know how to take pills." He said with a grouchy tone.

"Well, you may not like it but I promised Kristin I would watch out for you and I intend to keep my promise. You can just keep your bad attitude to yourself." Frankie said with a snap.

He popped the medication into his mouth and washed them down with a big swig of water. Crossing his arms over his chest, he stared over at Frankie for several seconds before his gaze moved to the table in front of him. "I'm sorry. I'm just worried about them. Most of them have never been out there like this before. We don't know who's maybe out there keeping an eye on them with bad intentions."

Feeling her tone soften, she got up from the chair and placed her hand on his shoulder as she said, "They are going to be just fine. They are all watching out for each other. Just like we are." Patting his shoulder a few times, she left the kitchen and slowly hobbled down the street to her own house. She had said they were going to be just fine but in her own mind she wished she could really believe it.

∙∙∙

The boys could hardly contain their enthusiasm. They had been making plans non-stop since finding out they would all be staying together for a while. Brian was more than ready to leave the hospital. He was hoping to start remembering things but, in the meantime, it would be fun to be with his new friends.

Everyone had left to go get their stuff ready for all the plans tomorrow. Simon had promised to be back later and stay the night again so Brian wouldn't have to be alone. Brian was starting to get restless and bored. All of the monitors had been removed and he didn't have any more tubes coming out of him so for that he was thankful. Even though he was still weak, he felt like he wanted to move around now that he had so much freedom.

His door had been open for a while and he could hear the chatter of nurses, visitors and other patients outside his room. The muted sounds of televisions were almost like white noise. He watched people pass by his door and everyone looked like they had some place they needed to get to in a hurry. He wasn't used to so much commotion. Getting more restless by the minute, he decided to move around a bit. He slowly headed out his door. Looking around double checking his room number to make sure he remembered how to get back, he started walking down the hallway. He told himself that he would look out the window at the end and then head right back. No one would even know he was out of his room.

His mind wandered for a moment and from somewhere deep in his memory, he pictured looking out a window into darkness. He wondered what was outside that window in his memory.

He had made it three doors down and was already feeling worn out and tired. Deciding he wouldn't make it all the way down the hall and back, he slowly turned around to head back to his room. A nurse was leaving the room in front of him so he stopped to let her pass. As the door slowly closed behind her, Brian could see a boy laying on the bed inside the room. In the few seconds he had to focus on the face of the boy before the door completely shut, he had enough time to recognize him. It was Joshua. It all started coming back to him. The walls started tilting and he could feel himself breathing harder.

Brian felt strong hands behind him hold on to his shoulders to steady him. The man said, "Nurse, could we get some help here?"

She was kneeling in front of him doing a quick assessment when Brian saw Wray rapidly walking down the hall toward them. "Brian. What's going on buddy? Can you walk back to your room?"

Brian turned and with a little help from Wray and the plain clothes police officer who had been following him closely as he began his stroll down the hallway, he made his way back to his room. The nurse followed and got him all settled back in his bed.

The officer quietly updated Wray about the incident then left to go back to his post across the hall. Wray sat on the edge of the bed next to Brian. He picked up the boy's slim wrist and felt his fast, pounding pulse. In almost a whisper Wray asked him, "Brian, did you see Joshua?"

Brian's eyes locked in to Wray's and Wray could see the fear. "You're safe here Brian. I promise. Do you remember what happened?"

Wray could see Brian swallow. Turning his head away from Wray, Wray could see the tears start falling from his eyes.

CHAPTER 16

RJ could have continued walking all night. This was the best day of his life. The air was so refreshing. The smells were different with each step he took. There were so many different kinds of trees and leaves and plants. He was starting to hear more birds chirping and insects buzzing. These were all just things he had read about or saw pictures of and now he was actually seeing and hearing them. He took it all in with complete joy.

The view of the sun setting with the light ricocheting off the water was amazing. Kristin had forgotten how beautiful sunsets could be. She enjoyed watching RJ experience it. It couldn't have been more perfect for his first night outside the cave. The air was warm but the slight breeze made it feel comfortable.

The leaders of the group had been following what appeared to be somewhat of a trail. It made sense that someone had to get food and supplies to them from somewhere. Whoever had been supplying them had been careful to cover their tracks because following the trail proved to be tricky. With daylight slowly fading, they decided to set up camp. Each given their duty in preparation for the night, the neighbors went about their tasks and everyone seemed to be in their own little world pondering the events of the day and wondering what tomorrow might bring.

Even though they had brought food along, they knew it was limited so a few of the members went out looking for food and a clean water source. One neighbor had a lot of knowledge about what berries were edible and had stopped along the way to pick some food for the night. Every little bit helped their food supply last since their number of days out here were unknown.

Fires were being built. Make shift tents and coverings were being built. Everything was going along smoothly when off in the distance there was a scream. A loud scream of pain. No one moved. They all looked wide eyed at each other. Two members of the group ran toward the sound. Kristin told RJ to stay with the neighbor standing close by and the neighbor nodded her agreement that she would not let him out of her sight. Kristin grabbed her bag of limited medical supplies and ran after the others.

As they approached the area where the noise had come from, they started calling out. Nearing the edge of a steep drop off, they heard a muffled cry for help. Leaning over to get a closer look, they noticed it was quite a distance down. One of the neighbors ran back to camp to get a rope. Kristin was calling down and trying to get answers from the injured individual. After several repeated tries to get a response, they heard a voice call up one more time. "Help!"

Looking at each other, Kristin said to her neighbor, "That sounded like the mayor."

Not speaking but nodding in agreement, they were each trying to make a mental plan to get down the embankment when the other town member got back with the rope. Kristin said, "I should go first and see what's wrong before we try to pull him up.

We might need more help pulling if you want to run back and get a few more people to come."

Kristin's neighbor said, "I will go first to make sure it's safe and if he needs medical attention then I'll call you down, ok?"

Agreeing, she paced a little circle waiting to hear something. They hadn't heard him call for help since realizing it was the mayor. Several townspeople gathered with Kristin as they waited to hear word from below. It seemed like hours even though it was only a few minutes before hearing a call from below, "Kristin, can you come down?"

With the help of a rope and several friends, she made her way down to the injured mayor.

"I'm glad you're here, Kristin. When I got down here, he was still awake but now I can't get him to respond. He appears to be bleeding from a wound on his head plus his leg is twisted kind of funny." In the dwindling light, Kristin made an assessment and plan of treatment.

As they were about to begin their struggle back up the steep incline, the neighbor leaned over and in a hushed tone said, "I need to tell you something though. Kristin, before he lost consciousness, he told me someone pushed him from behind. We have to help him but we have to do it in a hurry because I think we all may be in danger."

Simon had been called by a nurse at the hospital and was told wait until morning to visit Brian. Unsure what caused the change of plans, he couldn't help but be worried about his new friend.

Ron and Simon were finishing up a quiet supper. It had been a while since they had been alone and had time to discuss the events of the past several days. They had both seemed a little preoccupied. Simon was the first to bring up the subject they had been thinking about but were not wanting to voice.

Simon began with hesitation. "Dad, I want to ask you something."

"Sure. Anything." Ron answered.

"All those years in the cave, we thought we were down there for our protection because of the plague and everything was contaminated on the outside."

"Yes." Ron replied trying to keep the anger from rising inside himself. It seemed with each passing day he was feeling more hostility about the situation they had been placed in.

Looking at his hands which he had placed in his lap to keep them from trembling, Simon kept on in hopes of getting the question answered that had been on his mind for several days. "If everyone on the outside was safe, where is mom? I understand if she was told we were dead that she might not stay around here but do you think she might still be alive? Where is she? How do we find her?"

"We are on the same page Simon. I have begun searching for her. I am not having very good luck but Richard and his team are searching also and I have no reason to believe she is not alive out there somewhere."

Feeling sick to his stomach, Simon asked a hard question. "Do you think since she thought we were dead, she might have...you know." Simon kept swallowing to keep from showing too much emotion.

Ron's heart was breaking for his son. "Simon, if she was told we were dead, I'm sure she struggled for a long time. Our hope should be that she did move on with her life and maybe start a new family. It certainly wouldn't mean she quit loving us. She was given false information. You are her first born. She loved you like crazy. No matter where she is now, I have no doubt she thinks about you every day."

"Dad, don't you think she would have come to find us? The story was all over the news. She had to hear about it and guess it might have been us."

Ron had been struggling with the same thought. He knew his wife would have been there if she heard the news. It didn't matter where her life had taken her or where she ended up. She loved them and she would have been there by now to see them. Something wasn't right. He could feel it.

After a few moments of silence with each of them in their own thoughts, Ron finally said, "I give you my word that I will search every day for the rest of my life until I find your mom. No matter where that search takes us."

With the topic finally out in the open, Simon felt a little better. After a quick discussion about the plans for the next day, each of them went to their rooms in the hopes of a good night's sleep even though they both knew it was probably unlikely.

■ ■

Wray and Anne had taken turns staying with Brian during the night. He had still not spoken and his health seemed to be taking a turn for the worse. Wray was afraid he would have to hook him back up to fluids if he didn't start drinking again.

After a restless night of tossing and turning and waking up in fear from nightmares, Brian was relieved to see the sun coming through the window again. Night was the worst because it reminded him of the dark cave after lights out.

Richard had been in to talk with him about what he remembered but Wray hadn't let him stay for too long. Brian was afraid to talk about it. He felt like if he didn't say it out loud, maybe it didn't really happen.

Anne had been watching him wake up and continue his silent stare out the window. She was thankful that she could be here hoping to give the sweet boy some comfort. Richard and Wray had each told her it was ok to try to get him to talk or at least to drink or eat.

214

"Brian?" She spoke his name quietly. He turned his gaze from the window to her face. Her eyes looked so kind. He had never known his own mother. He hadn't really realized until a few days ago that he even missed it. But right now, he would give anything to have a mom of his own looking at him with kind eyes.

Anne continued in a quiet voice, "I know you saw some bad things. You don't have to talk to me about it. But I want to tell you something. I have only known you for a few days and I know you are a good, kind person. I'm sure the people who were with you loved you very much." She had to stop for a minute because it almost took her breath away thinking about the poor elderly people whose bodies had been stacked in a pile. It made her sick to think that Brian might have been the one having to stack the bodies. Continuing with her appeal to Brian, she stated, "I'm sure they would want to see you eat and get better so you can get out of here and have a normal life playing outside and having friends and learning new things every day."

Brian looked back out the window as he remembered his old friends telling him to stay strong and making him eat their share of the meager rations that dwindled every day. He moved his eyes back to Anne who sat patiently as his mind took in what she said. She was right. He nodded his head.

Anne smiled as she slid a big glass of water across the night stand toward him. "Well, I would say this is one of those rare opportunities where it is acceptable to have chocolate ice cream for breakfast. What do you say?"

215

His smile reached his eyes as he nodded his head again. He wasn't ready to talk yet but he would eat.

●●

Betty was just getting started with her day when her boss came in sounding impatient and annoyed as he finished up a conversation on his cell phone.

"Betty, we have an urgent matter at hand." He stated, looking like he wanted to throw his phone at the wall.

"Ok. What can I do to help?" Betty asked knowing whatever it was would probably involve a lot of work on her part.

"We need to find a replacement in accounting ASAP." He said with irritation.

"Ok. Is someone sick?" She asked with concern.

"No. Sue didn't show up this morning. When someone went into her office to talk to her, it was cleaned out. She took all of her files and computers. It's going to be a nightmare. Do what you can to get it somewhat up and running as soon as possible. The other staff over there will help you. I hope I don't need to remind you to keep this under your hat. Word of this gets out and it will be a messy road. I'll check in this afternoon." With that he turned on his heel and stormed out of her office.

This was too much of a coincidence. Knowing her job was on the line, she hesitated for only a second before calling Ron. She knew somehow this had something to do with his search for his wife.

CHAPTER 17

Wilderness expert and tracker, Randy, arrived at the police station bright and early. Richard met him at the door and quickly brought him in to brief him on the latest developments and show him specifically what he was looking for on the lake map. Having a plan in action and communication in place, Richard sent him on his way along with several of his officers to start the hunt for additional caves.

Richard hadn't been sitting at his desk for more than a few minutes when there was a knock on the door. "Come in." Richard called out wishing he had thought to grab a cup of coffee before continuing his work.

One of the detectives working on the case entered the room but didn't bother sitting down as he quickly relayed his new information. "We have identified the individual leaving room 203 and trying to contact Jacob outside the hospital."

Crossing his arms over his chest and leaning back in his chair, Richard said, "Good work. His name?"

Richard wasn't prepared for the answer. It almost took his breath away. "His name is Winston Ellison. He is the son of the man in room 203."

They were getting close. Richard could feel it. Once the pieces started falling into place, they would come together quickly. Hopefully it was quick enough to prevent finding another cave full of dead bodies.

It had been an exhausting night with little rest for Kristin. With a lot of work from multiple people, she had been able to get the mayor back to the camp site. She tended his wounds and reset his leg. She was quite certain no one would willingly volunteer to be her assistant ever again after witnessing resetting a leg. Most everyone in the camp would never forget the sound it made.

They had agreed as a group that half of them would stay put for the day with the other half continuing on the journey to get help. After a day of rest and with a lot of continued help, the mayor would be able to be moved with care.

RJ was content staying with Kristin's group and was being entertained by the frog he had found by a stream near their camp. The frog would have to do as a pet until he could get his dog.

Richard had spent most of day following leads and making inquiries. He had just sat down to consider how to proceed with the information that Ron had given him about the missing accountant from the hospital. Obviously, the computers had some information someone thought was important if they had disappeared. He knew they would still be able to retrieve the information they were looking for but it would just take a few more steps this way.

Lost in thought, he was startled back to the present by his cell phone ringing. Still slightly distracted, he answered on the second ring.

If it wasn't such a serious situation, he would have thought it was a joke. Randy spoke the words that Richard had been waiting for but had not expected so soon. He was elated and fearful at the same time. "Hey man, we found a door."

Getting Randy's location, Richard dashed out the building and ran to his car. He met the state helicopter at the landing pad of the hospital. Wray and another member of the medical staff met him at the door as he was jumping in.

With everyone's adrenalin pumping, it seemed to take hours to get to their location. They had sent more help by foot but Randy said the terrain was difficult. It would take the other officers a while to catch up once they got to the end of the driving road. He had spotted one clearing that wasn't too far away from the entrance which was just enough space for the helicopter to land.

Upon arriving at their designated spot, everyone exited the helicopter and hunching over they quickly ran to the edge of the woods where Randy and his team of officers were waiting for them. Randy explained that it appeared the door had been tampered with. No one had entered yet. Knowing back up was following shortly, Richard decided to go in with the team he had. No one knew what to expect. They had to be prepared for anything.

Pushing the door as far as it would budge, they were able to maneuver through the opening. Flashlights in hand, they headed forward following the wall. They had made good progress and were adjusting to their dark surroundings. Up ahead they spotted some dull light. They pushed forward with renewed determination knowing that if there was light, there probably was – or had been – life.

They were almost to the edge of what appeared to be a town when they heard voices yelling from several places in front of them. "Stop! Do not go any further. We have weapons and will use them."

∙∙∙

Brian was feeling much better even though it was difficult to process his returning memories. His friends had been in to see him during the day and they had enjoyed some more time outside. He was looking forward to getting out of the hospital but because of his setback earlier, he was going to have to stay for one more day.

He had started hearing hushed conversations after the helicopter had left a while ago and he was curious to know what was going on. Everyone was being so nice to him but he felt like they were acting differently. Like they knew something about him.

After sitting alone in his room with some time to think, he had made a decision. Simon was going to come back in about an hour to spend the night on the roll away again. He was happy that he didn't have to be alone. But before Simon came back, Brian wanted to go see Joshua again. This time it wouldn't be such a shock. He wanted to make sure his friend was ok. Doctor Wray had told him that Joshua still hadn't woken up yet but that he was getting better every day.

He didn't know if the nurses would let him in Joshua's room so he was going to have to make sure no one saw him. He walked to his doorway and peeked out. Everyone was busy doing something but there was one nurse that he knew would see him if he tried to slip by her. Just at that moment, a call light came on outside a room down the hall and she immediately headed in that direction. He took action and quickly made his way down several doorways and slipped into Joshua's room. He stood inside as the door quietly closed behind him. He waited with a pounding heart feeling sure someone would step through the door and make him leave. After a minute with no one entering, he slowly headed toward the bed. He stood staring down at his friend. Joshua was the only other person who knew what they had been through. He really wished he could talk to him.

Brian's gaze traveled over the machines surrounding Joshua. Even with all the tubes and wires surrounding his friend, Brian thought he looked much better than the last time he had seen him in the cave. He was actually surprised that Joshua was still alive.

"Joshua." Brian whispered quietly.

After getting no response, he leaned over closer to his ear. "Joshua. It's Brian. Can you hear me?"

One of the machines that was beeping seemed to start beeping faster. Maybe it was Brian's imagination. He just knew someone was going to come in any second and his chance would be over.

"Joshua. Please wake up." He spoke a little louder.

Brian gasped with surprise and took a step back as Joshua opened his eyes and looked at Brian's wide, fearful eyes.

Brian watched as Joshua started looking around the room. The beeping started getting even faster. He made eye contact with Brian as Brian stated, "You are in the hospital. We were rescued."

Joshua tried to lick his dry lips. Brian leaned down to hear what he was trying to say.

With hardly a sound, Brian knew what he asked. "Jack?"

Joshua looked with pleading eyes toward Brian. "Jack?" He mouthed again with his eyebrows creasing with concern.

Brian shook his head. "No. That's why I need you to wake up and talk to me. I don't know what to do. I don't know who to trust. Please. I need you to tell me what to do."

They heard the door open. Standing in the doorway was the plain clothes police officer assigned to watch Brian.

CHAPTER 18

Richard held up one hand and shined a flashlight on himself with the other. "We are here to help. May we continue forward?"

From somewhere off to the side, a voice called out, "Where do you come from and how did you know where to find us?"

"We come from Blue Water and I'm with the police." He gestured to the others. "This is Doctor Lindstrom and Nurse Lindsay from the Blue Water hospital along with Randy who is actually the one who discovered your door. Behind us are more officers from Blue Water and the county. There are eight of us total. We have been looking for you. We have located two other caves similar to yours. We are here to get you safely back home."

"Did the others send you?" Asked a voice from the opposite direction of the first voice.

Looking over at Wray, he replied, "No. Like I said, we have been looking for you. Who would have sent for us?" Asked Richard with confusion.

"That Randy guy who found the door, send him forward to talk to us. The rest of you stay where you are." Hollered a third voice.

Getting a nod of approval from Richard, Randy headed toward the town.

After about ten minutes Randy called out for the others to come ahead. Randy filled them in with the details of how they had been cut off from food and supplies and that approximately half of the town escaped and were going to send help when they found it. Knowing they couldn't have gotten too far in less than two days, Richard radioed in for search parties.

Gathering what they could carry, the group that had been left behind in the cave began their journey to the outside. Medics came to accompany the elderly who needed help. Frankie had checked on Ben and they were both looking forward to meeting up with Kristin and RJ to hear about their adventures. No one had expected to be rescued so soon.

· ·

It was late in the evening when the group that had been found in the woods reunited with the rescued townsfolk from the cave. They had been taken to a large fellowship area attached to a church in Blue Water. Everyone was enjoying a hot, hearty meal that the community had quickly prepared when the news spread of the arriving group. Everyone was overjoyed and talking over each other when Frankie called out loudly to stop talking.

"Where are the rest of us?" She asked with urgency.

Looking around the group, Ben chimed in, "Where are Kristin and RJ?"

One of the men found in the woods looked around the room. "Didn't you find the other group?" He asked with surprise.

Richard walked over to him. "What other group?" He asked with a sinking feeling.

"The mayor got hurt so we split up. Half of the group stayed with him."

Frankie could feel her mouth go dry. "Where is Kristin?" She asked anxiously.

"Kristin?" Richard asked as the possibility started sinking in. "Is she a nurse? About 35 to 40 years old?"

"Yes. Where is she? Where are the others?" Frankie started feeling panicky.

Things were quickly starting to make sense and Richard was not liking the way direction they were heading. He ran from the room and called into headquarters. "Send out every available unit. We have to find another group in those woods. They can't be too far from where we located the first group."

∎∎

Kristin was so thankful to have been rescued. The nicest group of hunters had found them and brought them to a shelter. It was much easier to care for the mayor and they had been assured that help would be called for the other group of neighbors separated in the woods and for those left behind in the cave. RJ had quickly fallen asleep when they arrived at their shelter. Kristin watched him sleep and was about to doze off herself when she heard another helicopter overhead. She hadn't heard the sound of a helicopter for over a decade. It seemed strange that there would be one flying over this desolate area at this time of night. But she didn't know how things worked out here these

225

days. It never occurred to her that they would be searching for her group.

Kristin's eyes were getting heavy when she heard the door open. Sitting by the door was one of the men who had rescued them and graciously offered to stay close in case anyone needed anything. She could just barely make out what he said.

She fell asleep hearing him say, "Everyone is settled in for the night. I'll let you take over. See you tomorrow, Winston."

The Broken Window

Carol Shackleford

CHAPTER 1

Richard paced the room while reaching up to rub the tight muscles of his neck and shoulders. It had been two days since locating the group of people in the third underground town. The discovery had been a mix of emotions. While everyone was elated to have found a majority of the residents who were all healthy and in good spirits, the rest of the group was still unaccounted for. Richard's team along with help at the state and federal level were unable to locate the missing. The woods and surrounding areas had been scoured from one end to the other with no signs or evidence of them. It was as if they had disappeared.

Richard called together a briefing with everyone involved in the search. Using a large white board, he impatiently scribbled out a summary of the information they had accumulated so far. It was going to be a long meeting. There were a lot of pieces to this unreal puzzle and so far, none of them were fitting together.

● ●

RJ could not believe his good fortune. Not only had he made it out of the suffocating walls of the cave, but he was in a place where he could enjoy being outdoors and much to his surprise and delight, there was a dog. He was told the dog's name was Duke but RJ called him Alaska when no one was around. He thought for sure the dog was getting used to his new name. Alaska had started following RJ around wherever he went.

Kristin watched from a distance as her son played with his new canine friend. It was a pleasure to see him so happy with his new freedom. The mayor had asked to speak to her privately. Due to his injury from being pushed down a steep embankment, the mayor was uncomfortable and agitated. He didn't want to stay inside the shelter so she had gotten him settled outside while still being able to keep a watch on RJ. Although Kristin had been overjoyed to be free of the cave and being rescued by the hunters, the time had passed where she was feeling relaxed. She was starting to feel uneasy about their situation.

"Thank you for taking care of me the last several days, Kristin." The mayor began. "I am feeling much better and feel like I should be good as new before we know it." Kristin noticed his eyes roaming the area around them. He seemed hesitant about continuing. In a hushed tone he continued, "You are the only one I can talk to without raising suspicion. I will act like I am discussing my leg. Pretend like you are checking it over."

Kristin kneeled next to him and started putting pressure on different areas of his injury. She was surprised by his secrecy. "Should I be concerned?" she asked him quietly.

"I'm not sure. I feel like we are being watched every second. I don't understand why we are still here. The members of this hunting party have every excuse in the book for why we can't leave yet. But they come and go as they please. They claim they are trying to find our neighbors but I don't believe them. We need to get help for the others still in the cave. I'm sure they are getting worried about us."

Kristin nodded in agreement. Continuing her fake assessment on his leg, she asked, "What do you want me to do? It's not like we can call a meeting because I feel like they wouldn't allow it. Should we try talking to them more forcefully or try to leave or what? I'm open to any suggestions. I feel like we are on borrowed time here. There is a reason they are keeping us and I don't think it's in our best interest to stay."

"Agreed. We outnumber them so let's get our friends on board and make a time to take over. If we are wrong, no harm done. Let's plan seven o'clock tomorrow morning. Talk to as many people as you can. We yell a code word then take charge. What's our word?"

Without hesitating, she quietly said, "Code Blue".

"Got it." He was feeling better about having a plan. Just then he noticed a hunter heading in their direction. Kristin also noticed him out of the corner of her eye and patting his leg said in her normal tone, "Looking good mayor. You'll be running a marathon in no time."

The hunter walked by and smiled at them but his smile didn't reach his eyes. Kristin wondered if he was here by choice or because he was doing a job.

Richard began the team briefing in a clear, loud voice. "This is what we know as fact right now. We have located three underground towns. Town number one had one hundred residents. Everyone is currently safe and accounted for. We believe part of the reason this town was initially discovered is because one of our boys from Blue Water crossed into the Yellow Zone and fell into the lake where he made eye contact with a member of the underground town. The Yellow Zone has been disassembled and we have not received any reliable information from them about further prisoners at different locations.

"Town two had one hundred residents who were all over the age of 80 plus an additional two residents aged ten and thirteen. All one hundred of the elderly residents perished in the cave due to either natural causes, poisoning or starvation. The two boys remain in the Blue Water Hospital and although both are regaining their health, neither have disclosed any information about their time spent underground."

Looking around the room, everyone was paying close attention to Richard's information and taking notes. Every person in Blue Water had been impacted by the underwater window discoveries. Whether it was housing and caring for the folks discovered or providing meals and help with locating family, everyone had come together to help.

Continuing his rundown of current information, Richard went on, "Town three had 200 residents. One hundred three of these residents were safely rescued from the cave. Ninety-seven of the residents had escaped and once outside had split into two groups. One group was found with 56 people. The remaining forty-one residents are unaccounted for. The missing folks range in age from 13 to 51. We have reason to believe they were being hunted by the despicable people who are behind these underground caves."

Reaching into his folder, he pulled out an enlarged picture from surveillance video. "You have each received a copy of this person of interest. His name is Winston Ellison. Study this picture. Get to know it. Look at it until you can see him in your sleep. We believe he is the person who has all the answers we are searching for. Call for backup before confronting him. He knows he has a lot to lose if he is captured. Most likely, he won't go down without a fight."

• •

Brian and Joshua had been sitting in Joshua's room for most of the morning. Brian knew his new friend Simon was going to be there to visit soon. Brian wanted to get something off his chest before Simon's arrival, but he was afraid to start the conversation. Staring down at the floor, Brian began with the same question he had asked Joshua for the past two days. With hesitation, he asked again, "Would you want to go outside? You can see what fresh air feels like. I bet there are a lot of birds out there today."

Joshua had his head back against the pillow. He gave a negative reply by just barely shaking his head. It didn't feel right to him that he should be able to go outside when Jack couldn't.

Brian was starting to feel frustrated with him. "Joshua, why can't we just tell them? They can help us. Maybe they can get to the others in time to save them."

Joshua turned and stared out the window. "What would we tell them? They wouldn't believe us. And even if they did, we don't know where they are. What if the person we tell is not on our side? They might take us back there. I'm getting stronger every day. Another day or two and I can get out of here and we will find them ourselves."

Brian looked at him with pleading eyes. "Another day or two might be too late. I really do trust Simon. He was just like us. He was in a cave almost his whole life. Now he has a normal life. We can too. I know it. That police officer that found us, they call him Richard. He is looking for them. We can help him find them. Please Joshua."

Their conversation was interrupted by the door opening. The nurse was in to check on both of the boys. As the door was closing behind her, there was a quick knock on it. Simon poked his head around the half-opened door. "Knock, knock, anyone home?" Simon asked with a cheerful voice.

Simon stepped into the quiet room. He stood off to the side while the nurse quickly did her work. She closed the door behind her when she left. Simon felt awkward standing there being watched by Brian and Joshua. Joshua turned his head and looked at Brian. He took a deep breath and let it out slowly. "Ok."

Brian couldn't believe his ears. He stood up and nodded his head vigorously. "Ok." He said beaming. He turned to Simon. "Can you get Officer Richard to help us?"

• •

Jack was feeling desperate. He knew their time was running out but he didn't want to let anyone down. He was supposed to be in charge here. He was the oldest. Everyone had always looked to him for all the answers. Their food supply had just about run out. The man who brought their supplies and food had quit coming. Jack had realized a while ago that something wasn't right and had immediately started rationing food but it would soon be completely gone.

Everyone gathered for each meal at the picnic area around the window. They had been sharing meals together since their first weeks in the cave together. Now it was just natural but there was a change in the atmosphere during their time together. It was the day to let everyone know their circumstances. It broke his heart knowing how distressing the news would be.

The last time he had called a meeting after mealtime was to discuss the disappearance of Joshua and Brian. They had disappeared in the middle of the night and to this day he struggled with wondering what he could have done differently to keep them safe. Since that time, they had arranged taking turns to have one person in each of the ten cabins stay awake all night to ensure there were no intruders.

When Jack arrived at the picnic area, everyone was already seated and ready to begin their meal. Jack made eye contact with the meal preparers and he could tell they knew their situation was dire. He cleared his throat to get everyone's attention. Straightening his shoulders just a little bit to try to appear confident, he began, "I'm sure you have noticed that your meals have seemed like smaller portions. This is true. Our resources have been suspended and I am not sure when or if they will begin again."

The chatter of multiple voices could be heard from each table. He felt like he was going about this all wrong. How do you tell your neighbors that they might starve? Holding up his hand to temporarily silence the voices, he continued, "We will be trying to make our food last as long as possible. Please be patient. We all have to sacrifice a little right now. We have been through struggles before and we will get through this too. Remember, we are all in this together." Smiling to hide his fear, he tried to be reassuring as he cheerfully gestured to the serving table.

The group got up and in their usual orderly fashion, went to get in line for their food. The line started with the youngest and ended with Jack who was the oldest town member at age 26.

Richard had just walked back into his office after the cave briefing. He was frustrated with the lack of new information. Every way they turned seemed to be a dead end. Instead of sitting down at his desk, he paced the room while searching his mind for what direction to go with the investigation.

The phone on his desk rang, breaking his concentration. With annoyance, he grabbed the receiver and answered with a gruff, "Yes?" He couldn't believe it when he was informed that Joshua and Brian had agreed to talk with him about their cave. "Be there in five." He said before grabbing his file and rushing out of the room. Finally, we might be getting somewhere, he thought to himself.

■■■

CHAPTER 2

Brian felt almost fully recovered after being found near death in the cave. He still didn't have a lot of strength so Simon pushed Joshua in a wheelchair for his first dose of fresh air. Brian was almost giddy with anticipation. He remembered how exciting it had been just mere days ago when he had his first excursion outdoors. They had arranged to meet Richard out in the courtyard.

As they came to the door leading outside, Simon noticed that the wind had picked up since he arrived for his visit. It had been bad upon his arrival but now it seemed even stronger. At least it was not raining and the temperature was still favorable. Brian opened the door and Simon slowly pushed the wheelchair into the wind. It almost took Joshua's breath away. He looked around almost fearfully at the bending tree limbs.

"Maybe this wasn't such a good idea." Brian said to the others. "Honestly, Joshua, it's not usually like this." He was disappointed that this was his friend's first experience being outside. The sky was dark and the air was heavy and damp. "It looks like a storm is definitely brewing." Simon stated. Before they could go any further outside, Richard appeared at the door followed by the boys' doctor.

Brian's face lit up. "Dr. Wray, look at the sky. Is it going to storm?" He had become close to the man he believed had saved his life. Wray had made him feel safe with his constant care.

Wray looked up at the clouds rolling in and nodded his head with a look of confidence in his assessment. He pretended to lick his finger and hold it up in the air. "I'm not a weather forecaster but I would say that it is one hundred percent likely."

Richard chuckled and said, "Why don't we take this into the conference room. Before I talk to you, Wray has some news to share."

With curiosity, the boys followed Richard and Wray into the conference room. Wray began right away sensing the boys' eagerness. "I understand that you have decided to share information about where we found you in the cave. That's great news! I also have great news. You boys," he gestured toward Brian and Joshua, "are well enough to be discharged. If you continue at the pace you have been, you will be good as new in no time."

Brian looked nervously at Joshua. "Where are we going?" he asked quietly.

Wray could have kicked himself for not coming at this from a different angle. This was supposed to make them happy, not anxious. He quickly explained, "Of course, you will stay together. You will be staying with my family until we can locate your relatives. Simon is welcome to stay too and you know my son, Jacob and nephew Lincoln. Now, if you feel more comfortable staying in the hospital for a few more days, that can be arranged also. You two talk about it and let me know this afternoon. How does that sound?"

The boys nodded their agreement. Wray continued, "I'm going to let you talk to Richard. If you need anything at all, you just have someone come find me."

The news made Joshua even more eager to share information with Richard in the hopes of finding his neighbor friends and Jack. Hopefully this Officer Richard was as trustworthy as Brian claimed he was.

∎∎∎

Kristin was worn out from secretively making plans with as many neighbors as she could. Each one was in agreement and more than willing to participate. They had been kept in the cave for over a decade and now they were still being held hostage. She was trying to figure out where the safest place would be for RJ during the takeover. She watched with amusement as her son was trying to teach the dog to roll over.

RJ was glad for the distraction of Alaska. He knew he might be bored otherwise. It was great being free from the confining walls of the cave but he felt it had just been replaced by the confines of the forest and the shelter. There was a new tension he could feel. No one was really complaining but he knew people were starting to wonder why they were still here. He thought often of his elderly neighbor Frankie that they left behind in the cave. She and numerous others weren't physically capable of making the journey into the unknown. How long would they be ok in the cave without help? He leaned over and began one of his secret talks with Alaska.

Rubbing his neck and ears, RJ began sharing his concerns with the furry listener. He leaned his forehead against the top of the dog's head and was whispering in his ear. All of a sudden, Alaska tensed up and lifted his head from its listening position. One of the hunters had walked up behind RJ.

"Seems to be a lot of quiet talk around here today. Anything you want to share with me, kid?" the man asked gruffly.

Before RJ could respond, Kristin was standing next to him. RJ now had a better understanding of why his mom wanted him to stay within her eyesight. She smiled at the hunter with a smile that RJ could only describe as forced and fake. "RJ, why don't you show me the tricks you have been teaching the dog."

The hunter glanced down at Alaska with a look of disgust on his face. "That dog is too stupid to learn any tricks. You're wasting your time." He shot Kristin a look that RJ didn't understand but made Kristin stand a little taller. He spit on the ground next to her feet before turning to storm away.

Kristin was grateful that they were making their plans to get out of here in the morning. Everyone was on edge and it was only a matter of time before someone snapped.

*****

Jack was sitting at one of the picnic tables staring through the window into the clear water behind the glass. Everyone else had left the area after their meal. He leaned his elbows on the

240

table and dropped his forehead into his clasped hands. Closing his eyes, he tried for the hundredth time in the past several days to formulate a plan. Ten years ago, when they first arrived, he and several of the other older kids went searching for an exit and found nothing. They didn't have any light source so they felt their way all around the side of the cave. It had been terrifying and disappointing to have come back to report that they were indeed stuck down here. The ten years had seemed to go fast and slow at the same time. When Jack focused on today and tomorrow it went fast. When he would day dream about the past, before arriving down here, it dragged on. Everyone had given up hope long ago that they would ever get out of here. The horror stories of the outside being ravaged by disease and death had convinced everyone that they were better off being safe down here.

Watching a fish slowly swim toward the window, Jack couldn't help but smile when the fish seemed to stop and stare at him through the glass. Wouldn't it be wonderful to have the freedom of this fish to just turn around and swim away? Shaking his head, Jack was ashamed of himself to be jealous of a fish for an instant.

There was a fine line for him these days between concentration and panic. If he focused too much on their dire circumstances, he felt like his chest would explode. But doing nothing was not helping. Jack got up and started walking circles around the picnic table area. Maybe the person delivering the food and supplies was just sick. Surely other people knew about them and someone else would start taking over the deliveries. What kind of horrible person would just knowingly let all these young people die? But what if they were able to finally get out of here and there was no help on the outside? No way to survive out there either? Before going about his daily duties, Jack had one final thought. It was the same question he asked himself hundreds of times each day. Were his brother, Joshua, and their friend, Brian, still alive out there somewhere?

■■■

Simon sat quietly at the table listening to Richard ask Joshua and Brian dozens of questions about the cave they had been found in and about the cave they were taken from. Richard tried to be delicate about how he worded the questions about the deaths of the elderly people in the cave where the boys were found barely alive.

Neither of them remembered how they arrived at the new cave. They had been lovingly accepted and cared for by their new neighbors. The boys did their best to then, in turn, care for them. It had been difficult watching their new friends die right before their very eyes. Richard couldn't imagine what these two boys had witnessed. The only thing he could do now was try to find the other cave where hopefully they wouldn't be too late to save some lives.

Richard learned that there had been 50 young people in the cave the boys were taken from. Joshua had a brother, Jack, who was the oldest member of the town at 26. He had taken charge from age 16 and had taken care of Joshua and Brian as if they were his own children. Brian was the youngest and had been just an infant when they had arrived at the cave.

They had been informed, just like the other caves, that the outside was not safe. They had been in contact with only one person who would come and go but they didn't know how he got in or out. This person would deliver their food and supplies and give them medicine if they were sick. He took care of their medical needs like the time one of the neighbor girls tripped while enjoying a game of tag and sprained her ankle.

Richard continued his questioning. "Do you know what this person's name was?"

Nodding their heads, they both said in unison, "Doctor O."

Taking in a slow breath, Richard dug through his file and pulled out an old hospital staff photo of the missing Dr. Olingham who had delivered some of the babies at Lancer Memorial Hospital. Two of those babies, Lincoln and Simon, had then been found in one of the caves a decade later.

He placed the picture on the table in front of them. They both glanced at it. Brian answered first. "He doesn't have as much hair and he looks a lot older now but that's definitely him."

Joshua nodded in agreement.

Richard looked for a piece of paper in his file again. He read the names of the other three babies born around the same time

Lincoln and Simon had been born at Lancer. "Do you know these names?"

Shrugging his shoulders, Joshua replied, "We don't know most kids' last names because they were too young to remember them; but yes, there were kids by those first names down there."

"Does the name Winston Ellison mean anything to you?" Richard asked hopefully.

Looking at each other they both thought about it for a few seconds. Brian answered with certainty, "No. That's a strange name. I think I would remember it."

Richard felt disappointed but quickly glanced over as Joshua made a questioning noise in his throat. "Hmmm. That's funny."

Joshua felt everyone's eyes on him. He felt his cheeks start to blush with embarrassment.

Richard waited expectantly. "What's funny?" He asked hopefully.

Joshua smiled and bent his head as he scratched the back of his neck. "Well, a night or two before we were taken from the cave, I heard Doctor O. mumble under his breath as he left the room. He said a cuss word followed by Winston. I just thought maybe Winston was a cuss word too."

■ ■

Ron felt as though he would leave a permanent trace of his pacing on the living room carpet. He was surprised it wasn't worn through already. He felt like every road he had taken in the search for his wife had come to a dead end. Although he knew the police had all of their team working on it, he was becoming overwhelmed with frustration. He tried to keep his actions in check when Simon was around. Ron was thankful to know that the hospital staff along with undercover officers were keeping an eye on Simon while he was visiting his new friends at the hospital.

As he was turning around to begin another lap in the living room, the phone interrupted his thoughts. Glad for the distraction, he picked up quickly.

"Hey, dad. It's me." Simon said cheerfully.

Ron had to smile. "Me who?" He joked.

"Very funny." Simon replied with a chuckle. He hesitated before continuing. "I have to ask you a question but before you think about it, I want you to know that I really want you to say yes."

Ron could hear the seriousness in his son's voice. "Is everything ok?"

"Yes. Everything is great." He took a deep breath before continuing. "Brian and Joshua are getting released from the hospital today and they are staying with Dr. Wray. You remember him. He is Lincoln's uncle. And Lincoln is staying there too and you know I haven't seen that much of him since we've been out of the cave. Especially since I have been visiting Brian so much at the hospital. I think Brian would be really more comfortable with me there because he trusts me. And it would just be us boys in the basement and we won't go anywhere and I promise we will be good and you won't hear a bad thing about us. And"

Ron interrupted his ramblings. "Simon."

"Yea?"

"Have a good time." Ron grinned as he thought of the look on Simon's face right now. "Will you have Doctor Wray call me when he has a chance?"

"I will. Thanks dad! I'll see you tomorrow." Simon said with enthusiasm. "Bye."

"Bye." Ron said. As he was reaching to hit the hang up button on the phone, he overheard Simon holler, "He said yes!" right before the connection ended when Simon hung up on his end.

It made him happy to know his son would have a good time with his friends tonight. It was good for him to have a distraction and be around other kids his age. Plus, this way, Ron could focus all of his energy into locating his wife.

· ·

The hunters that were originally considered heroes for rescuing the group lost in the woods were now thought of as enemies. Everyone could feel the tension in the air. In discussions among themselves, the hunters had agreed that this was getting extreme. They had been following orders and doing their jobs but it was taking too long. They now felt that they were here for the wrong reasons. Their boss was supposed to be back to camp in the morning and they had agreed to confront him about their concerns. All of them had agreed except one. He was trouble and they all knew it. They just called him Jones because no one used their real names here. Jones was a ticking time bomb waiting to explode. None of them wanted to be around when that happened.

It was quiet in the shelter as everyone settled in for the night. Even though there was a solid plan in place, each town member was thinking through the next morning and wondering if the takeover would actually work. Even if it did, it didn't mean they were safe. How many other people knew they were here? And how far away were they from potential help? What if there was no help?

Alaska was curled up at RJ's feet. Kristin was watching them from her cot just feet away. She quickly closed her eyes and pretended to sleep as she felt the presence of someone walking up behind her. She tried to control her breathing but her heart was beating fast with nervousness. The person stopped right next to her head and she could feel their eyes on her face. Hoping it was dark enough so they couldn't see her trembling eyelids, she tried not to swallow the lump in her throat. It seemed like time stood still as she waited for him to leave.

Eventually, she heard footsteps walking away. She opened her eyes just a slit to make sure the coast was clear. The first thing she spotted were Alaska's eyes looking right into the back of the person leaving. Even in the dim light she could tell he was tense. His eyes moved to look at her. She smiled at him. She could hear his tail thump against the bed a few times before he laid his head back down but she could still see the whites of his eyes as he kept watch. Knowing he was on their side made her think she might be able to relax a little but she doubted she would be able to sleep. There were too many questions bouncing around in her head.

∎∎

Richard had stayed up most of the night going over the information the boys had given him. It was difficult to imagine what they had gone through. It seemed like with each answer came dozens more questions. He did know for sure that there were 48 young people and children who needed their help. There was definitely at least one more cave. There was an all-out search being held for Winston Ellison and Doctor Olingham. Certainly, either of them would be able to lead them to the cave. However, if Brian and Joshua had been taken, who was to say the others were even still there?

First thing in the morning, he would call his friend Randy to see if he had any leads from his search of the specified lakes and surrounding area. His team was getting spread thin between looking for the group lost in the woods and the group stuck in the cave. The lights flickered as he was about to get up and head to bed for a few hours before sunrise. The storm had been raging for hours. Richard looked out into the dark sky as it would regularly light up with large bolts of bright zapping energy followed directly with rumbling thunder. He had been so distracted with his thoughts; he hadn't even realized that the strong winds had done some damage. Looking out, he noticed a large chunk of the tree in his front yard had fallen and was just feet away from taking out the mailbox. He was thankful it had at least fallen away from the house. He would still be able to get out of the garage in the morning. Hopefully the storm wouldn't delay the searches in progress. He considered the folks who were out in the woods. At least one of them was injured. He wondered how they were faring in this weather.

Dragging himself into his bedroom, he dropped down on the bed in the wrinkled clothes he had been wearing for almost 24 hours. He was asleep almost instantly but vivid dreams of people running through storm ravaged woods made it a restless few hours.

■■

CHAPTER 3

Kristin was awake when she started hearing her neighbors getting up for the day. She wondered if any of them had slept or if they had been up thinking, planning and re-planning their day like she had been. Looking around, she noticed everyone was on high alert. Slight eye contact along with barely perceptible nods were enough confirmation that the plan was going forward. She made a sweeping glance of the area and noticed four of their captors were spread out in different sections of the room.

Several of the townspeople made a trip outside claiming to be checking the weather this morning. She knew it was so they could take inventory of any threats from outdoors.

RJ was still resting quietly but Alaska was wide awake and taking in the activities around the room. She went over and bent down to quietly talk to the dog. She touched her nose to his large, wet nose. "Listen," she said in barely a whisper. "I need you to stay with RJ and stay calm. It's probably going to get loud and rowdy in here but you have to stay with RJ. Keep everyone bad away from him. Do you understand?" Alaska's big eyelids blinked at her a few times.

She moved her gaze to RJ's face and saw his expression was a mix of excitement and fear. "Mom?" He asked so many questions with that one word which was barely audible to her ears.

Kristin continued to pretend to whisper to the dog but she was actually addressing RJ. She scratched Alaska behind his ears and he pushed his head against her hand to get her to scratch a little harder. "RJ, I need you to listen closely. Stay here. When things start happening, I want you to get under the cot and do not come out until I come to get you. Do you hear me? This is more important than anything I have ever asked you to do."

Starting to feel like something bad was about to happen, RJ began to feel panicky. "Mom. Stay with me. Tears started forming in the corner of his eyes. Please. Stay here." Just as he was reaching for her hand, he heard commotion by the door heading outside. Someone hollered "Code Blue!" Suddenly, there were sounds of fists hitting flesh and angry words flying all around the room. Before he could process what was going on, Kristin practically pulled him off his cot and shoved him underneath. "Mom!" He yelled as she stood up and pointed her finger from Alaska to RJ. "Go now!" She demanded and Alaska jumped off the cot and lay pressed up against RJ's side. "Mom!" He yelled as the noise around him got louder and louder.

"You're ok. I promise. I won't let anything happen to you." Kristin hollered as she got up and ran into the kitchen.

RJ watched from his limited view under the cot as the fighting continued. He jumped and held his breath as his mom's cot which had been right next to his flew into the air as one of the guard's bodies slid to a stop close enough for him to reach out and touch. RJ felt Alaska tense up even more as a growl started in his throat. With the guard face down on the ground, two of RJ's neighbors worked together to tie his hands behind his back. Then they taped his ankles together so he would quit kicking at them. They picked him up and dragged him over to lean again the wall near two other guards who had been restrained in the same manner. They ran out the door as they heard a neighbor calling for more help.

Kristin had been helping restrain one of their captors and was just getting her breath back when she was grabbed from behind by her wrist. She winced from the pain but was even more startled when she felt a gun in her side. Her heart was pounding in her ears as she made eye contact with RJ still under the cot. His eyes were full of tears and she could hear him calling to her. She watched him try to scramble out from the cot but was thankful that at her pleading eyes and shaking head, he obeyed her and stayed where he was.

She was repulsed as she heard Jones' voice in her ear, "You're coming with me. You're my ticket out of here." She watched RJ trembling with fear and uncertainty as she was being dragged from the room.

▪▪

Richard rolled over to look at the clock beside his bed. It was almost 8:00. He jumped out of bed. He couldn't believe he had slept so late. He looked out the kitchen window as he started a pot of coffee. Luckily the storm had passed. Waiting for the water in the shower to get hot, he started planning his day. There was so much to do. He didn't know how to prioritize it since all of it seemed so important.

Within five minutes, Richard was showered, dressed and quickly shoveling in a piece of tasteless, dry toast. He poured his coffee into a travel mug and started for the door. He was surprised to hear a loud knock on the front door. Who could that be? He yanked the door open to see one of his officers who had been working closely with him through the whole case.

"Sir. We have some news. Thought you should be the first to know." The officer said in a very official tone.

"Continue." Richard said. This had to be important in order for him to come to the house instead of calling or waiting for him to get to the station.

"Sir. We have in our custody a doctor Olingham. He said he's ready to talk."

∙∙

Jack had been up all night pacing the floor of his tiny room. Rather than stay inside staring at the same four walls, he decided to take a walk to the window. As he got closer to the window, he thought there must be a mistake with what time he thought it was. There was only one clock down here and it had always kept good time as far as they knew. It should be early daylight but the water was dark. He walked right up to the window and stared into the darkness. He could see faint light toward the surface but upon inspection, he discovered the water was very murky with a lot of floating debris. There didn't seem to be many fish around. It could only mean one thing. There must have been a heck of a storm last night.

Jack used to enjoy listening to storms. The thunder and lightning were energizing to him. His mom would worry about the roof getting damaged by hail and she would listen closely for the tornado sirens even though they would rarely go off. The hall bathroom was apparently her safe place if she thought a tornado was getting close. She always said it never hurt to be prepared and have a plan. His dad would try to reassure her that it would all be ok. With sadness, he realized it had been a long while since he had thought about his parents. He felt like he had really let them down when Joshua and Brian had disappeared. His parents wouldn't have let them be taken. He stared out into the effects the storm had on their natural light. It would probably be dark most of the day. Just like his mood.

· ·

Ron had made a decision last night. He checked in this morning to make sure Simon was ok after the storm. Wray had assured him the boys had made it through the night just fine. Between being in a basement and having the tv loud and their even louder chatter, they barely noticed the weather. Ron made arrangements for Simon to stay all day with the other boys.

Packing some supplies, food and water, he headed to his car to drive to the woods where someone had last seen his wife. He couldn't wait another day. He had spent over ten years missing her in her presumed death. He would not spend another day knowing she was actually out there somewhere. What if she needed his help? He was going to find her. And he was going to find her today.

∙∙

Kristin struggled to keep her footing as she was being dragged out of the shelter that everyone had originally assumed was meant to keep them safe. Now they knew it had been meant to keep them hidden. Making a quick assessment of her surroundings, she had made a mental note that there were three captured hunters inside the building and she could see two more outside. How many more were there?

She watched as her neighbors looked on helplessly. From off to the side, she heard a familiar voice. It was the mayor. "Please, take me instead." He pleaded.

"Right! With your messed up leg? What a nuisance! I should have pushed a little harder so maybe you would have broken more than your leg." There was an audible gasp among everyone. Some of the town members felt shame for not believing the mayor when he said someone had pushed him. They thought he had tripped and fallen off that cliff because he was being careless.

255

Pulling a little harder on her twisted wrist, Jones continued to pull Kristin toward a stand of trees.

From around the side of the shelter, one of the hunters started walking forward. He spoke up loudly as if finally finding his voice. "Jones! Let her go. This isn't our fight anymore. We were brought here to do a job and obviously we were misled as to the reason for that job. Look, no one has gotten hurt. We can all just do the right thing now." As he spoke, he continued to slowly walk toward Kristin and Jones. "Don't do something you can't undo. Just let her go and we'll get to the bottom of all this. No one even remembers why we are here."

"Shut your mouth. You've been a problem ever since we got here. Thinking you're better than the rest of us." Jones was getting agitated and Kristin could feel it on her wrist.

"Jones, let's just all walk out of here together. Come on." He was getting closer and Kristin could feel the tension in Jones.

"Stop right there, superhero. You don't call the shots around here." Jones took the gun from Kristin's back and started swinging it toward the townspeople. "None of you call the shots around here. I'm here because you're the problem." He was starting to get more agitated.

Kristin could hear a loud roaring in her ears. She was afraid she would pass out from the pain in her wrist or from fear.

The hunter took one more step in their direction and Kristin heard a loud gunshot right before she hit the ground.

Richard made it to the station in record time. As he burst through the door, the person at the desk called out, "Room Two". Nodding his thanks, he headed in that direction. Stopping to take a deep breath, he had to remind himself to take it slow and not make any simple mistakes in the haste to find those kids. Taking four or five breaths in through his nose and out through his mouth, he bent his head from side to side to work out the kinks that were already forming in his neck. He had to be at the top of his game. "Here we go." Richard said to no one in particular.

Richard entered the room with another detective that had been on the case from the beginning. He immediately recognized Doctor Olingham from the photos in his file. He took a seat opposite the doctor. "I'm Detective Mansell with the Blue Water Police Department. This is Detective Edmonds also with the BWPD." He gestured with his head toward Edmonds in the seat next to him. Starting the process, he said, "Please state your name."

"Doctor William Olingham". Stated the doctor calmly. "I am here to cooperate in any way I can."

Already knowing the answer to his question, Richard asked him, "Did you come here on your own or were you encouraged to speak to us?"

"Well, I was just about to come in to talk with you when I was determined to be driving in excess of the posted speed limit. Apparently, the nice fellow who pulled me over recognized me as being a wanted man. Can you imagine that?" Doctor Olingham asked with a serious expression.

Richard nodded. "Well, however you got here, I'm glad to hear that you are willing to cooperate. There are dozens of lives at stake here. Can you start by telling me as a matter of urgency, where the underground cave is located so we can try to save those lives?"

Looking up at the ceiling as if thinking about it for a minute, Doctor Olingham replied, "I don't think I can tell you where it is."

Richard was about to go across the table after this guy when he continued. "But I can show you."

■ ■

CHAPTER 4

All of the townspeople watched in horror as Jones waved his gun in the air with a wild look in his eyes. The hunter who had confronted him had taken another step forward when Jones shot him. Kristin fell at the same time and everyone was confused by the flurry of activity. Jones had just grazed the hunter's shoulder so the slightly wounded man continued with a huge leap forward to tackle Jones to the ground. After that, several of the others went forward to retrieve the gun, tie up his hands and feet and get him away from Kristin.

She responded right away to their inquiries. "I think I just fainted. I'm fine. Please help me up." Knowing her wrist was broken but not worried about that at the moment, she got up and ran into the shelter. She pushed RJ's cot out of the way and pulled her sobbing young son into her arms.

RJ looked up into her face and between long gasping sobs, he said, "I.....thought.....he.....killed ....you."

Kristin held him tight to her. "Thank you for staying here like I told you. I'm sorry you were scared. But look who stayed right here with you the whole time. I can't believe it." Kristin looked over at Alaska who thumped his tail against the floor before jumping up to lick their faces.

RJ chuckled between his gasping hiccups. This made Alaska even happier and he almost knocked them both over with his enthusiasm.

Kristin looked around at all of her neighbors who had gathered around. Most had tears in their eyes. With a big smile she called out loudly, "Let's get out of here!"

Everyone started gathering up the supplies they thought would be needed as they finally continued their journey to get to freedom. She looked around for the man who had been shot. He probably needed her medical attention. Grabbing her bag, she went back outside with RJ right on her heels and Alaska right on his. She found him leaning against a tree with several townsfolk watching over him.

As she walked up to him, his face showed concern. "Are you ok? I'm so sorry Jones did that. That's not what we were here for. He's a bad egg."

Smiling at him, she leaned down to inspect his shoulder. "I'm fine. Thank you for your bravery. That took a lot of guts. He was unpredictable and I'm so thankful that you didn't get hurt worse." She instructed one of the neighbors in the cleaning and bandaging of his bullet grazed wound." As soon as he was all fixed up, Kristin then instructed the neighbor in the bandaging of her own wrist along with a make-shift sling to help hold it above her heart in the hopes of relieving some of the swelling. She didn't know if it was broken but it was already severely swollen and bruised. Taking some anti-inflammatory medication, she was ready to finally get on their way back to civilization.

Richard was starting to feel like they were being played as fools for thinking William Olingham was really going to take them to the cave. With his patience wearing thin, he was about to change his strategy when William called out, "We have to park here and walk the rest of the way."

Still not trusting him, Richard stayed a close distance behind William as they started trekking through the woods. They were all surprised by the amount of damage caused by the storm the prior night. Climbing over fallen trees and with debris everywhere, it was slow going. It almost appeared like possibly a tornado or straight-line winds had come through. It was fortunate there were no houses around.

After trudging through the difficult terrain for almost thirty minutes, William stopped and slowly looked around. He rubbed his hand across his mouth several times as if thinking. Shaking his head, he stated, "This doesn't look right. There is so much damage, I can't find the entrance."

Not trusting himself to restrain the urge to grab William by his shirt, Richard took several steps back. His team started searching the area for any signs of a hidden entrance. He expected it would be well camouflaged like the other caves had been but with this storm damage, it might be almost impossible to find. That's assuming that William was telling the truth about this being the right location.

Hearing the static of his radio, his attention was re-focused.

"This is Mansell, go ahead." Richard spoke into the transmitter attached to the top of his shirt.

"Hey man, this is Randy. Our guys have spread out in the area and we found a decent-sized lake. Looks pretty deep. Want me to send divers down?"

"Yes. As soon as possible. Thanks. We'll keep looking for the entrance here and then meet you at your location after."

"Copy that."

Richard looked over at William who had a smug look on his face. "I told you it was around here." He said with satisfaction.

Richard walked away so he wouldn't punch him.

∙∙

Winston was furious that no one was responding to his calls. Now he had to make a special trip out to the shelter to see what the problem was. He knew there had been a storm last night but that had never interfered with his contacts before. He had intended to forego his planned visit to the shelter. Someone was going to have to answer for this. He didn't have time to be following up on his orders. Especially when he could feel the pressure closing in on him. He had received information that indicated Doctor Olingham was in custody. He had been helpful in the beginning but Winston knew he would sing like a canary if he felt threatened at all. He had always worried more about himself than the experiment.

Winston already had several people on a mission to take him out at the first opportunity. Hopefully that was before he said too much to anyone.

. . . .

Kristin and her neighbors were making the final plans to leave. The man who had been shot asked to speak to the group. Kristin quickly agreed. She felt like they should be able to trust him after he put his life on the line for her. First, she inquired, "I'm sorry but I don't know your name."

Smiling slightly, he answered, "Dave."

"Ok, Dave. You have our attention." Kristin said with curiosity.

"I don't know what your plans are but I wanted to offer my services to you." He gestured to the whole group. "I'm sorry for this. I honestly don't think any of us had a clue that it would go this way. Except maybe Jones. I was wondering if you wanted me to stay here to guard everyone until you send someone or would you want me to show you the fastest way out of here? This is a tricky area. It's almost impossible to get into or out of through the thick overgrowth. There is really just one small spot that is passable. I can show you or just give you the best directions that I can explain."

Kristin exchanged glances with the neighbors and everyone nodded their heads. "We would be happy for you to show us the absolute quickest way out of here!" Kristin said with obvious relief.

263

"Good. It's about a two-hour hike. I'm ready when you are."

With Dave leading the way, everyone else followed closely behind. Kristin felt a little bad about leaving the hunters tied up with no way to get food or water until someone came to get them. However, they couldn't chance them escaping and being able to catch up with them.

Looking over at RJ, she was pleased to see him smiling and ready for a new adventure. She hoped today wouldn't haunt him for years to come. Looking down at her wrist and feeling her heartbeat in the pain of it, she was quite certain it would haunt her.

■■

Ron had been scouring the woods for hours. It felt like a dead end. He could hear nothing but birds, bugs and branches. But he did feel good that at least he was trying to do something. He was tired of waiting for news. He knew his wife was out here somewhere.

Out of the quietness, he suddenly heard loud rustling. It was coming from behind him. He listened closely. He could hear a person. He wasn't really speaking out loud. It was more like mumbling. Ron hadn't come upon anyone in his search today. Not sure why he reacted like he did, he quickly and as quietly as possible hid behind the trunk of a large oak tree.

As the person came closer, Ron could tell that he was in fact mumbling to himself. He sounded irritated. Ron slowly peeked his head around a large branch to see if he could assess the situation at all. The man was walking right towards him. Ron got a good look at his face even though the man was looking at the ground in front of him. With confusion creasing his forehead, he slowly pulled his head back around the tree. Where did he know this guy from? He certainly looked familiar.

Winston didn't know he was being watched as he fumed at the waste of time to get all the way out here because of the incompetence of his crew.

Ron watched as the man continued to make his way through an unseen path to some destination. He was almost out of sight when the memory came to him. This was the man from the picture Officer Richard had shown him when doing inquiries about where his son had been born. He has to know something about his wife. Why else would he be out here? He stepped out from behind the tree and as quietly as possible began to follow this mysterious, mumbling man.

■■■

Richard and his team had searched every square foot of area where there could have been an entrance but other than sections of land that had recently had trees almost uprooted, they had covered all the possibilities. They were now heading toward the lake and hoped that the divers were on their way.

If it had been anytime other than during an investigation, Richard would have stopped to admire the beautiful view when they reached the edge of the woods which overlooked a breathtaking view of a lake with reflections of the sun glistening off of the surface of the water. It was like a hidden gem. Being careful to watch their footing, they one by one made their way down a rocky slope towards the water. Richard stared into the cloudy darkness wondering if there was even the slightest possibility someone was right on the other side of a window down there. From a distance the water had looked blue and clear but up close they could see evidence of the storm from the previous night. Right below the surface it was murkier with run off from the heavy rain and scattered debris from tree branches. Leaves were gathering in the areas where the slight wind was pushing them into large clusters.

Meeting up with Randy, he got an update on the search and where they believed the window had the best chance of being. Richard asked the one question that he really didn't want the answer to. "Randy, even if we find the window, if we can't find the entrance, how will we get to them?"

Randy nodded his head and quickly tried to reassure his friend, "I've got all of my team and all of yours working on that very question. I am extremely confident that if this is in fact the place, we will get to them. One way or another."

Richard hoped he was right. Time was running out. And it was running out fast.

■■■

Dave had been leading the group from the shelter through thick brush and rough terrain. Kristin looked back at the two men on either side of the mayor, helping him along. She called ahead to Dave. "Dave, I think we should take a little break to hydrate and let everyone catch their breath."

Looking back at the exhausted group, he quickly agreed. He could only imagine how tired they must be. Certainly no one had slept last night in anticipation of this morning's take over. He had to admit, they did a good job. These people worked together incredibly well. Not wanting to overstep his bounds, he was hesitant to ask questions but his curiosity was getting the best of him.

Dave went over to sit on a fallen tree trunk next to Kristin. She had finally sat down after checking on the mayor's broken leg. They both watched with humor as RJ and Alaska kept running around and jumping over anything that got in their way. It was hard to tell who was having more fun. The smile on RJ's face was equally matched by the constant wagging of Alaska's large tail.

Dave looked at Kristin. "Isn't it funny that kids find entertainment and joy in what we would consider obstacles?"

Kristin chuckled. "Yes. They are resilient for sure. He is just so happy to finally know what it's like here on the outside."

Dave thought that was a funny choice of words. "Outside?" he questioned.

Still watching her son, she answered, "Yes. He was born in the cave. That's where he has lived his whole life. He has wanted to get out here since the first time he heard about it. And he has really been wanting a dog so this is all like a dream come true for him. Whose dog is that anyway?" She glanced over at Dave. His face was pale and it looked like he might pass out.

Kristin quickly reached over to steady him. "Dave, are you ok? Let me take a look at that bullet wound. It might be getting infected. I thought I had made sure it was cleaned and covered well." She was about to get up and grab her bag when he shook his head. "No, I'm fine. How long have all of you been in a cave?" He was trying to wrap his head around what she was saying.

"About ten years." Kristin took a deep breath and let it out slowly. "Ten long years."

Dave was about to ask another question when it all of a sudden got very quiet. RJ and Alaska had quit running around. Alaska was standing at attention with his hair sticking up on his neck. The people close to him could hear a low growl in his throat. He was staring into the woods. Everyone looked around at each other trying to make a plan without knowing what the plan should be.

Kristin motioned with her hands for RJ to lower slowly to the ground and get behind the tree that was off to his left a few feet. He looked at his mom then glanced at Alaska. Looking back at his mom, he saw her eyes with their very serious "Don't you dare!" look in them. He did as she instructed and had just crouched behind the tree when he heard a familiar voice mumbling in the distance. That was the sound of the man who had kept them at the shelter.

Making quick gestures to each other, the townspeople made a silent plan of action. No one was very confident with their plan since they didn't know how many others would be with Winston. Dave quickly understood what to do and watched in amazement as everyone disappeared into the woods without hardly a rustle. Dave started taking a few steps toward the sound of Winston's voice.

As Winston stepped through the brushy growth and saw Dave, he didn't know whether to feel relief or anger. "Why has no one been answering my calls?" He looked around and not seeing anyone he asked, "Where is everyone else? And why, may I ask, do you have blood all over you?"

Dave looked Winston in the eye and said quietly, "There has been an incident."

■ ■

CHAPTER 5

The divers finally made their way to the lake. Since there was no access to the lake from any roads, it was more time consuming to get all of the equipment to the scene. Luckily the days were getting longer with sunlight and it was a good day to be out. The storm had left behind clear skies that reflected the slow moving, random white puffs of clouds off the water.

Unknown to those on the water side of the window, those on the inside were starting to feel the effects of the lack of food. They had gathered for a mid-day meal instead of a separate lunch and supper. There just wasn't enough food for three meals a day. There had been very little talk or discussion among the increasingly weak young town members.

Instead of feeling his 26 years, today Jack felt like he was 100. The weight of the world was on his shoulders. He hadn't been sleeping. He was hungry, irritable, exhausted and if he was being quite honest with himself, he was feeling very hopeless.

Everyone had disbursed the area to do their chores even though several of them thought it was a complete waste of time at this point. They had all been doing their part and staying together in their plight but Jack could feel his neighbors starting to fracture. Tempers were flaring. Greed would start to rear its ugly head soon.

Something caught his eye at the window. He got up and walked over to look into its dark depth. It had cleared a lot over the day and he could see farther out. He guessed that meant the storm was past. It was light at the top so he imagined it was a sunny day. His mind wandered to the feeling of sun on his skin. It was almost at a point that he couldn't really remember things like that anymore. He felt guilty for his thoughts. At least he had the memories. Many of these kids down here had no memories at all of being outside. Closing his eyes, he imagined what it would be like to sit behind the wheel of a car. Maybe a convertible. The top down and the sun on his face with the wind blowing his hair in every direction. He had been just about to get his driver's license when they arrived at the cave. He never imagined it would be 10 years and he would still be here. Maybe it would be better to put all those thoughts of the sun from his mind. At this rate, the next few weeks would be difficult at best and would end with a lot of pain and sorrow.

Looking back out to the water, he thought he saw a flash of light in the distance. "Great", he thought to himself, "I'm already starting to see spots from lack of food. This is happening faster than I thought it would. Or maybe I'm just tired." Feeling discouraged, he spun on his heel and headed away from the window to go check on their supplies knowing it was wasted time because nothing had changed.

No one was there when an underwater flashlight shined its light through the window into their picnic dining area.

Richard and Randy were standing by the water's edge in anticipation of the diver's return. Richard had just been in contact with the team still searching for the missing members in the woods. It wasn't possible that they just disappeared into thin air. Richard was looking forward to getting back to questioning Doctor Olingham. Maybe he would have answers regarding the other discovered and possibly some undiscovered caves too.

Looking over in the direction of the doctor, Richard wasn't sure if the look of distress on his face was concern because this was the correct location of the window, or because it wasn't. Either way, Olingham was going to jail. Richard hoped he understood that his cooperation would go a long way in determining how long that jail sentence would be. A determining factor would also be if any of these kids had died on his ten-year watch.

Startled back from his distraction, everyone was anxious as bubbles started surfacing indicating the diver's arrival. It seemed as though no one was breathing waiting for the news. There was a huge sigh of relief when the diver reached his hand into the air and gave a thumbs up signal.

■ ■

Kristin could hear RJ breathing next to her. It sounded so loud through the tension in the air. She was amazed that everyone had taken cover so quickly and it appeared that Winston didn't suspect that he was surrounded by his prisoners.

Winston was annoyed at the news that there had been some type of incident. This whole ordeal was getting out of control. He was starting to feel the pressure closing in on him. It was really only a matter of time before the authorities started piecing things together. If they hadn't already. How could it be unraveling so quickly? All of his research was about to be for nothing. People he employed who he thought would never turn on him were starting to get nervous. Even with the incriminating black mail he had on some of them, he knew they would give in to pressure and throw him under the bus.

At least he didn't have to worry about his dad letting the cat out of the bag. Winston was somewhat impressed that his dad had kept his mouth shut for so long. He knew it must make him an awful person to be relieved that his dad had died taking their secret with him. He had almost felt bad the last time he saw his dad laying in the hospital bed pleading with him with his eyes. His final words had been a whispered, "Too far." He hadn't taken it too far. In fact, in his opinion, he hadn't taken it nearly far enough.

With a huff of disgust, Winston demanded, "What kind of incident?"

Dave gestured back toward the way Winston had just come. "Why don't we head back to town and I'll tell you all about it."

"I can't go back to town you idiot." He started past Dave and headed in the direction of the shelter. "Obviously there is an issue out here that needs my attention. Come on."

Dave knew if he headed back toward the shelter, the people he had helped to escape would not be able to finish finding their way out of here. There was the risk if Winston released the others he had worked with, they would surely come looking for his newly freed companions. And if Jones got his hands on any of them, it wouldn't end well.

Struggling to think of a good excuse to go in the opposite direction of the shelter, Dave stood in his spot and knelt down on one knee. He put his elbow on his raised knee and put his head in his hand. "I don't think I can make it. I think I lost a lot of blood. I'm feeling really weak. You go on ahead. I'll meet you at the entrance."

Winston sensed something was suspicious. He walked over and roughly pulled the shirt away from the bullet wound. "What's this? How did this happen?"

Not sure how to proceed, Dave just replied, "Jones."

Winston cursed under his breath. "I knew he would be a loose cannon. Well, suck it up. You're coming with me. We have to get those people out of the shelter and I need all the help I can get."

As he took a few steps away from Dave, a sudden movement in the trees caught his attention.

Dave quickly got up and started walking toward the shelter. "Ok. Let's go. I'll be fine."

Winston put his hand up in the air as if to silence everything. He cocked his head to one side listening intently.

Dave laughed nervously. "The squirrels out here are the size of cats. Better get a move on so we can get back out by dark."

Winston took his gun out of its holder on his belt. He shot into the dense brush and called out impatiently, "Come on out. Right now!" He recognized two individuals from the shelter as they slowly exited the brush with their hands held slightly up in the air. Again, he cursed under his breath. He pointed the gun from them to Dave. "Get over there with them. How many of you are out here?" He started waving his gun wildly around. He pointed to the left of Dave and shot into the brush again. "Get out here before someone gets hurt." Several more people emerged from their hiding places.

Just as Winston was about to shoot into another area, a streak of fur ran at him from the side. Before he had a chance to turn his weapon toward the moving target, Alaska jumped and grabbed Winston's gun toting arm in his strong jaw. Winston dropped the gun and cried out in pain. Before he could even look back up from the dog's fierce gaze, all of the town members who had been his prisoners first in the cave and then in the shelter were standing over him. Dave had grabbed the gun away from him and several others were searching him for other weapons.

Kristin was standing with RJ on the edge of the group. She called out to Alaska, "Good boy."

Alaska let go of Winston's arm and trotted over to Kristin and RJ. He looked up at them and thumped his tail into the dusty ground. RJ dropped to his knees and hugged the dog and rubbed

275

him roughly around his ears just the way he knew was his favorite because the dog pushed his head into the rubbing hands as if to indicate to rub harder.

Feeling like she couldn't handle much more excitement for one day, Kristin called out to all of her neighbors, "We literally aren't out of the woods yet. There could still be more trouble."

The mayor, with the help of friends, turned back toward where they were headed. "Dave, would you lead the way out of here?" He gestured toward several of the people closest to Winston, "You got him?"

They nodded and started forward each holding tightly to him even though they knew he had nowhere to go.

Halting the group, Kristin stopped them momentarily as she quickly walked one of them through how to clean and bandage Winston's bite. Her anger and dislike for this awful person who had obviously had much to do with their imprisonment was overshadowed by her compassion as a nurse to care for a wounded patient.

This day was starting to take its toll on everyone but especially on Kristin as she could feel the pounding in her wrist. She had to get it taken care of soon. She was starting to feel light headed again from the pain.

They were about to start their journey again through the narrow trail of thick brush when they heard a branch crack just ahead. Everyone was on high alert and ready for another fight when Ron stepped out into a small clearing in the woods.

Jack was exhausted and emotionally drained but his brain would not shut off as he stared at the ceiling. He had often had restless nights in this small area he had called his bedroom for over a decade. It had been even harder to sleep after Brian and Joshua had been taken. Jack's mind worked over every possible scenario in his imagination of where they had disappeared to. None of them were good scenarios. Everyone had retired extra early this evening. They were trying to conserve what energy and strength they had for the coming days.

He knew he needed rest in order to stay somewhat focused and attentive to everyone's needs. Closing his eyes, he tried to will himself to sleep but only ended up staring at the back of his dark eyelids.

CHAPTER 6

Brian and Joshua had been enjoying their new friends and all of the new experiences they never knew existed outside the cave. But as the day wore on, they started feeling restless. Every day people had been around asking questions and trying to find clues about the location of where they had been kept underground for so long. Why had no one been around asking questions today? Surely they hadn't given up the search.

Simon wondered where his dad had gone today. He had kept his plans rather secretive. Simon knew his dad would never give up the search for his mom. Meanwhile, he wanted to keep his new friends distracted.

Lincoln and Jacob could feel the anxiety in everyone. They spoke to each other about it quietly trying to come up with a plan to lighten the mood. Jacob had an idea and without drawing attention to himself, quietly left the room to go upstairs to talk with his parents.

Wray had been at the hospital most of the day working but he was supposed to be home early for supper. Jacob discussed his plan with his mom and she said she would discuss it with her husband just as soon as he walked in the door which should be any minute.

With some sense of accomplishment, Jacob headed back down to his friends.

After about 15 minutes, they heard a voice call down the stairway, "Hey boys, will you come up here please?"

Jacob really didn't know if his plan would be acceptable or not but he was anxious to find out. They all exchanged glances of curiosity as they headed up the stairs.

Wray and Anne met them in the kitchen. "Have a seat." Wray said as they entered the room.

Sitting at the table with questioning looks, Wray tried to hold back a smile. "We thought about grilling out and making burgers tonight. What do you think?"

They were all ready to be outside and get some fresh air. Even though they were free from the cave, they still had to be cautious about someone with bad intentions keeping a watch on them. They all nodded enthusiastically.

Wray put his finger over his lips and wrinkled his forehead as if thinking a deep thought. Speaking slowly as if the thought were just coming to him, he continued, "What would you think about after eating those burgers, we go to the field and watch the baseball game tonight?"

It was comical to see the expressions on their faces. It was almost as if he had asked them if they wanted to get on a rocket and fly to the moon.

Anne watched them with happiness and nervousness. She had been assured that there would be extra plain clothes officers all around them at all times but she couldn't help being a bit cautious. She had to admit that seeing those huge smiles and hearing their enthusiastic responses was worth whatever they had to do to make it happen. She made eye contact with Jacob and he nodded his head at her as a show of acknowledging her part in making this happen. She winked at him in return.

As she started preparing for their barbecue meal, she could hear their animated voices talking about their evening plans. She wondered what else she could do to make this a fun night to take their minds off their worries.

■■

Kristin pushed RJ behind her as everyone held their breath waiting for the next confrontation. No one recognized this as someone who had held them at the shelter.

Ron held his hands up by his shoulders. He was shaken up by what he had just witnessed. Alaska, not feeling threatened by this new stranger, trotted over to him and sniffed his legs. Ron bent down to pat his head while keeping his eyes on the one person he had been waiting to see for over ten years. He stepped out of the shadow into the clearing.

No one spoke or made a move as they waited to see what his intentions were. After a minute of silence, they all noticed the eye contact between this new arrival and their Kristin. Did they know each other? That didn't seem possible. What would he be doing here in the middle of the woods?

Kristin could feel the breath leave her lungs. She could see him but she didn't believe her eyes. Starting to blink rapidly as the tears began coursing down her cheeks, she reached up and covered her mouth with her non-injured hand. Removing it, she began taking in deep shaky breaths. Her hands were trembling.

As Ron took another step forward, a loud anguished cry escaped her. She felt like she was moving in slow motion as she started toward him. Ron began moving forward and as they met after several steps in the middle, he grabbed her in a giant hug as she threw her arm around his neck. He closed his eyes with pure joy as he bent his face down into his wife's hair and took a deep breath. She clung to him as she sobbed uncontrollably.

After several minutes they moved apart just enough to look into each other's eyes. They didn't need to speak. Their communication with their eyes said everything they needed.

Even though no one in the group knew who this man was, they expected that it was certainly her husband. She spoke about him to everyone and they all knew how desperately she missed him. Most of the group was choked up from the loving reunion. But they all held their breath and listened closely as RJ stepped up behind his mom and asked quietly, "Mom?"

That one word hung in the air as each person, especially Ron, processed what that meant.

Kristin stepped to the side of her husband but continued to hold his hand. "RJ, this is Ron. Your dad." She looked into the surprised eyes of her husband. "Ron, meet your son, RJ, Ronald Junior."

Ron and RJ stared into each other's eyes as what Kristin said sunk into their minds.

RJ smiled the biggest smile of his life as he proclaimed loudly and with excitement, "I knew you would come to find us, dad!"

Ron looked at Kristin's tear-streaked face and tender eyes. She smiled and let out a sound that was half laugh and half cry. Ron dropped to his knees and took the young son he didn't know existed into his arms. RJ gave him a fierce hug back. And then in typical RJ fashion, he made Kristin laugh when he pointed at Alaska and exclaimed with pride, "Look dad, I got a dog!"

This was definitely a moment that would be talked about in endless detail as the town members all looked on with not a dry eye in the crowd. Except for Winston who knew things were going from bad to worse for him.

∙∙

Richard waited impatiently as the diver got to shore and began his description of the underwater window.

Richard started shooting questions at him. "Could you see through the glass?"

The diver, knowing Richard from previous cases they had worked together, knew Richard preferred short and to the point answers. "Yes."

"Were there any signs of life?"

"I didn't see anyone at the time but it appears to be some type of eating area. There are multiple picnic tables and trash cans. It was very neat and orderly."

"Was it just one area or could you see buildings or other sections where people could be? Like sleeping quarters?"

"I could only see a little way in because it was pretty dark inside. All I could see were the tables."

"How far down was the window?" Richard asked as his mind started going in several directions.

"About fifteen feet."

Richard looked around for Randy and hollered out to him at the edge of the woods. "Randy? Has your team had any luck finding a way in?"

Randy shook his head and yelled back, "Negative."

With a sense of urgency, Richard made a quick decision. He asked the diver, "How soon can you get what you need to start draining this lake and how long would that take?"

Scanning the lake from shore to shore he responded, "I could get everything I need and have it started by tomorrow afternoon. It would take about three days to get to the window and that's if we don't get any rain."

Richard looked into the water and wondered what they would find on the other side of that window. "Get it started. Thanks."

Three days was a long time without any resources. Would it make a difference for those on the inside to know people were attempting to get to them? They would try to make contact again in the morning.

Doctor Olingham was standing at the edge of the woods. He had done his part. He helped them find the cave. Surely they would take that into consideration. He was doing the math in his head of exactly how long these kids had been without adequate food. Starting to feel nervous, he started designing a plan of excuses that all started and ended with Winston.

●●●

Brian thought maybe he had never tasted anything so good as a hamburger from this fire outside. It was in a little container that they called a barbecue. Sure, he had tasted hamburger before but this, well this was unbelievable. Between bites he said to Simon, "This is even better than ice cream!"

Simon agreed wholeheartedly.

"Doctor Wray, you sure are a good barbecue cooker!" Brian said. It was so nice to be outside. The air smelled so fresh and clean. It was warmer than he was used to and he could feel a dampness on his arms and face. It was different than sweat from running around or playing too hard. It was from the air. He wondered if anyone else felt it.

Wray smiled and accepted the compliment with pleasure. He glanced around the group of boys who were all connected in such a bizarre way. He was grateful that Brian and Joshua had been rescued in time and that they seemed to be adjusting to their new environment with ease. Making sure the grill was turned off, he got up to start gathering the empty food plates from the table. "Hey guys, grab a few things and take it into the kitchen then get ready to go to the game."

Anne smiled as everyone pitched in and made quick work of clean up. She spent a few minutes tidying up the kitchen then called her sister-in-law, Clara, to see if she and her husband Samuel would be at the game. Clara answered on the second ring. "Hi Anne! Yes, we are planning to go but might be a bit late. Samuel just got home from work. Are the boys super excited?"

"Oh yes! They are so cute. It will be good for them to get out and about a little. Do you and Samuel want to come over after the game? I am planning a little surprise for the boys."

Clara felt such happiness hearing Anne's excitement. "We would love to. Is there anything I can do to help or anything I can bring?"

"Nope. It's nothing big. Just something I thought everyone would enjoy. I can't wait to visit at the game. I haven't seen you as much as I would like. I still can't believe you are really here. It's like a dream."

Clara felt the same way. Her heart swelled with thankfulness. With a chuckle in her voice, she said, "I know. I can't wait to see you. We will be there soon."

The boys were walking through the kitchen on their way outside. "Lincoln, I just talked to your mom. She and your dad will be meeting us at the game."

"Cool." He replied flashing her a smile.

She couldn't help but notice the quick glimpse of sadness cross Brian's face as he followed closely behind the other boys. She stepped quickly next to him before he made it to the doorway. She put her arm around him and gave him a little squeeze. He leaned into her and let out a small breath. Reaching around her waist he gave her a quick hug before running a few steps to catch up to the others. Looking back at her, he gave her a genuine smile that went right to her heart.

It was a bit of a walk but they all agreed it would be nice to get the exercise. They were taking turns throwing the baseball to each other as they each somehow knew right when to race ahead to catch. Wray and Anne were following closely behind the boys on the deserted streets. They were lucky to live on a road without much traffic. Wray reached over and took his wife's hand. This had been a busy several weeks and he missed spending time with her. As she turned to look at him, out of the corner of her eye she saw Brian, who had been walking on the other side of Wray, reach up and take Wray's other hand. It was just for a second then he ran up ahead with the other boys. Wray swallowed the lump in his throat as Anne tried to keep the tears from showing in her eyes.

Unsure what the future would hold, they both knew it would be a difficult day if this sweet boy ever had to leave their lives.

Ron, Kristin and RJ held back and let Dave, along with the rest of the group, lead the way out of the woods and back to civilization. They were all surprisingly quiet, each in their own thoughts. It was not an easy journey through the narrow pathway hardly created through the dense brush.

RJ had so many questions but he was trying to store them up to ask when it was easier to hear the answers. But the one main question burning on his tongue had to be voiced. Kristin's tears had hardly had a chance to dry up when RJ brought forth the question that had plagued his thoughts for as long as he could remember. "Dad?"

Ron slowed down so he could give more attention to his son instead of concentrating on the steps he took over the rough terrain. He smiled at RJ and felt his heart swell. It was like he was looking at a younger version of Simon. He could hardly wrap his head around the idea that this whole time he had another son and didn't know it. It made him feel a little better knowing Kristin had been blessed with RJ to help her through her experiences just like he had had Simon. "Yes?"

RJ was almost afraid to ask in case the answer wasn't a good one. He hesitated. "Dad? I was wondering….. is my brother alive?"

Kristin's eyes welled up with tears again as she also waited for Ron's answer. She didn't realize she was holding her breath.

Ron grinned and joyfully replied, "He sure is! And he is going to be over the moon when he finds out about you."

RJ couldn't hold his excitement in any longer. He started talking at a fast pace. "His name is Simon and he is thirteen years old and he looks just like me and he is a great big brother who will be my friend and want to protect me forever. Dad? Does he have a dog?" He looked over at Alaska who had been keeping step with him the whole way. Reaching down to touch his head he whispered to the dog, "Don't worry, if he does, I will still love you the best." Alaska looked up at him with big eyes and a few big tail wags.

Ron enjoyed seeing the affection between his son and this gentle dog. He had no idea it was such a recent bond. "No. He doesn't have a dog. There were no animals down in the cave."

Everyone stopped in their tracks. Kristin's face went ashen. "The cave?" she asked as her throat started to feel tight.

"Yes. We were taken to a cave. We were just rescued about a month ago. We have been looking for you ever since."

The whole group was chattering to fill in to those further away who hadn't heard what Ron just said. They were all in disbelief. They had just assumed that they were the only ones who had been prisoners.

Dave was the last to hear the news since he was the furthest away. He pushed his way through the narrow line of people and didn't even feel the branches and brambles scratching him as he finally reached Ron. He asked somewhat breathlessly, "Were there any kids with you in the cave?"

"Sure. We had several." Ron answered.

"Any kids by the name of Jack or Joshua?" Dave stared intently into Ron's eyes.

● ●

Taking the boys to the baseball game had been a huge success. It had been such a pleasure to see them so carefree and animated. Anne thought it was the most she had seen Joshua talk since she had met him. She and Clara had been able to have a nice visit while watching closely over the boys. Their husbands had also had a chance to catch up on the events of the past several weeks. Wray gripped his brother's shoulder with his strong hand. "Samuel, I still can't believe you guys are here. I am so ashamed of myself that I believed all the lies they spewed when you disappeared. I should have found proof. Demanded more answers. We were just so heartbroken that we didn't question things like we should have. I'm so sorry."

Samuel furiously shook his head. "No. There was no way to think that this possibly could have happened. There was so much planning and deceit involved. Whoever is behind all this already had all the answers they needed to keep their sick plan moving ahead. We can't look back. We look forward and work towards getting things back as normal as we can." Looking over to his nephew, Samuel tried to lighten the mood. "But I will tell you this."

He smacked his brother on the shoulder. "I'm glad you never taught Jacob to swim!"

The sky was almost dark with stars starting to blink in the clear, cloudless night. Crickets were chirping and there were several excited voices talking over each other about the baseball game. It had been a close one with the home team finally pulling out a win in the bottom of the ninth inning.

As they arrived back at the house, Anne told everyone to head to the back yard. She went into the house to retrieve the ingredients for the smores as Wray started to build a bonfire. All of the boys stood close by as Wray lit the kindling. Their eyes lit up at the sight. Although Jacob had seen bon fires plenty of times in the past, his eyes were lit up at the sight of his friends. There were so many things he had taken for granted over the years. Something as simple as a bonfire was an absolute treat for these guys. He looked into the fire trying to imagine seeing it for the first time. The sound of the wood crackling and the colors of the flames as they danced around in different directions as if trying to see which flame could reach the highest. Jacob held his hands out toward the fire. The night had been getting increasingly cooler. It was just enough heat to take the chill off without getting too hot. The others each slowly reached out their hands and Jacob enjoyed the smiles on their faces at the feeling of the heat.

Taking a deep breath in, Joshua stated, "I love the smell of it."

Wray chuckled. He said, "It's one of a kind. But don't get too close to the smoke when you breath in like that or it will make you choke and I'm off duty tonight."

They were all laughing when Anne returned with the smores supplies. She handed each of them a long skewer and they all pulled a chair a bit closer to the fire. As directions were being given as to how to make a perfect smore, Anne claimed, "You shouldn't watch Jacob as an example because he tries to start his marshmallow on fire on purpose every single time." She grinned as she looked at Jacob out of the corner of her eye.

He bent his head down to hide his smile. "Well, it takes too long otherwise!" he replied feeling convinced that he made a good argument.

● ●

Jack had been lying in bed staring at the ceiling for hours. Going to bed early to conserve energy had just worn him out more than if he had just stayed up. He decided to take a walk to the window. Staring out into its dark depth, he suddenly had a memory as clear as day. He remembered being in a boat with his dad. He was young. Probably younger than Joshua. They had been sitting in the boat for what felt like days to Jack. He hadn't had a bite all day. He was feeling restless and as he looked back at his memory, he knew he was probably not acting very nice.

His dad could sense his discontent. He could almost hear his dad's voice. "Jack, some days the fish just don't bite. If they bit all the time, it wouldn't make it special when they do bite. In every part of life, you have to take the bad with the good. Nothing is perfect. Otherwise, the almost perfect moments in your life wouldn't mean so much." No matter how hard he tried, Jack couldn't bring back the memory of the rest of the day. He wondered if he ever did catch a fish that day? Trying to shake off the heavy feeling the memory had left with him, he turned away from the window to leave. Here lately, he would like to feel that there was at least a little good to take with the bad. It seemed like good was a thing of the past.

As he started on his short journey back to his sleeping quarters, he heard a noise. It was coming from the dining preparation area. He knew before he got there what he would find. Knowing it didn't make the disappointment any easier. As he rounded the corner, he saw two of his neighbors stealing what little food was left. He quietly walked back to his bed with an even heavier heart than before. He could have confronted them but he knew that the guilt they would feel in the morning when they witnessed their friends discovering the food was gone would be punishment enough.

Feeling completely exhausted and not wanting to deal with what lie ahead in the morning, he finally fell into a fitful sleep.

• •

The smores had been a big hit. Anne was sure that Brian got more chocolate on his face and hands than in his mouth but she had enjoyed the way he rolled his eyes into his head with each bite like it was the best thing he had ever tasted. She couldn't believe he was the same age as their daughter Jillian. Jillian was a tough cookie though. She had actually taken all of the recent changes in their lives in stride and Anne thought she probably really enjoyed the added commotion and constant drama.

Everyone was starting to get quiet as the long day began taking its toll. The air was crisp and cool and the fire was starting to die down. A few yawns were being heard from all directions. Anne was just about to get up to start getting everyone headed for the house when they all collectively gasped in surprise as a big dog ran from the side of the house and started around the circle of people at the fire. Wray and Samuel were about to lunge for the animal when it barked and frantically wagged its tail as it put its paws up on Simon's lap. From the darkness they heard a voice holler, "It's ok. He's friendly to good people!"

With a sigh of relief, Wray and Samuel headed in the direction of the voice they both recognized as Ron's. Simon smiled and got out of his chair to greet his dad as he came around into the back yard. He stopped in his tracks as he noticed that his dad wasn't alone. There were shadows of two people behind him. His dad stepped out of the dim light to let it shine on a woman. Everyone in the group looked from Ron to Simon to the woman who was only slightly lit up by the stars in the sky, the slight sliver of a moon and the light from across the back yard. Simon took a few steps in their direction as she stepped towards him. He stopped and looked at his dad as he shook his head in disbelief. He could hardly get the words out of his mouth. "You found her."

Kristin couldn't move forward. Her sobs were making it hard to stand up. She couldn't believe her eyes. Her boy was so grown up. Ron put his arm around her and motioned for RJ to come along. He guided her shaking body toward Simon. He was staring at her and felt like he was moving in slow motion as he met her in a hug and she clung to him as she continued sobbing.

RJ was a few feet behind them but as he slid up next to Ron he stated loudly, "What a crazy day! My mom has cried more today than I have seen her cry in all my whole life combined."

It took almost a full minute for his words to sink into Simon's mind. He pulled back slightly from his mom's hug, "Your mom?"

RJ nodded big and slow in exaggeration. He reached out as if to shake Simon's hand. "Yep! Hi. I'm your brother RJ."

Simon didn't know if he was holding his mom up or she was holding him up.

∎∎∎

CHAPTER 8

Richard met the divers and the team that had been assembled to drain the lake at first light. There was a crew that was supposed to get an excavator in to start digging a trench to help drain the water into a lower lying area along with several professional grade water pumps placed in separate areas of the lake. It was going to be a slow process. They were already running behind where Richard would like them to be since it was so difficult getting the excavator through the miles of woods.

With the generators loudly pumping the water, Richard was discussing the plans that had been made with the diver who was going to go down again to see if he could make contact with anyone in the cave. Jumping into the water, the diver reached up to grab the signs that had been made to help communicate with those on the other side of the window.

Richard and some others gathered around a computer screen that showed the image from the camera that had been attached to the diver's head. It was hard to get used to recognizing what was on the screen but as the diver continued down, the water became clearer and they could make out what appeared to be the side of the lake wall. Everyone was hoping to see some signs of life. It would be awful if they were just days or hours too late.

Everyone had gathered at the picnic area with stomachs growling and attitudes starting to flare up. Jack was feeling very hopeless and almost panicky as he addressed the group. The individuals who usually prepared the meals had come to him early this morning to let him know of the missing food discovery. He knew they had been talking among themselves about it and he hoped they didn't think he had some kind of magic cure.

Getting everyone's attention he loudly cleared his throat. He could tell that his voice wasn't nearly as strong as it was a week ago or even as strong as it was yesterday. When there was silence, he slowly scanned each town member's face and made eye contact with all of them. The two culprits who he knew stole the food were the only two who wouldn't look him in the eye. At least they had the decency to be ashamed, he thought to himself. He rubbed his hands together to try to tame some of his nervousness. He didn't think this would be so hard. He felt so many emotions at the same time. Anger. Fear. Despair. This responsibility was overwhelming. He didn't want to do it anymore.

Shaking his head as if to clear it back into focus, he began addressing his neighbors. "As I'm sure you know, we had a few selfish individuals who made a decision to eat the rest of our food. We don't need to discuss this any further. They know who they are and their actions can't be changed. The consequence for all of us is that we have no more food. Things are about to get extremely tough. I am asking you to please, please ..." Jack's attention had been drawn to the window. Everyone followed his gaze as a hand appeared on the glass. As a face became visible there were several reactions. There were screams of fear and there were yells for help. Several kids ran over and started banging on the glass.

It appeared obvious that this person was trying to make contact with them. Jack went to the front of the group and stood almost eye to eye with this person. He appeared to be a diver. He was floating in the water and his hand on the glass seemed to be holding him in place. Jack called to one of his main helpers to go get a marker and paper. Jack slowly mouthed the words, "We need help!". The diver nodded his head in understanding. Jack continued, "No food." He rubbed his stomach and shook his head. Jack all of sudden noticed the camera attached to this person's head. He looked into the camera and said, "Joshua? Brian? Do you know where Joshua and Brian are?" Looking back at the diver, he could tell that he hadn't been understood. He grabbed the paper and marker that had been brought to him. Writing "Joshua? Brian?" on a piece of paper he held it up to the window. The diver slowly shrugged his shoulders.

All of the kids were leaning in and trying to get a peek at the diver. One of the kids read aloud as the person on the other side of the window held up a sign against the glass. They read,

"Help is coming.

We have to come through the window.

It will take several days.

Is everyone ok?"

Jack nodded in understanding then wrote on his paper and held it up.

"Zero food. Please hurry."

The diver turned his sign around. The reader spoke aloud again to say,

"We will have to break the glass.

Stay far back.

Wear light clothing. Nothing heavy.

We will help. Do not try to get out by yourself.

One at a time."

Seeing the nods of agreement, the diver gave a thumbs up sign then headed back toward the surface.

Feeling reenergized again, everyone started talking all at once. Jack looked at all the happy faces. Hope had been restored. Just in time.

■■■

Richard had also been reenergized. But seeing those kid's faces through the bleary camera made him realize how serious this situation was. He was relieved to know they were all still alive but it was difficult learning that they were starving. He could see it in their gaunt faces and drawn, dark eyes. And there was no quick way to get to them. Making sure everything was on its fastest pace at the lake site, he headed back to town to get more answers and share a lot of good information. They would be preparing for another round of guests to Blue Water. He was certain the town would welcome these missing kids with open arms.

●●

Brian had been awake for quite a while. He felt terrible about not being super happy for his new friend Simon. He was reunited with his mom and a brother he didn't even know he had. He had a whole family and now even a dog. It just didn't seem fair. He thought of all the nice old people who had cared for him and then been taken away. He turned his head and looked at Joshua and Lincoln still soundly sleeping. As his eyes kept scanning, he noticed Jacob looking at him in the quiet semi-darkness of the basement.

Jacob whispered so he didn't wake up the other two. "Want to go see what's for breakfast?"

Brian nodded and felt his dark mood lighten a little bit. They each were trying to be quiet as they made their way across the basement. Just then Jacob kicked the small squishy baseball they had been throwing around last night and it flew across the room and bounced off the wall. Brian looked over at Jacob with big eyes as Jacob covered his mouth with his hands to stifle the laughter that was bubbling up. Trying not to laugh and wake up Lincoln and Joshua, Brian ran as quietly as he could up the steps. He rounded the corner to the kitchen and almost ran right into Anne.

She was startled for just a second but had gotten quite used to boys running through the house without looking where they were going. Jacob followed right behind and almost ran right into both of them. Jacob stopped in his tracks and with laughter in his voice still, he said, "Morning mom."

"Good morning to you! And to you Brian." She said as she reached over to tussle his sleep messed hair.

"Mom, what's for breakfast?" Jacob asked. He almost blurted out "We're starving," before he quickly remembered that Brian had in fact been starving just weeks ago. He was happy he caught himself in time.

Anne answered, "Well, I was going to make pancakes and scrambled eggs but I thought I would wait until everyone is awake. Your dad, even though he was gone most of the night at the hospital, came by a little bit ago and dropped off a box of donuts as a treat."

Jacob and Brian's eyes lit up. "Maple?" they both asked at the same time.

"Is there any other kind?" Anne asked with a laugh. "I think I may have to start feeding you all nothing but bran cereal for a month after all this sugar lately." She teased as she got each of them a glass of milk to enjoy with their donut.

"What are we doing today?" Jacob asked between bites.

"Well, Uncle Richie just called and said he wants to talk to all of us later this morning. I told him we would go down to the station and save him a trip."

Brian looked confused. "Who is Uncle Richie?"

Anne answered, "Officer Richard. He's my brother. Jacob's uncle."

"Wow. This is a small town like we lived in. Everyone knows everyone." Brian said. After thinking for a minute, he asked her, "Are you going to stay with us when he asks questions?"

"I will if that's ok with you." Anne answered with a melting heart.

Brian looked relieved. "Yah, that would be ok." Anne smiled at him and he thought that maybe no one in the whole world had a nicer mom. Did he even have one? He had to try not to like Anne too much because it wouldn't be right to like her more than his own mom.

Hearing a commotion coming up the stairs, Anne prepared for more breakfast eaters as she got the milk back out of the refrigerator.

• •

Getting back to his office, Richard called a meeting for a quick update from the team that had been assembled to track families of the people in the caves. Most of those who had already been rescued had been reunited with their families but now there was another group that had just arrived and more that should be rescued within the next 72 hours.

It had provided a lot of hope for those who had thought they had lost loved ones a decade ago to a plague. Plus, now it was known that some had just been taken and presumed missing for this long. Richard had been firm about not allowing the town to be taken over by people and news stations that just wanted a quick story.

There were two people who could give him a lot of answers if they would be cooperative. He had a feeling that Doctor Olingham would be agreeable since he was just a puppet in this crazy show and he had already been helpful in locating the cave with the kids. The big break was getting Winston in custody last night. It had been a complete surprise and Richard accepted it gratefully. So far though, Winston had refused to talk. He was meeting with his lawyer at the moment but Richard was itching to get to him for questioning.

Richard was just about to get up to get a cup of coffee when the phone on his desk beeped with a call from the front desk. He picked up with a quick, "Yep?"

"There is someone here named Dave who was with the group that arrived last night. He would like to speak with you if you have a minute."

"Sure. Send him in." Richard was aware of this individual and was very interested to hear what he had to say.

Before Dave could even lift his hand to knock on the door, it was opened wide. Richard introduced himself with a handshake and gestured for Dave to take a seat at the desk. Richard cut right to the chase. "You are fortunate to be on this side of the jail cell my friend. All of your buddies are behind bars. But you have about fifty people who would swear you are an angel. I think you have a lot of explaining to do." Richard leaned back in his chair and gave Dave his full attention.

Dave nodded in agreement. "I have a lot to say but first I want to say that those were not my buddies. I never met any of them before." He leaned forward and clasped his hands together rubbing his palms into each other. "I need to know if any of the kids you found are named Jack or Joshua. Jack would be 26 and Joshua would be 13." He started slightly rocking back and forth in his chair as if nervous for the answer.

Richard was slow to answer. "Maybe you could tell me why you want to know."

Dave looked into Richard's eyes with desperation. "They are my sons. I've been looking for them for ten years. Please. Do you know them?"

Richard remembered the first time he saw Joshua. He was barely alive. He wondered if Jack was the young man standing behind that glass asking about Joshua and Brian? Knowing Joshua would be coming to the station at some point this morning, he decided it best to get to the bottom of this right away.

Ron felt like he was in a dream when he woke up and his family was finally all together. It had been late when they got home from the hospital. Kristin's x-ray had confirmed a broken wrist and it had taken a while for the hospital staff to get it all fixed up. Everyone had been exhausted and exhilarated at the same time. Kristin had been amazed at how much had changed in technology at the hospital. She said that everything she ever really used in the cave fit into one bag just like the old days. Not wanting to disturb her sleep, he crept quietly out of the room and entered the living room where the boys had each taken a couch. Alaska slept on the floor at RJ's feet. As he walked in, the dog's head rose in greeting. Ron whispered to him, "Do you have to go outside?"

Getting up and slowly stretching, the dog quickly went toward the door with a wag of his tail. Ron went out the door with the dog and sat on the front step as Alaska took his time sniffing out each and every tree and bush in the yard. He heard the screen door open behind him. He didn't have to turn around to know it was Kristin. She came and sat down next to him on the step. Smiling a big smile, she leaned on his shoulder and said, "Good morning husband." Her voice was still sleepy.

"Good morning wife." He said with a grin. He put his arm around her and kissed the top of her head. "Did you get enough rest? How is your wrist feeling this morning?"

He felt her nod her head against his shoulder. "I crashed last night." She held up her cast and moved it back and forth in the air. "It feels a lot better than it did yesterday. It was a simple fracture so it won't take long to feel good as new." Sitting in each other's company each thinking their own thoughts, Kristin finally asked, "I wonder what the boys think of meeting each other? I wish I could have seen Simon's face. I bet it was priceless. My tears got in the way of my vision."

"I was thinking the same thing," Ron replied with a chuckle. "I'm sorry you had to go through all that stuff in the cave alone. Did you have any trouble delivering RJ without a doctor?"

"No. I was an old pro after all. And I wasn't alone. I really did have a lot of support through the years."

Ron nodded in agreement. "As did I. But it wasn't the same. It wasn't you."

"It wasn't you. But we managed to make it. I've got you now."

"Yes, you do." Ron said pulling her closer. They both sighed with contentment..

∙∙

Jack had encouraged everyone to try to relax and save their energy for their departure out of the cave. All they could do was stay hydrated with water since there was no food but seeing that face on the other side of the window gave everyone renewed energy. It could still be several days though and everyone had already been slowly getting weaker.

With nothing to do but wait, they all decided to take shifts of either sleeping or staying in the picnic area to report any further activity in the water.

What would await them on the outside? Most of them had never allowed themselves to think about it. It seemed too painful to make those dreams and plans. Jack decided to let his mind wander and was deep in his thoughts when one of the youngest of his neighbors interrupted his daydreaming.

"Jack, some of us were wondering..." She hesitated as if debating whether to ask the question or not.

"Go ahead." Jack said with patience.

"Some of us were wondering if you could tell us about the outside? You would remember the most of everyone since you are the oldest. Some of us don't remember anything at all. Would you tell us? You've never talked about it."

Nodding his head in agreement, he went to sit on the tabletop of one of the picnic tables. As he started telling of his memories, he would often glance out the window at the water. "Well, what I miss the most is the sunshine. It was warm, sometimes even hot. It could get so bright that you had to wear something called sunglasses." His audience was hanging on his every word. He held up his hand as if to block the sun from his eyes. Then he pretended to take out a pair of sunglasses and put them on his face. "And if you get the right pair of sunglasses, they make you look really cool." He ran his fingers through his hair and stuck out his bottom lip as he bobbed his head up and down in exaggeration. Everyone started to laugh.

As the stories continued, he wondered if the diver was making any progress on their rescue. Their complete lack of food would catch up with them quickly. He would do his best to keep their minds occupied so they had less time to think about how hungry they were.

• •

Richard listened with all of his attention. He was glad he asked Dave for approval to record their conversation because it was almost too much to absorb. Dave had shown him Jack and Joshua's birth certificates and the most recent pictures he had of them. Richard had no doubt that they were indeed the boys that Dave had been searching for.

Unlike most of the prisoners they had discovered, Jack and Joshua had disappeared from several states away. There had been no stories of a plague taking their lives. Jack, then age sixteen, had been watching his little brother while his parents went out to run some errands on a Saturday morning. When they arrived home a few hours later, the boys were gone. After they had searched everywhere and checked with all of Jack's friends, they notified the police who started an investigation into their disappearance. They were never seen again. But Dave and his wife never gave up hope and had continued looking for them.

Dave remembered hearing about the plague that had devastated so many people's lives but he was dealing with his own tragedy and didn't think anything more about it. It wasn't until he heard talk of people who had been held captive for over a decade and had been discovered in caves that he decided to travel here to see what he could find out. Once in the area, he listened everywhere he went for clues. He knew the children that had been rescued had all been reunited with family or had always been with their families underground.

One evening while he was in a dark, quiet, roadside bar about 100 miles from Blue Water, he was listening to the hushed voices of conversations and something caught his attention. He had been about to leave with another night of no leads when two men came through the door and each took a seat at the bar. They both ordered a drink and were quiet as they took in their surroundings. Dave made sure to keep his face hidden from them and swayed back and forth a little as if to indicate that he had certainly had too much to drink. He leaned his head forward onto the palm of his hand as if holding it up so it didn't hit the bar. His ears were laser focused on what the two men were saying. They talked about their job starting the following day which involved making sure some people who were under surveillance didn't leave their shelter in the woods. They weren't anticipating any trouble. The pay was incredible for the only responsibility being to keep the people at the location and keep their own mouths shut.

Dave was intrigued. When the men left the bar, he snuck out after them and followed them to their cheap, dingy hotel. He waited in the shadows all night and was waiting for them in the morning. He caught one of them outside his room grabbing a quick smoke. Dave strolled by and struck up a conversation with him. Dave said he was down on his luck and was looking for work. The man thought he might be able to help him out for a small fee. He went back into his room to make a phone call and came out to offer Dave a job with the agreement that when he got his first pay, he would give the guy a hundred dollars. Dave grumbled as he shook the man's hand but inside, he was thrilled at the possibility of a lead actually heading somewhere.

Richard listened to the details of being at the shelter and the disappointment he felt that his boys weren't there. But he actually felt like he had to stay if for no other reason but to protect these people from the unstable group who was guarding them. He told Richard what little information he had about Winston and about each of the guards along with what he had learned about the individuals in the cave. It all made sense. It all matched up. Richard asked Dave if he would mind staying a while in one of the conference rooms across the hall.

Dave agreed with a heavy voice, "I have nothing else to do. No place to go. No one to go home to. I've got nothing but time."

Richard got Dave settled into the conference room with a cup of coffee and a bag of potato chips from the vending machine. He was just walking back into his office with his own cup of coffee when his sister along with Jacob, Lincoln, Brian and Joshua came strolling down the hall. It was hard for him to keep any expression from his face as he led all of them into a room big enough for them all to sit down.

Richard started by saying, "There have been some developments."

· ·

Simon woke to the sound of voices. As he quickly started remembering the events of the past evening, he listened closely to the sound of his mom's voice. It might be his imagination but he really thought he remembered it. It was very gentle. Soft and yet it carried strong confidence. He couldn't believe this wasn't a dream. He had spent a good amount of time in the waiting room with his brother last night while his mom was getting the cast on her wrist. It almost made him sick to his stomach as RJ explained what had happened to cause the injury.

Excited to see everyone, he jumped out of bed and eagerly headed toward the sound of the voices. They were in the kitchen and just as Simon entered the room, the screen door opened and Alaska came trotting in followed by RJ who was three steps into the room before he stopped in his tracks and quickly turned around just as the door slammed behind him. "Oops." He said as he sheepishly looked at Kristin. She just smiled and shook her head.

RJ got a glance of Simon and almost knocked him over in his enthusiasm.

Kristin walked over and hugged him for several minutes. There was so much to catch up on. Not worried about how to even begin, it all just started.

"What are we going to do today?" RJ asked with excitement.

"Well, for starters, we thought maybe we would eat some breakfast and then at some point go see Frankie and some of the other neighbors who have been so worried about us." Kristin answered.

Simon tried not to laugh as RJ began, "You see, Frankie was our next-door neighbor....." No one was worried that there would ever be a lack of stories or details with RJ around.

∙∙∙

Richard looked around the table at the interested faces peering back at him. They were looking for information. He was on information overload. Hardly knowing where to begin, he looked from Brian to Joshua. "First of all, how are you boys doing?"

They both nodded and replied at the same time, "Good."

"Feeling stronger every day?" He asked.

They both nodded in agreement again. "Yes."

"Would you mind if I spoke to Anne alone for a minute?" Richard asked the group.

Everyone was in agreement as Richard and Anne left the room to go into the privacy of Richard's office. Anne noticed the look of anxiety on Brian's face as she left the room. Jacob noticed too and tried to distract him by asking questions about what he wanted to do after they left the police station.

Richard quickly filled Anne in on Dave being in the next room and his connection with the whole investigation. He told her he was going to introduce Joshua to Dave and wondered if she thought he would be ok going in with just Richard. She thought he would be all right even though he might not remember what his dad looked like, surely he and Jack had talked about him. She voiced her concern that Brian may find it difficult since his friends were finding their families and he had no idea where that left him.

Anne asked quietly, "Do you have any updates about Brian's parents?"

"Absolutely none." Richard replied.

"Well, Wray and I want him to stay with us regardless of where everyone else goes." She said protectively. "Is it ok if I talk to the boys about Dave when you take Joshua in to see him?"

"Yes. Don't mention the other cave though. Not yet." Richard requested.

"Of course. Will you get to them in time?" Anne asked with concern.

"It's looking promising. We are doing everything as quickly as possible. I will keep you posted on everything. Will you stay around here until we decide where Joshua will go?"

"You bet. Have you been eating or sleeping? You look absolutely worn out. What can I do for you?" Anne asked. She was worried that her brother was going to work himself sick.

Smiling, he answered, "You are helping so much by taking care of the boys. Maybe later, you could make some of your award-winning meatloaf and mashed potatoes and bring me a huge serving? If I'm not here, you can leave it in the fridge."

Feeling pleased that she could do something productive to be helpful, she nodded with enthusiasm. "And oatmeal carmeletta bars for dessert?" She asked with a grin.

Tipping his head to the side and rolling his eyes back, he said, "I can taste them already. Thanks sis. You're the best."

Laughing as she got up to leave the room, she gave her usual reply to his compliment. "I know."

▪▪▪

Richard walked in behind Anne in time to see the look of relief on Brian's face. She sat down at the table and said, "Joshua, Officer Richard would like to see you for bit. Are you ok with that?"

With a look that could only be described as panic, Joshua asked, "Am I in trouble?"

Richard tried to ease his mind by answering, "Of course not. Unless you have robbed a bank that I don't know about?" He raised his eyebrows and put a comical expression on his face.

All of the boys laughed and Joshua got up from his seat to follow Richard from the room. Once in the hallway, Richard stood outside the door of the conference room which held Dave. Joshua looked at him with so many questions running through his mind. The first one out of his mouth was, "Did you find Jack and the others yet?"

"We'll talk about that. First, I want you to meet someone. He has been searching for you for a long time. I do one hundred percent believe he is who he says he is. I will stay in the room with you the whole time. If you ever feel like you want to ask me some questions privately, just rub your ear and that will be our signal, ok?"

Having no idea what was in store for him, he nodded his agreement as Richard reached over to turn the knob and open the door to where his father sat waiting for Richard but not expecting to see his son.

Richard walked into the room and stepped to the side as Joshua walked in behind him. Joshua made eye contact with his dad and he heard his heartbeat in his eardrums. He knew instantly who it was. He looked just like an old version of his brother. He looked up at Richard and Richard gently put his hand on the boy's shoulder. "Joshua, this is your dad."

Richard felt a lump in his throat as he looked at Dave and said, "Dave, this is Joshua."

Dave felt as if time stood still. He slowly took several breaths in and out. He blinked rapidly and his mind raced. "What?" He looked at Richard, "Where?" He stood up. "What?" He took the dozen steps across the room and knelt down on one knee in front of his son so he didn't tower over him and make him feel intimidated. "Joshua?" The name came out in a hoarse whisper. He placed his hand flat on his son's chest over his heart. "Joshua. You are so big. I have been searching for my little boy and here you are, nearly a man."

Joshua threw his arms around his dad with no hesitation. "Dad, Jack told me every day that if you and mom were still out there somewhere, you would be looking for us. He never believed that you were dead." He looked around the room. "Is mom with you?"

Dave's expression became one of pure sorrow. "No. I'm sorry, Joshua. Your mom was killed in a car accident five years

315

ago. But she was right by my side every day looking for you guys. She never gave up hope." He sighed with the sense of loss but brightened as he said, "She would be so happy right now." Now it was Dave's turn to look around the room as the full impact of the situation hit him like a slap in the face. "Where's your brother? Is he waiting for us somewhere else?"

They both turned to look at Richard. Richard gestured toward the laptop he had on the conference table. "Take a seat. I have to show you something."

∙∙

Jack had been telling stories for hours and then they began taking turns talking about what each person wanted to do when they got out of the cave. Several of the younger kids decided to get up and go to their cabin for a while to sleep. They had agreed that the more they slept, the quicker time would go before they were rescued.

As they stood to leave the picnic area, one of the girls swayed back and forth and just as Jack was reaching his hand out to call attention to those standing near her, she fell and hit her head on the edge of the table. Jack rushed over to her limp body and hollered for someone to get the first aid kit and some towels. He knew she had passed out from weakness and hunger. But that was the least of her problems right now. The wound on her head was deep.

With the first aid kit and clean towels in hand, Jack began to do what he could for the injured girl. He had to stop the bleeding and then most likely stitch it up. He hated doing stitches. He had only done them three different times. At least those times he had done it on a full stomach. This time he was feeling weak and queasy. As he pointed toward the cabins and asked for someone to go get a few pillows, he noticed his hand was trembling.

∎ ∎

Ron and Kristin were sitting on a park bench watching Simon and RJ throw a ball for Alaska to retrieve. They would sometimes throw it to each other instead of to the dog which would cause the dog to jump in the air then crouch down with lots of tail wags in anticipation of the next throw. Every time he did it, the boys would almost fall to ground with laughter.

Watching their boys with pure joy, Ron and Kristin still couldn't believe this was their life. They were finally together. There was so much to talk about and so many plans to make but for now they were just enjoying each moment.

They had met earlier in the day to reunite with some of their friends from the cave. Kristin was happy to see that everyone was doing fine. She had worried so much about the elderly people in her group after she had to leave them behind when they escaped. It made her day when Frankie had looked Ron up and down with discernment. She had stated, "So. You're Ron.

I'm sure you know how lucky you are to have this here special lady in your life again. And that boy. He will keep you on your toes, that one. They're a precious treasure. You all will be a good family." Frankie nodded her approval then turned and dear 91-year-old Ben winked at Kristin before he shuffled off alongside Frankie. Her favorite neighbors had become the best of friends and were good company for each other. Everything was falling into place.

■ ■

Dave and Joshua watched with curiosity as Richard started playing a video clip which appeared to be taken under water. It started out a bit murky but as they got used to it, they could make out where the rocky wall met an opening. Joshua was certain it was the window he had spent so much time looking out from the other side. Coming into view were all of his friends who he hadn't seen in so long. They looked different but the same. Then Jack came through the crowd to the window.

Joshua sucked in his breath as he saw his brother's tortured eyes.

Dave asked Richard without taking his eyes off the computer screen, "When was this?"

"This morning." Richard replied.

"Why do they not have food? Why can't you go get them?" Dave demanded.

"We are working on it. Would you two like to go with me to see the progress being made in their rescue?" Richard asked.

Dave and Joshua both stood up ready to do anything they could to help get to Jack faster.

● ●

Jack had given instructions to have signs made and ready for if the diver came back. Signs that stated their dire situation. He had been able to stop the bleeding from the injured girl's head wound. With shaky motions, he had succeeded in suturing it closed. His concern was that she still had not woken up. He didn't know what to do. Everyone was starting to feel the fatigue of hunger. It hadn't been that long with no food but it had been entirely too long with rationed, dwindling portions.

Jack was slightly comforted with the fact that everyone had seemed to pull together instead of turning on each other which was basically what he had expected. That diver had come just in the nick of time to give everyone hope again. He couldn't help but wonder if hope would be enough to get them through the next couple days until they could get out of here.

● ●

Once they arrived at the lake destination to check on progress with the water drainage, Richard excused himself from the group to make a few phone calls checking on the interrogations of Winston and Doctor Olingham. They were getting a lot of answers and were feeling fairly confident that there were no other caves or locations with prisoners.

The guards who had been with Dave all seemed to be clueless about the details of why they were actually there. They had been enticed with a large, easy paycheck with no questions asked. Richard felt disappointed with the fact that it was so easy to find people to do stupid things for money. The guards had all agreed on one point though. Once they had gotten out to the shelter, no one dared go against Winston.

As he was making his calls, Richard was also taking note of what was going on at the dive site. The excavator had finally made it through the heavily wooded area and was starting to dig the trench to divert some of the water. The pumps were moving the water as fast as they possibly could. It was working. It was just a little slower than Richard would like.

....

Dave and Joshua sat on the ground against the large trunk of a tree watching the progress being made to save Jack. Dave had shown Joshua the few pictures he had brought with him. They were well worn from being carried around for so long. Joshua stared at the picture of Jack as a 16-year-old. He looked so young and care-free. He had never really thought about everything that Jack had lost when they ended up in the cave. He felt a deeper respect and pride building for his brother.

320

Joshua lost his thoughts staring into the water. He had seen this water thousands of times from the other side of the window. It was interesting to him that he had never thought much about this side of the window. It wasn't what he would have expected. As he searched his memory, all he ever really thought was that it was just a wide open, dangerous place out here. Looking at all the people working hard to rescue his brother and friends and sitting here with his dad in the middle of some thick, deep woods, he felt like it was anything but wide open or dangerous.

His mind wandered to Brian and he wondered how his young friend was coping with all of this news. He remembered opening his eyes for the first time in the hospital and seeing Brian's scared eyes willing him to wake up to tell him what to do. He felt confident that Brian was in good hands now and turned his attention back to his dad. There was so much to say that it was almost overwhelming.

With all of the commotion going on, no one had really paid attention to the sky. Joshua looked up to see dark clouds rolling in. He hadn't been on the outside for very long but he did know that it usually meant a storm was brewing. Having been taught in the cave by the older kids and by books, he was certain of one thing. He didn't know if it was math or science but he did know that if it started to rain, the drain pumps would have a harder time keeping up with getting the water out. That was not good news.

Lincoln had gone home to have supper with his dad and mom. It had been quiet in the house with Simon, Lincoln and Joshua gone. Brian had not said much since Joshua had been reunited with his dad. Brian could hear Anne and Jacob's sister, Jillian, talking in the kitchen. It sounded like they were setting the table. It would be time for supper soon. Brian had never eaten such good food. It sure did smell delicious. He could hear Jillian running up the stairs to her room. He didn't know girls liked talking on the phone so much. Wouldn't you run out of things to say? He didn't think he could ever get used to talking into that small box you held up to your ear.

Anne poked her head into the living room where Jacob and Brian were watching tv. She asked, "Any takers to help me make dessert?"

Jacob glanced at Brian. Jacob made a sour face and stuck out his tongue. "Pass." He said.

Anne looked at Brian with a smile and raised her eyebrows in a questioning gesture.

With some hesitation, he turned to Jacob and asked, "Do you care?"

"Go ahead. Whatever it is, put in extra chocolate for me." He grinned.

Brian headed to the kitchen behind Anne. "It wasn't my job in the cave to make any food so I won't be much help." He said self-consciously.

Anne looked at him with a soft expression. "We all have to start somewhere." She opened a drawer near the stove.

Jacob yelled from the living room. "Remember, extra chocolate!"

Shaking her head, she chuckled out loud. Tousling his hair she asked, "I think you might be on board for extra chocolate, too. Yes?"

He nodded vigorously.

"Well, we are making something to take to my brother and he likes extra chocolate too so let's get started. First, we have to unwrap all these caramels. The chocolate comes later." She was happy to see that Brian was starting to look more relaxed. Brian enjoyed himself as he unwrapped, measured, poured, stirred and finally put the end result into the oven at the same time as the meatloaf came out of the oven.

Somehow, as if it was timed perfectly, Wray walked through the door. He stood inside the door and took a slow breath to enjoy the aroma. "Do I smell meatloaf?"

Brian smiled a huge smile. "Yep."

"One of my favorites." Wray replied. "I want to hear about everyone's day. Brian, would you go tell the others that supper is ready?"

Brian nodded happily. He went into the living room to get Jacob and was about to head upstairs to get Jillian when Jacob stopped him. "You don't have to actually go up there." He told

Brian. Then he put his hands around his mouth and yelled loud enough for the neighbors to hear. "Jillian. Supper."

Brian turned around with wide eyes to look into the kitchen just in time to see Wray and Anne both trying to cover up their laughs. Wray said loud enough for Brian to hear, "We're going to create a monster."

Brian felt like part of a family. He didn't let himself think past this meal. He enjoyed the conversation and joking and ease he felt around all of them. He felt a bit of pride when the timer went off and Anne declared, "Oh, it sounds like Brian's dessert is ready."

Jacob sounded off from his chair, "Did you remember…"

Brian finished in unison with Jacob, "the extra chocolate." He grinned. "Of course! It's the best part."

CHAPTER 11

With the storm rolling in, Richard knew it would delay the rescue. Although it had only been the better part of one day, he made the decision to send the diver down again and see about getting a little more detailed information about their circumstances. They suited up the diver and attached the camera to his head along with giving him a few more signs for communication.

Richard advised him to make it quick because the storm would be here soon.

It seemed as though the group behind the window had been waiting for him. They swarmed around the small area and he could see them all talking at the same time. He thought they were just excited to see him but quickly learned the reason for their animation was more of a desperate plea for help. One child gathered up some signs that had been pre-written. They held it up against the window giving him time to read it before moving on to the next sign.

There had been an injury and more kids were getting ill. Some could not leave their beds. This would definitely change their rescue strategy.

The young man who appeared to be in charge, whose name was apparently Jack, came to the window and everyone stepped aside to let him through. He mouthed the words as he looked directly into the camera, "We need help very soon."

The diver let his signs drop from his hand. He couldn't show them the message that rain was coming and would most likely delay them. He could read the anguish in each of their faces. He slowly nodded his head in understanding.

Jack placed his fingers against the glass and the diver slowly raised his hand against the pressure of the water to tap his fingers against his side of the glass in a show of support and hopefully encouragement. As he resurfaced to the beginning drops of rain, he wondered if this was going to go from a rescue mission to one of recovery.

∙∙∙

Dave couldn't believe his son was so close but not reachable. A number of people had gathered around to watch the exchange on the video through the computer screen. Richard turned to the person in charge of the draining operations. "Get this going faster. I don't care what you have to do or who you have to call in to help. Do it now."

The image of his brother's hand up on the glass was frozen in Joshua's mind. Dave placed his arm around Joshua's shoulder. Joshua stood a little taller and said with confidence, "Jack is tough. He is the strongest person I know. He's going to be ok." He glanced at the people around him and continued. "But let me tell you something. Unless you have been there, you don't know what it feels like to starve. It's an awful place. They are just barely holding on." He looked right at Richard. "Please save them."

∎∎

With supper done and dishes completed, Anne left to take food to the fridge at the police station for when or if her brother made it back tonight. She had watched Wray and the kids out playing basketball in the driveway as she backed out onto the road. The rain had been holding off but it looked like it could start at any minute. She was glad the station was close by and she was delivering the requested meatloaf within minutes.

As she was walking out of the break room at the back of the building, she noticed someone was being escorted out of an interrogation room in handcuffs. The man looked right through her. His face was expressionless and his eyes held a darkness she had never witnessed before. She felt a shocking feeling of disgust toward this evil person. She knew instantly that this was the man behind all of the indescribable horror inflicted on so many innocent people. Feeling herself start to tremble from the inside, she quickly turned and went back into the break room. There were a hundred different thoughts and visions crashing around in her mind. She hadn't seen pictures or known most of the victims but she had heard things. And she had seen Brian and Joshua and their struggle with their memories of what they had seen and been through. She had missed a decade of life with her brother-in-law and sister-in-law and nephew.

Overwhelmed with all the emotions and fear she had felt waiting for the investigation to lead to this person's arrest, she leaned against the wall and finally let herself feel. She hadn't wanted to break down in front of the kids. She hadn't wanted them to know she was afraid each minute of the day that something bad would happen or someone would try to take one of them because they knew too much. Feeling her knees get weak, she slowly slid down the wall and sat on the floor with her knees pulled up to her chest. Putting her arms around her legs and putting her forehead on her knees, she sat in a curled ball on the floor and cried. She cried for the deaths of the elderly folks in one cave and for the fact that Brian and Joshua were there as some of them closed their eyes for the last time. She cried for the childhoods lost and the parents, siblings, relatives and friends who had believed their loved ones had left this world in death a decade ago. She cried until all of her tears were shed.

And then she pulled herself together and drove home to her family to enjoy every minute she could with them. As she returned to the driveway and cheered on the game of basketball HORSE, she watched Brian interacting with everyone. She knew that in a short amount of time he had become part of their family. She would do everything in her power to protect him just like she would for Jacob or Jillian.

As the skies opened up and it started pouring rain, they all ran inside before getting soaked. The kids went to the basement to find a movie to watch. Wray and Anne stood at the back door looking out at the rain already starting to puddle by the garage. Wray tilted his head and with a critical eye, he asked her, "Are you ok?"

Wrapping her arms around his middle, she nodded her head and said, "Yep. I'm tougher than I think I am." Leaning against her husband, she felt safer than she had since the day Jacob fell into the lake and discovered the first window.

■■

The lake level was rising instead of lowering. Richard felt the pressure of time pressing on his chest. Knowing they had to work within hours instead of days, he called in every possible favor and started making demands on people he knew weren't used to getting told what to do. As he noticed the sliver of moon reflecting off the water, Richard looked up to see that the sky had cleared. Looking to the East, he could see the line where the clear sky collided with the dark, rolling sky. It had passed much faster than they had expected.

He could hear the voices of rescuers along with the sound of running equipment. With the blinding light of another excavator slowly making its way to another digging spot, things were starting to move along at an urgent pace. Everyone had been touched by the sight of those kids on the other side of that glass. Even with the setback of the rain, it was now a possibility that tomorrow by this time, they would be able to start bringing the kids up.

Knowing he couldn't do anything else at this location tonight, he headed back to the station. His fatigue was almost painful. He called the hospital to make sure they had arranged for extra staff to be on hand at a moment's notice starting tomorrow night. Even though the lake was some distance from Blue Water, it was still the closest town with a hospital. Some medical workers would be on scene but hopefully most of the kids would be able to withstand the travel before getting full medical attention.

As he ate the meatloaf at his desk, he didn't really taste it. He was under the same roof as the monster who had orchestrated this chaos. What in the world would possess a person to do such terrible things? His team had concluded that Doctor Olingham was just a pawn in the bizarre game of Winston's. Richard would try to get a few hours sleep tonight so he would have a clear head to ask Winston some serious questions in the morning. And he wasn't about to start playing his game.

As the sun rose and made a spectacular display across the water's surface, the crew at the lake was feeling optimistic about their progress. With the additional help brought in last night, they had worked around the clock to make it to the window in rapid fashion. The forecast was agreeable for the remainder of the day and plans were being made for the rescue of the kids by nightfall.

∎∎

The town of Blue Water was beginning to prepare for the reception of almost fifty kids and young adults. They had started setting up an area with cots for individuals to stay if they were released with a clean bill of health from the hospital. The residents were bringing in lots of food, clothing, bedding and hygiene items. The unit assigned to reuniting families was fully staffed and ready to start searching the group for the dozens of missing or presumed dead from the window of time a decade ago.

There was a lot of pacing, planning, preparation and positivity throughout the entire town. Many of the previously rescued folks were present and willing to lend a hand in any way. They had been so appreciative of the gracious welcome upon their arrival to the outside that they wanted to continue the trend.

Ben and Frankie had arrived at first light willing to be put to work but mostly just trying to encourage others and give helpful suggestions. As RJ walked into the large facility, his attention was drawn almost immediately to his two favorite previous neighbors. He ran across the room and instantly started talking a mile a minute. Ben and Frankie could hardly keep up. They were so pleased to see how quickly the boy had adapted to his new surroundings.

RJ looked at Frankie with a sparkle in his eyes. "I know you only saw my real town model a few times but don't you think this is so much better? I mean, how could I know what all was out here? There is so much!"

Frankie looked deep in thought and said, "Well, you sure did a good job trying to think of everything but I do think this real stuff is pretty good." His enthusiasm was contagious. He said his good byes and quickly ran off to talk to others. Kristin approached just seconds later. She pulled up a chair right next to them and instinctively grabbed Ben's wrist to feel if his pulse rate was too high. Ben chuckled and said, "You're off the clock now. My health is great. Don't worry about me." He motioned to her cast. "I did hear a few more details about your little run in with a ruffian. I'd like to get my hands on him! How is your wrist?"

Kristin waved her good hand in the air as if swatting a fly away. "Almost as good as new." She smiled and reached over to take Frankie's hand in hers for a minute. "And how are you doing my friend?"

With a new light-heartedness that Kristin had never seen in her before, Frankie replied with a very slight grin, "You know me. Always right on the edge of being a grouch."

Sitting just feet away, Ben made a noise that sounded like agreement.

Shooting him a fake ferocious glare, Frankie said, "Oh, so now you can hear everything?"

Kristin tried to keep a straight face. She had missed these two dear people. "Once we get this newly discovered cave sorted out, Ron and the kids and I want you guys to come over for supper."

They both nodded in agreement. Ben said, "We'll bring dessert. How about ice cream?"

Frankie looked at him like he had just spoken a string of curse words. "Ice cream? With your diabetes? You can't be serious."

Ben looked at Kristin and innocently asked, "What? It's like frozen milk. I need calcium for my brittle bones, don't I?"

Kristin smirked at the look on Frankie's face. "Well, it's hard to argue that point, isn't it?"

Frankie wasn't about to give in. "Well. A scoop maybe. But I'll be watching." Changing the subject as quickly as possible, she asked Kristin, "So, where is that good looking husband of yours?"

Ben raised his eyebrows in exaggerated surprise. "Good looking?"

Frankie enjoyed the banter. "What?" She asked. "They are just kids. Look at them." She reached over and patted Kristin's face. Kristin reached up and held Frankie's hand there for several seconds. She let it go before it embarrassed her.

Kristin answered her question. "My extremely good-looking husband," she looked at Ben and winked, "is helping make arrangements for transportation from the lake to the hospital. We are going out to the site later today to help out. I can't do that much with my hand being useless but I can help with assessments. Those poor children have been through so much. They will be happy with the welcome they receive I hope." She glanced around the room with amazement at the endless work this town had gone through with each group of new arrivals.

Frankie scanned the room and took a deep breath that she let out slowly. "Let's hope that the rumors we are hearing about it being the last cave are accurate. Enough is enough."

Ben and Kristin couldn't agree more.

∙ ∙

Richard entered the room with authority. Winston's attorney sat next to him across the table from where Richard pulled up a chair. Not wanting to take the wrong approach, Richard had given it a lot of thought. Even though he had slept only a few hours, they were enough to refresh him and give him clear thoughts. He knew Winston was incredibly smart, wicked and had a huge ego. Richard decided to work his ego a bit.

"I have to give you credit. You almost pulled it off. Can you tell me what you think of the outcome?" Richard asked.

Winston lifted his shoulder in a half shrug as he bobbed his head side to side as if contemplating the answer. "Well, I think it would have worked out just fine if that kid had stayed behind the fence like he was supposed to. I understand he is your nephew. That must give you a bit of a sense of victory."

Richard replied with an even tone. "Yes. He is my nephew. I don't really think victory would be the right word." He waited to see if Winston would continue or if he would have to start asking more questions.

Winston crossed his arms and leaned forward onto the table making direct and piercing eye contact with Richard. "Answer something for me. Why should I tell you anything? Maybe you should just work for the answers."

Richard was prepared. "Fair. I'll get the answers. It may take a while but I'll get them. I do have an opinion that I can't prove yet. Maybe you will enlighten me." He watched Winston's face. His expression revealed that he did enjoy feeling like he was in charge and had the knowledge that Richard was seeking. Winston just stared at him so Richard continued. "I think you didn't mean for anyone to die. I think things started getting out of control and you didn't know how to stop it."

Winston's chin lifted just a touch. Richard knew he was correct. Richard continued with questions. "Can you tell me if there are any more caves that we have not discovered yet?"

Winston replied, "No. They have all been found."

"Good. That's good." Richard didn't know what the answer to the next question would be. "Why did you do it? These people's lives will never be the same. They have lost ten years of their lives because of you. They can't get that back."

Winston leaned back in his chair and feeling confident in his superiority, he decided to share his findings. "Well, you see, it was just an experiment of sorts. I had an opportunity for access to my father's computer files while I was caring for him after his first heart attack about fifteen years ago. It just made me think that groups of people are predictable. So, over the course of several years, I developed some control groups on which I wanted to test my theories. It was not that hard to get individuals to help me along the way. Most people have secrets, skeletons in their closets, you might say. It didn't take much to convince them to help me. Either blackmail or offering a lot of money did the trick. You can tell who has a weak character and they are easy to get on your side. I don't think any one of my employees turned on me. Well, except until right at the end. That Dave fellow surprised me. However, to be fair, I didn't hire him directly so that's my fault and it sure enough did come back to bite me."

Richard had to hold back from asking him questions. He was speaking pretty freely at the moment. Richard would just let him continue. His arrogance would keep him bragging on himself.

"There were a few bad eggs in the groups but for the most part, people really pulled together. Their true character came through. As I expected, the elderly folks were more accepting of their new life in the cave. They tended to believe the stories about the virus more easily that the younger ones. Most of them could still remember stories as the bubonic plague went around. I guess they decided they were happy to have lived a good life and had a lot of memories to carry them to the end."

"The kids were the most resilient. Most of them quickly got used to their new lives and weren't old enough to remember what they were missing on the outside. They were cared for by others and became like a large family."

Richard couldn't help but interrupt with a question that had been on his mind for days. "Why were Joshua and Brian taken from their cave and brought to the cave with the older residents?"

Winston shook his head with annoyance. "The elderly folks had started getting sick and a few were dying and they were all getting weaker by the day. They needed someone there to help take care of them. But I needed it to be someone who wouldn't ask a lot of questions. Unfortunately, those folks were smart. They started figuring out that there must be people on the outside. We had no choice but to quit providing them with the necessary supplies to keep them going. A few of the more inquisitive folks had to be helped along with a bit of terminal medication."

Richard asked with a mix of anger and disgust, "So, you knew they would all die? Including Joshua and Brian?"

"That's just how the experiment played out. I hadn't planned on it but that's the cost of these things." He continued on with his dialogue as if it was important to him to get some of his conclusions heard.

"The cave with the mix of ages along with those separated from family members fought more in the beginning. They questioned everything. Those in their 30's, 40's and 50's missed the outside and felt like they were being cut short of what they deserved out of life. It was all very predictable. Although I did think we could break them easier but they stuck together and it made them stronger." With a look of disappointment, Winston finished his explanations. "It's a shame it all got derailed. I could have learned even more given extended time."

Since Winston seemed to be willing to answer his questions, Richard continued. "How did you get the individuals into the caves? Did they go willingly?"

Winston puffed up with pride as he summarized it all by simply saying, "Just a little bit of the right kind of drug and they were out cold giving us plenty of time to get them settled into their new environment. It was almost the easiest part."

Trying hard to contain his rage at this person's self-involved tribute to his so-called research, Richard continued to act impressed. "Did you maintain files on each of the individuals in the caves?"

"I did." Winston looked at Richard as if he was obviously of lower intelligence.

"With your research complete, it would help our team greatly if you shared those files so we could reunite families in a timelier manner. Would you consider that?" Richard could feel his jaw clench with the request. It would certainly move things along faster which was the ultimate goal.

"It's possible." Stated Winston feeling like he still had all the power. "But I think I would be more willing to give you that information if the person who interrupted my plans asked me for it. I think your nephew should be the one to ask me." With a deep smile of satisfaction spreading across his face, Winston leaned back in his chair. He looked Richard in the eye and with a smirk in his voice, he said, "Your move."

■■

CHAPTER 13

Ron and Kristin stopped to drop the boys off at Wray and Anne's house for the day so they could go help at the lake. Everyone had been sitting outside waiting for their arrival. The kids all ran off to the back yard followed by a very excited Alaska. He wasn't used to getting this much attention and was enjoying every minute of it.

Kristin watched them all disappear around the side of the house. "Are you sure you don't mind the dog being here? He is good about staying outside and not wandering."

Anne smiled and replied, "I don't mind one bit. It's fun to have him around and he and Bosco seem to get along so it's no problem at all."

Wray was watching Kristin's movements with her injured wrist. He asked with concern, "How is your wrist feeling?"

"Good as new." Kristin answered. "A little bulky but that's ok."

"Are you sure you will be ok helping out at the lake?" Wray asked.

Grinning at Ron, she tipped her head toward him as she answered Wray's question. "I have made a pledge, an oath, a promise and a guarantee to this guy that I will absolutely, under no circumstance, do anything to cause further damage to said wrist."

Simon came running around the corner of the house. "Mom! Oh good, I caught you before you left." He ran to the car and opened the back door. Reaching in he pulled out a grocery bag. "I almost forgot the chocolate ice cream. I promised Brian I would bring it."

Kristin couldn't hide her smile as she said, "And here I thought you were glad we hadn't left yet because you wanted to say good bye."

Simon had a quick flash of guilt cross his face before realizing she was only joking with him. "Well, of course that's why I'm glad you're still here. The ice cream save was just a perk." With a serious tone taking over, he said, "Good bye, mom. Good bye, dad. Good bye Doctor Wray. I hope you have a successful time at the lake."

Kristin gave him a quick hug as they headed toward the car. "Take care of your brother."

Right at that moment, RJ came zooming around the corner and almost crashed into Simon. "Will you be on my team for dodgeball? Whatever that is. Oh yea, ice cream." Waving with exaggeration, he hollered, "Bye guys!"

Simon made eye contact with his mom. "I'll take care of him." He said with a chuckle.

Anne held out her hand to take the grocery bag from him as he took off for the back yard to join the others.

"Thank you!" Ron and Kristin called from the car as they backed out of the driveway. Knowing the kids were in good hands allowed them to focus all their attention on the task at hand which would be making sure all the young ones were taken care of when they got out of the water. Hopefully there would be no unexpected surprises.

■■■

Jack had come running when all of the commotion started in the picnic area. There were shouts and hollers and cheers. As he arrived, they were all pointing to the top of the window. They could finally see a small space at the very edge where the water was lowering. It was happening.

Gathering all of the kids to a space far enough from the window to be out of the way, they discussed the plan again and started arranging themselves in order of youngest to oldest except for the girl with the injured head who still hadn't woken up and two others who were so weak they couldn't walk by themselves. They would be first in line. There was an incredible amount of energy within the group. No one had stopped to ask what would happen once they got outside. Jack's first question to the rescue team would be if they knew anything about Joshua or Brian.

Slowly the water was receding. It was painstakingly slow for the viewers.

It was also painstakingly slow for Dave and Joshua to be watching from the other side of the window. News had spread quickly that they had reached the start of the window. The waiting seemed harder the closer they got.

342

Knowing they were in a time crunch; the team had agreed to start the rescue process before the water was completely removed past the bottom of the window. They had all the tools necessary to cut and break the window along with a thick rubber, weighted mat to put over the glass to prevent any injuries. Five rescuers would enter the cave to maintain order and hand the kids through the opening. Ten would be in the water to receive the kids and get them to shore. Each would get a quick examination on shore before being sent to the hospital. Numerous ambulances would take the injured and ill while several vans would handle the others. It was now just up to the water pumps to keep up the pace of removing the water.

After what seemed like days instead of hours, the time had come to finally break the window. Seeing that the kids on the inside were at a safe distance, it went smoothly and before they knew it, the five rescuers were in the cave and gently handing the unconscious girl through the opening to the waiting crew on the outside. After that, it went like clockwork. Everyone was efficient in their roles and in no time, it was down to the five crew and Jack. He turned to glance at where he had spent the last ten years. Life was about to begin again and he was ready.

· ·

Richard had arrived at the lake to help with the rescue. It was all proceeding better than anyone could have hoped. While maintaining focus on the mission at hand, in the back of his mind he couldn't help thinking about Winston's request. They were getting court orders and warrants to search several places they knew Winston had been. With the help of Doctor Olingham, they might be able to find even more. They were so close. Justice would be served but no kind of justice could give someone back ten years.

Richard was standing just feet away to witness Jack set his feet on dry land.

Jack looked up at the sky and took a deep breath of the fresh air. The wind was rustling through the trees and he looked down at his wet skin for several seconds as he watched the wind dry the water quickly. As he looked back up, his eyes rested on the brother he had spent so many hours thinking about. Not knowing whether he was dead or alive. There was a man standing with his arm around his brother. He looked at him closely and felt the air leave his chest.

There were too many emotions to put into words. No one spoke. Dave and Joshua walked over to Jack and they put their arms around each other and just let the moment wash over them. There were no words to describe it. A huddle of three. There was no past, no future, just this minute in time. This minute that they would each remember in their own way. Questions could wait. Answers could wait. This is more than they could have dreamed.

Several days had passed since the water rescue. As expected, the town had graciously accepted each new resident with open arms. A picnic followed by fireworks at dark was the plan for the evening. The gathering was growing and everyone was enjoying the sun washed early evening.

. . . .

Richard had arrived feeling like a heavy weight had been lifted from his shoulders. He just had an exhilarating conversation with Winston. As they sat across the table from one another, Winston had asked his usual question with the anticipated hint of arrogance in his voice.

"So, when will I be talking to your nephew?"

Today, after receiving word of a successful warrant search for his files, the investigators had finally found what they were looking for. Today, Winston held no cards.

When asked the usual question, Richard smiled and replied, "As I have said, that won't be happening."

"Well, if you want to know where my files are, you will bring him in here and he will ask me for them." Winston said patiently as if talking to a six-year-old.

Richard shook his head slowly. "No. You don't have to worry about it anymore. I do want to thank you for keeping such good records of all of your victims. Excellent organization. You

345

even kept track of everyone on your payroll. Some might consider that a bit risky."

Winston visibly tensed up. His conceit wouldn't let him believe that he had lost control of the situation. "Not possible."

"You have made our investigation so much easier. Gosh, we sure do appreciate it. You have a good evening. You just might be able to hear our fireworks from here. If you listen closely." Richard stood up and placing his palms on the table and leaning forward toward Winston he raised his eyebrows and said, "Checkmate."

∙∙

The gathering at Blue Water Lake was becoming more alive with each passing minute and with each additional town member arriving. It had not taken long for the fence that had surrounded the lake to be taken down. No one had been able to get a good view of it for so long that most residents had almost forgotten what it looked like. Several people who were very handy with woodworking had crafted a beautiful trellis entering a newly planted memorial garden in honor of those who lost their lives while in the cave.

There was a trail down to the shore of the lake with a large observation dock extending out over the water. The trail with built-in steps had a small directional arrow pointing to the water that named it Bosco Way. As far as Jacob could tell, it was pretty close to the exact spot where he had been chasing his dog where he lost his footing, falling into the lake only to discover the very first window.

Not sure how to feel about the memories, Jacob chose to distract himself with a game of football. He called all of his new friends together. Brian watched him as he started running off to start the game. After several yards, Jacob slowed down and turned to glance behind him. "Brian! Come on!" Jacob slowed his pace as he watched Brian look over to Anne and Wray. "Go." They both laughed and said at the same time. With excitement, Brian followed Jacob to join the others. Richard had informed them earlier today that a file had been found on Brian. He had been taken from a hospital under the care of Doctor Olingham after his mother had died in child birth. There was no father's name listed on his birth certificate. He got lost in the paperwork and no one ever really questioned his whereabouts. It made Anne so sad to think about. She and Wray would see to it that there were never any questions about that anymore. They would know his whereabouts. They had decided to wait until the active day was over and everyone had gotten rest tonight before discussing with Brian what he thought about being adopted by them.

Samuel and Clara were sitting with Wray and his family. It had been wonderful for them to be able to spend so much time together since being rescued from the first cave. It seemed like a life time ago. Lincoln had been spending a good part of his time at the town gathering looking down to the water. Had it really been just a short time ago that he saw the surprised face of a boy on the other side of his underwater window? It was that face that had given him the courage to find his way to the outside.

Simon and RJ raced to see who could get there first. Simon could have easily beat RJ but he had to continually slow down as Alaska kept darting in front of him unaware that it was a race and not a game just for his entertainment. Kristin and Ron shared a moment watching their two boys together. They would catch up eventually on separate events of the past but they were looking forward to each memory they would now make together.

Frankie and Ben were slowly making their way toward the rest of the group. Both had continually turned down help from others while grumbling to themselves that they weren't invalids yet. All the while they each kept telling the other to be careful and watch their step.

Dave had become quite good friends with Randy, who had helped to find three of the caves. Randy's wife was certain she knew of several nice women Dave might like to meet. Randy just rolled his eyes and tried not to encourage her. Dave wasn't interested in anything like that right now. He felt like he was just starting to live again after finding his lost boys. He noticed that Jack was with a small group of people around his age down by the water. Jack had gotten an excellent report from the doctor. He was surprisingly strong and healthy for someone who had been deprived of sunshine for years and of decent food for an extended period. He seemed to be comfortable in his new surroundings which pleased Dave to see. Joshua had joined the football game and was laughing and enjoying himself. It was like they had all been friends for a lifetime.

As the first fireworks lit up the sky, everyone's attention turned to the beautiful display of color. After the first few loud explosions rocked their senses, some continued to watch the sky. Some watched the joyful faces of young ones who had never witnessed the booming glory of fireworks. Some just watched the faces of the loved ones they had missed for all these years. As the night wore on and darkness descended, each individual at the Blue Water Lake gathering had their own story to tell. Stories that some would say were far-fetched and hard to believe. Is it hard to believe that with over 117 million lakes in the world, there wouldn't be any with a secret window?

THE END

Made in the USA
Columbia, SC
01 March 2023

2bd205cf-2f07-4226-a493-b7d8eb8252b1R01